He W
Come for Me

Nicole Abrams

Edited by: Scarlett @ Scarlett's Proofread Services

Cover Designer: Nicole Abrams

Synopsis

Held captive in chains with only my memory to keep me occupied, even though I had no memory of how I got there, or who took me. The one thing I held on to that kept repeating in my head was, "He will come for me. He always comes for me." Then, after what my mind believed to be months, I was finally rescued; by the boy I had a crush on at Brighton Academy.

Phoenix Stone. Who is ALL man now and my father's enemy.

Now, I've traded chains for walls. His words say I am a prisoner, but his actions don't. I soon learn I am not his captive in this war between my father and him; but his property. He says he did it to rescue me. To protect me from evils I couldn't understand. As secrets unwind, and my memories return, I begin to wonder…

Did I fall in love with my knight in shining armor or the devil himself?

Dedication

To the one who wants to be someone's obsession, even if they are morally grey.

Prologue

He will come for me. He always comes for me.

Chapter 1

My name is McKenzie... I suck in a deep breath, ignoring the rapid beating of my heart. *I'm twenty-three years old. I've been kidnapped. But he will come for me. He always comes for me.* I squeeze my eyes shut at the realization that I can't remember who *he* is anymore. But I say this mantra in my head everyday so I don't forget. Fear settles on my chest like a boulder. *What if one day I don't even remember my name?*

I shift uncomfortably on the cot; the springs dig into my back and hips. The chains around my wrists dig in and I try my best to hold in a whimper as they rub against my raw skin.

I'm going to die here. I'm going to die here, not knowing if there's really someone out there looking for me. Is there someone out there that misses me?

I jump when a loud bang erupts upstairs. There are shouts coming from above me and several pops. I swallow convulsively. *Is that gunfire?* I squeeze my eyes shut and curl into a ball, hoping this isn't how I die. "He will come for me." I cough, so I finish it in my head. *He always comes for me.*

There are voices outside the room I'm in and goosebumps break-out along my body. I curl even more into myself, hoping I die quickly. I scoff as a tear slips out of the corner of my eye.

Who am I kidding? I've been slowly dying since the day I was brought to this prison. I want my father.

I imagine being in the backyard of my childhood home and him pushing me on the swing that hung on the biggest tree. Me giggling and asking him to push me higher and him saying I'm going to fly away if I go any higher. Maybe it's my father that will rescue me.

The door behind me bursts open and I brace my body for what's going to come next.

"In here!"

I'm suddenly thankful I don't have the strength to roll over. I won't have to see how they kill me. Other people enter the room and I hold my breath, hoping they'll think I'm already dead. Although if they think that and they've killed the people upstairs, I'll be left here to rot.

"Fuck. I'm going to make every person suffer," a voice booms behind me.

"She's chained to the wall," another voice states.

I stay perfectly still, not sure of their intentions. Someone sits on the cot and I groan as it causes my sores to rub against the spring painfully. My heart beats wildly in my chest, afraid of what they're going to do next.

"Do you know where the keys are?"

It's the same voice that was booming, but he's soothing now. *Why?* I suck in a breath as my body shakes from my nerves. *Will he make me suffer too?* I try a few times to speak, but it takes me several tries before I'm able. It's been a long time since I've used my vocal cords above a whisper. I've learned how to stay as quiet as possible. The only time I allow myself to speak is when I try to remember, but even that is hard sometimes.

"Hook." I cough again. "Wall." My voice is cracked and raspy. There isn't a response, but there is movement, then the distinct rattle of the keys. A hand touches me and I jerk away.

"I'm not going to hurt you. I'm going to unlock your chains."

I force myself to stay as still as possible, but my body is shaking and I can't stop it. The man unlocks the chains around my wrists. He touches them and I cry out in pain. There's cursing, then he's lifting me from the cot and holding me in his arms.

My wrists are on fire, my throat is dry, and every muscle in my body aches. I hope they kill me quickly. Someone places a blanket over me and I sigh at the warmth it provides. I can't remember the last time I was warm. I'm sure my teeth have cracks in them from how often I shivered from the cold. I haven't opened my eyes once since I heard the bang upstairs. As warmth invades my body, I know in a matter of seconds I'll be asleep or dead. I'm not sure which yet.

So, I force myself to crack my eyes open to see who my rescuer is. At least I hope he's my rescuer. He might be taking me to another prison for all I know. Or maybe he's taking me somewhere else to kill me.

I blink several times before his face comes into focus. When it does, my heart fills with lead. His icy eyes collide with mine and the warmth that was enveloping me vanishes. I pull my chapped lips between my teeth as a different kind of fear envelops me.

"You," I whisper. His eyes narrow, but if he responds I don't hear him because darkness overtakes me.

The first thing I notice is how warm I am. The second thing I notice is the smell of lavender. Opening my eyes slowly, I stare at the ceiling, blinking until the sandpaper feeling goes away. *Where am I?* I swallow. *Does my prison have a gilded cage now?*

My name is McKenzie. I'm twenty-three years old. I've been kidnapped. But he will come for me. "He always comes for me," I say, finishing my mantra out loud. Someone shifts next to me and my eyes fly to the man sitting in the chair. He's reclined back in the chair, arm draped along the armrest with an empty glass hanging from his fingers. Staring at me with a blank look on his face. His jaw ticks as I return his stare.

He looks different, yet the same. His jaw is more defined, eyes are even icier than they were if that's possible, and his dark blond hair is longer than it was when we went to school together. He looks taller and has more muscle, a deadly force I would not want to cross, and my father's enemy, making him mine as well.

Now I'm his prisoner. He leans forward, resting his elbows on his knees, rubbing a finger along the rim of the glass. I try to swallow and realize how parched I am.

"Water?" I ask. He stands, places his glass on the nightstand, grabbing the cup on the nightstand, and places his hand behind my head to lift me. He brings the cup to my lips. I try to grab it to do it myself. I'm not helpless. He refuses to let me hold the cup, and I'm too thirsty and weak to argue. I don't take my eyes off him as I take a sip from the cup. *What if he's drugged it?*

"I haven't." My eyes widen and some of the water goes down the wrong way, causing me to cough. "If I wanted you dead, you'd be dead." His voice is deep and low. My eyes catch the bandages on my wrist, and track marks on my arm along with the IV. Everything comes rushing back. Sucking in a breath, I remember his eyes were the last thing I saw before I fell asleep. Or maybe I passed out.

"Why am I here?" His eyebrows cave in as icy blue eyes bore into mine. He leans back, placing the glass back on the nightstand.

"A doctor will be here in a few minutes to check you over." I lay back down as I study him. I finally have the freedom to get up and walk around, but I don't have the strength to do it. I eye him. Maybe he's giving me what looks like freedom, only to take it away when I get comfortable.

"You didn't answer my question."

I swear I see his mouth twitch like he wants to smile. "You don't want to know the answer."

I look away from him and back at the ceiling. *What is that supposed to mean?* I take in my surroundings. This is definitely a step up from where I was. It doesn't smell like death. The bed is soft and comfortable. Shifting, I grimace at how sore my body is. I look at what I'm wearing and realize I'm in clean pajamas.

"Did you change my clothes?" I'm not as dirty as I was either. I'm still not clean, but I can tell him or someone washed off some of the grime. When he doesn't answer right away, I turn to look at him. He's staring at me with that blank look on his face.

"No." Relief washes through me and I wait for him to say more, but he doesn't. The hard lines of his face get harder. He pulls a phone out of his pocket, tapping on it, then brings it to his ear.

"She's awake." That's all he says before pocketing his phone again. No greeting, no bye. I tear my eyes from him and take in my surroundings again. This room is huge. The bed is in the middle. There's a fireplace on the opposite wall with a television above it. The wall to the right of the bed looks like it might be all windows, but I can't be too sure because it's covered by curtains. There are two chairs, one is occupied, the other is empty. My eyes collide with ice again as he watches me take in everything.

"I need to go to the bathroom."

Will he let me go? Or, will it be like my last prison where I'm forced to hold it until I couldn't anymore or they remembered I was there and took me? Would he watch me as I went, or would he give me privacy?

He doesn't answer, but he stands and walks over to me, folding back the blankets and lifting me in his arms. I gasp and clutch at his shoulders.

"Can you grab the IV stand and pull it?"

I look from him to the IV stand. "I can walk."

He narrows his eyes, and I know this is not up for discussion. So, swallowing my pride and nerves, I grab the stand and pull it along. He walks slowly, so the stand doesn't fall over. After a few steps, I realize how weak I am. When was the last time I ate? I can't remember.

A cold sweat covers my body, and my chest is tight. Ignoring it for now, I focus hard on not losing my grip on the stand. I'm embarrassed at how slow he has to walk because he can tell how much I'm struggling, but he doesn't say anything. I'm sure if he had a third arm, he'd drag it instead of having me do it.

He walks to one of the doors in the bedroom. When he opens it and turns the light on, I stare longingly at the huge bathtub. The shower is also large, but I don't think I could stand long enough. He carries me to the toilet and I suck in a breath as he slowly lowers me to the ground. I sway, but he keeps his arm wrapped around my waist to steady me. *He's going to stay in here.*

"Do you need help?" he asks. I glance up at him. He is so tall. I stare at the tattoo that's peeking out of the top of his shirt. I wonder what it is. My eyes travel along the cords of his neck, along the hard lines of his jaw, up to his eyes. His full attention on me as he waits for me to answer.

"I'd like to try by myself. If that's okay?"

He nods once. "I'll be right at the door. If you need help, call out to me. Okay?"

"Okay," I whisper.

He slowly lets go of me, probably making sure I don't crumble to the ground. He backs up to the door, watching me closely before opening it and closing it behind him. Shuffling to the toilet, I relieve myself and slowly make my way to the large counter that has two sinks. I'm suddenly grateful he carried me because walking from the toilet to the sink was difficult enough.

I avoid the mirror as I scrub my hands, trying to remove the dirt from under my fingernails. Tears form in my eyes as I stare at the running water. *How did this happen? Why did this happen?* I don't even know why I was kidnapped or who kidnapped me. Unable to avoid it any longer, I finally look at my reflection and the tears I've been trying to hold back fall.

My silver hair hangs limply, looking dirty and greasy. The only unique thing about me. It was brown when I was younger, but when I hit puberty, it started turning silver.

Apparently I lost the pigment, but I was never mad about it. It's a beautiful color and I don't even need a box to make it this way. I always wonder how my beautiful mom and handsome dad made such an average-looking child. I wasn't average any longer because of my hair, but now with it looking so limp and greasy, the feeling creeps back over me of how I felt before it turned silver. My brown eyes look hollow, with dark circles under them. My cheekbones are prominent because I'm basically skin and bones. The weight I felt on my chest grows as the tears cloud my vision and the image in the mirror becomes blurry.

"Why?" I whisper. "Why did this happen?" I want to slam my fist into the mirror and break it. It would look like how I feel inside. Broken and falling apart.

"McKenzie?" The door opens behind me. I hang my head at his soft voice.

Why is he being so gentle with me? Is he luring me into a false sense of safety?

Turning to face him, he looks back at me with that blank look on his face. He doesn't react to my tears, simply stares at me. I guess I'm now the prisoner of Phoenix Stone, my father's enemy.

Chapter 2

He approaches me slowly, like he would a scared animal. I turn the water off and allow him to pick me up again. What little strength I had is rapidly decreasing and I don't want to fall at his feet. *Would he kick me while I was down?* I refuse to meet his eyes as he helps me back to the bed. There's a woman and man standing near the bed talking in whispers, but when they notice me, they go quiet.

The woman's eyes widen, but she schools her features quickly. "Miss Kenzie, how are you feeling?" I scowl at her. *What kind of question is that? And why is she calling me Kenzie?* That's reserved for friends only and I have no friends in this room.

"Like I've been kidnapped and chained," I reply. Her mouth falls open and Phoenix's grip on my waist tightens slightly. I drop my eyes to the floor, feeling slightly guilty for snapping at her. She's just doing her job. Phoenix helps me into the bed and the man approaches with a bag in his hand.

"McKenzie. I'm Dr. Chamberland." He takes a stethoscope and blood pressure cuff out of his bag. "I'm going to listen to your heart and check your blood pressure." I nod slightly as he does everything he needs to do, following his instructions when he tells me to take deep breaths. My hands are beginning to shake and the tightness in my chest gets worse.

What is wrong with me? Am I having a panic attack? Maybe it's anxiety?

Dr. Chamberland stands from where he was sitting on the bed and I raise my knees, putting my forehead on them, trying to calm myself. The shaking in my hands spreads throughout my body.

"McKenzie?" Phoenix calls out to me, but I ignore him. The bed dips and out of the corner of my eye I see his tattooed arm reaching out to touch me, but I flinch away. He pauses in midair, retracting his hand. "What's wrong with her?" His voice is hard as he addresses the doctor.

"I think she's having withdrawal symptoms."

I'm pretty sure they drugged me. My eyes drop to the inside of my arms, noticing the track marks again. Phoenix stands. I can't stop my eyes from following him. He begins pacing like a lion trapped in a cage. He balls his hands into fists, causing the veins on his arms to pop even more than they already do.

A flash of a tattooed hand pushing my silver hair behind my ear goes through my mind and I suck in a breath. Shaking my head slightly, I silently berate myself. *Don't fantasize about your enemy.*

There's another dip in the bed, but I ignore it. "Miss Kenzie?" I inhale slowly, my irritation, exhaustion, and everything else overwhelming me.

"My name is McKenzie, not Kenzie." I try to keep the irritation out of my voice, but her green eyes still cloud over with what looks like hurt that she hides quickly. She stands, rubbing her hands down her jean-clad legs. Something that feels a lot like guilt stirs in my stomach.

Does it really matter what she calls me? I glance around the room. I'm still being held captive; my cage just looks nicer. Even if it's not her fault, I'm not comfortable with her calling me Kenzie. Maybe that will change, but not today.

"Of course." I notice the doctor and Phoenix have stopped talking and their attention is focused on us. There's an unreadable look on Phoenix's face, but I ignore it.

"What's your name?" I ask her, still trying to ignore the uneasy feeling I have. She stares at me, her eyebrows scrunching at my question.

"I'm Clara." She swallows and looks at Phoenix before wiping her hands down her jeans again and offers me a small smile. "Are you hungry? I can bring you something." At the mention of food, my stomach clenches with hunger pangs. I can't remember the last time I ate.

"I would suggest starting off with some broth first before giving her solid food," Dr. Chamberland states. I scowl at him. I don't want broth. He notices my expression and his eyes soften. "Do you remember the last time you ate?" I shake my head slowly.

"Jesus Christ," Phoenix growls.

Clearing my throat, I look between the three of them. "Even when they fed me, it was usually bread and cheese." My voice is small. "I think. It's a little fuzzy." I don't want to admit how much I don't remember. What looks like concern flits across the doctor's face and he walks over, sitting back on the bed.

"What's the last thing you remember?" he asks. I begin rocking slightly, trying to ignore the shaking in my limbs as I try to recall my last memory before I was kidnapped.

"My father and I were going to a party. It was the first time he let me go with him to one of his parties." I try to bring back the memories from that night, but all I remember was the dress I wore because he gave me shit about it from the moment he saw me in it.

It was a little more low cut than I normally wear and it had a slit to the middle of my thigh. But I refused to change because I loved it and I was sick of being treated like a fragile china doll. I think. The dress was my choice, right?

"I don't remember anything about the party. My father and I argued all the way to the party because of the dress I was wearing. As soon as the driver pulled up to the door, I got out and put as much distance between us as possible." Looking up, I glance around at the three of them. Phoenix has his hands balled into fists again, Clara is worrying her lip, and Dr. Chamberland simply nods.

"I was at that party," Phoenix says. I narrow my eyes at him.

"You were?" I don't remember him being there. *Why would my father bring me to a party where his biggest enemy was?* "I don't remember," I whisper. He gets that blank look on his face again, so I look away and focus on the doctor.

"When is the last time you remember seeing Phoenix?" I tilt my head at him. *That's an odd question. Why would he want to know that?* Instead of asking, I think back. Clearing my throat, I hold my knees even tighter as another pang of hunger hits me.

"Ummm... I think at our high school graduation from Brighton Academy." I watch to see what reaction that will get out of Phoenix, but he doesn't react. Except for the tick in his jaw, he still has that blank look on his face.

"Clara, get McKenzie some broth," Phoenix says, changing the subject. Clara nods and scurries out the door. "Dr. Chamberland, what do we need to do while McKenzie goes through withdrawal?" Dr. Chamberland doesn't seem to be put off by Phoenix changing the subject.

"The IV will help. She's dehydrated and malnourished. It could help move along the symptoms, but there's no guarantee. Unfortunately, she's going to have a hard time for the next week, maybe longer." I swallow as I half listen to their conversation. They talk like I'm not even here, but I don't care enough to call them out on it. My eyes are beginning to droop. I wouldn't mind going to sleep because the urge to claw my skin off is becoming unbearable.

I think I must nod off for a few minutes because the next thing I know, Clara is shaking me slightly. "Miss McKenzie," she whispers. I open my eyes slowly, trying to focus on her, but I seem incapable of doing that. "Your broth is ready." She helps me get situated and puts a lap tray over my legs. My eyes finally coming into focus, I watch as Clara gets everything situated.

"Clara?" I ask. Her eyes connect with mine. "Thank you," I whisper. She pats my hand lightly.

"Of course." She places the bowl on the tray, with a small croissant that makes my mouth water, and a glass of water. I realize the doctor and Phoenix are no longer in the room.

"Phoenix had a phone call he had to take. Dr. Chamberland went to get everything he needs to complete an exam," she explains. I don't respond. Instead, I grab the croissant, tear off a piece, and dunk it in the broth. Closing my eyes, I savor the taste as I chew it slowly. Even if it is only broth and a croissant, it tastes amazing. A far cry from the bread and cheese they fed me where I was being held. Sometimes they would be moldy, but I'd eat what they gave me because I never knew for sure when they'd bring me food again.

The doctor comes in carrying his supplies. I watch as he sets everything up before picking up the spoon so I can sip some of the broth. But my hand shakes so badly it spills back into the bowl. I try again, but I can't stop my hands from shaking. The harder I try, the more they shake. Giving up, I tear off another piece of the croissant, dunk it, and eat it. Ignoring Dr. Chamberland and Clara, I pick my spoon up again and ladle some broth on it. Instead of bringing the soup to my lips, I lean forward so I only have to move the spoon a small distance.

I huff in frustration when barely any makes it in my mouth and wipe my chin from where it spilled. Finally lifting my head, I realize everyone's eyes are on me. Phoenix is leaning against the door, his arms crossed as he watches me. My eyes begin to sting from how helpless I feel. He pushes off the door and stalks toward me. Sitting next to me, he reaches his hand out and grabs the spoon, dipping it into the broth and brings it to my lips.

I watch him closely the entire time. Leaning forward, I open my mouth and close it around the spoon, never taking my eyes off him.

His icy eyes return my stare, but when the broth hits my taste buds, I close my eyes and hum.

So good.

"I'll make sure to let Phillip know."

"Who's Phillip?" I ask as he brings another spoonful of the broth to my mouth.

His lips press into a thin line before he replies. "He's the cook."

I eat a few more spoonfuls, but my stomach begins cramping. I scrunch my nose, deciding whether I should keep trying to eat or not, but a cramp hits again, so I take a deep breath and lean back.

"Kenz?" Phoenix leans forward, his hand extending toward me. I flinch just as he's about to push my hair behind my ear, reminding me of the flash I had earlier.

"Don't touch me." His eyes darken and his face turns to stone, but he doesn't reach for me again.

"What's wrong with you?"

"My stomach." I inhale. "But I'll be fine."

"That's why she should only have broth until she can tolerate solid food." Phoenix's eyes shoot to Clara. "Other than bread, of course," Dr. Chamberland finishes. Clara wrings her hands.

"Maybe the croissant was too much?" She asks, her eyes moving from Phoenix to Dr. Chamberland then to me.

"I liked the croissant." Another pang hits my stomach, but I refuse to show it because I don't want Clara to get in trouble.

Dr. Chamberland walks over with his supplies and sits down gently. "Maybe next time eat smaller bites," he jokes. Phoenix glares at him. I roll my eyes and give Dr. Chamberland a small smile. "I need to do an exam and make sure everything else is okay." I nod once as he shines a bright light in my eyes, looks in my ears, nose, and throat, tests my reflexes and pushes on my stomach.

I squeeze my eyes shut, hoping the pangs will go away soon. Dr. Chamberland pats my hand. "Your stomach isn't used to the food. It will acclimate quickly," he promises. "How does the IV feel?" I glance at Phoenix. His eyes never left the doctor as he did his exam. I shrug as I thumb the bandage on my wrist.

"Okay. I guess." *What does he want me to say?*

"I know it will be uncomfortable. Hopefully, we'll only need it for a couple of days. If you drink water and have as much broth as you can handle, we'll be able to take the IV out and move you to a better diet." Dr. Chamberland packs up. "Call me if you need me," he tells Phoenix before leaving.

"I'll go get another glass of water and take everything to the kitchen." Clara grabs the tray and follows Dr. Chamberland out. Phoenix doesn't move. He stays on the bed next to me. I feel his eyes on me, so I finally look at him.

"Can I take a bath?" He looks from me to the IV and I sigh. I forgot that quickly. I'm not shaking as badly as I was. I have a little more energy than I did earlier, but I'm still exhausted.

"I can help you take a shower," he offers. I swallow and shake my head quickly. "Didn't think so." He stands and runs a hand through his hair. "Dr. Chamberland will be back in the morning. I'll get him to unhook the IV so you can take a bath." He grabs the remote and hands it to me. "If you want to watch TV." He shows me how to work it and walks to the door.

"I'll be back in a bit to check on you. I'm sure Clara will be in and out checking on you, too."

I pull my lips between my teeth as I study him. "Am I your prisoner now?" I ask softly.

He places his hands in his pockets as he studies me for a few seconds. "Yes." He walks out of the bedroom and closes the door gently.

Chapter 3

I stare at the ceiling after everyone has left. Alone with my thoughts.

Why am I his prisoner? He didn't want anything to do with me at school. Why is he suddenly showing interest?

Sighing, I adjust myself and close my eyes, trying to ignore the sensation of wanting to claw my skin off. I have no idea what they drugged me with, but whatever it was probably helped keep me docile. It doesn't make sense why Phoenix wouldn't want to keep me docile as well. The last thing I think about is his tattooed hand pushing my hair behind my ear.

My eyes fly open and I suck in a breath when I'm met with unfamiliar surroundings. "My name is McKenzie. I'm twenty-three years old. He will come for me. He always comes for me." The room is dark, but it's not as dark as the prison I was kept in.

I try my best to calm my racing heart, but I'm unsuccessful. Closing my eyes again, I repeat my mantra. "My name is McKenzie. I'm twenty-three years old. He will come for me. He always comes for me." Wiping away a tear that escapes my eye, I'm reminded of the IV that's in my arm.

"Who is he?" I turn my head toward the voice and make out Phoenix's silhouette in the dark.

"What are you doing in here?" I ignore his question. It has to be the middle of the night. There isn't a clock in here, but I'm assuming it has to be.

"Answer my question first."

Pulling my lips between my teeth, I quickly release them because of the sting with how cracked they are. "I don't know," I whisper.

"You don't know?"

"I answered your question. Now you answer mine." He's not my friend. I'm not confiding in him.

"I have to go away for a few days." I squint at him, confused. That doesn't answer my question. "I came in here to check on you before I left."

"Why do you care?" He stands and stares down at me. I'm glad I can't see his glacier stare.

"You're mine. So I need to make sure you stay alive." With that, he stands and walks out of the room. I ignore the ache in my chest and the shaking of my hands as I watch him leave. *Of course I'm his. His prisoner.* I must doze off for a few minutes, because the next thing I know, Clara is nudging me because she brought me some broth.

"Sorry to wake you, Miss McKenzie, but it's getting late, and the doctor wants you to eat and build your strength up." *Guess I dozed off longer than a few minutes.*

"What time is it?" I ask. She helps me sit up and puts the table across my lap before walking over to the curtains and pulling them back. I squint at the sudden brightness, but I welcome it after the dungeon I was held in for god knows how long.

"It's almost lunchtime." I wasn't expecting that answer. It feels like Phoenix just left. "Mr. Phoenix said to let you sleep, but not sleep too long."

"God forbid his property not get healthy again." Clara doesn't respond, instead she grabs the broth and sits it on the table.

"Sorry," I mumble. It's not her fault her boss is an ass.

"Eat as much as you can, but don't force yourself." She begins dusting the room. I stare at the bowl in front of me minus the croissant. *Stupid Phoenix. I'm sure he's the reason I didn't get that.*

Grabbing the spoon, I ladle some broth and am more successful at keeping it on the spoon this time. My hand is still shaking, but not as bad as last night. After a few sips, I get frustrated because I have to concentrate so hard on my hand not shaking.

Finally giving up, I lay back against the headboard and sigh. A few days ago, I was shackled to a bed, not knowing if I was going to die there or not. While I may still be a prisoner, at least I'm getting treated better and I'm getting more than stale bread and moldy cheese.

"Would you like help?" I lift my head and catch Clara watching me. My face heats with embarrassment. I want to tell her I don't need help, but she obviously saw me struggling. I'm baffled by her concern. *Why does she care? Why is she being so nice to me?*

I finally nod. "Yes, please." She gently grabs the spoon and brings it up, indicating for me to take it. Leaning forward, I sip the broth and she smiles at me.

"I was able to get a few bites before I gave up," I admit. "I wasn't shaking as bad as last night." She pats my arm before dipping the spoon in the broth again.

"That's a good sign." She doesn't mention anything about me struggling. It makes me like her a little more. I eat a few more bites before I can't anymore.

"Am I not allowed to have a croissant?" I ask, feeling like I'm pushing my luck. She chuckles as she grabs the tray and stands.

"I told Mr. Phoenix you wouldn't be happy about not getting a croissant." I roll my eyes and she smirks. "I'll bring you one for dinner. It'll be our secret."

"Can I take a bath today?" I change the subject because I don't want to talk about Phoenix Stone.

"Yes. The nurse should be here soon and she can unhook your IV so you can take a bath. I'll wash your hair if you want me to," she says as she finishes dusting the furniture. Excitement flutters in my stomach at being able to soak in the bathtub. I never got showers or baths where I was. They'd hose me down every few days. It was degrading, embarrassing, and freezing.

I shiver, remembering how cold I always was and snuggle under my blanket. "Wait. There's a nurse coming?" Clara turns and gives me her full attention.

"Yes. The doctor will visit every few days, but Mr. Phoenix hired a nurse to take care of you full time until you're better." Picking at the bandages around my wrists, I think about how much thought Phoenix is putting into my care.

Is he going to use me to get to my father? Did he get me before my father could rescue me? Is my father looking for me? Is he worried? Was I kidnapped at the party we went to?

Sighing, I force myself to stop thinking about all the questions riddling my brain. I wish I could remember. *Why can't I remember?*

"Miss McKenzie?" I turn my attention back to Clara.

"Sorry. Did you say something?"

"I was saying I'll be back in a few minutes. Do you think you have the strength to go on a tour of the house?" I stare at her for several seconds before answering.

"I can leave this room?"

She chuckles. "Of course you can. You can even go outside with an escort. You just can't leave the grounds without someone with you."

"Maybe another day of rest before that."

As much as I'd love to go now, I know my limits and I wouldn't make it just yet. She nods, grabs the tray, and leaves. I suck in a breath and scoot to the edge of the bed. Resting for a few seconds, I drop my feet on the floor and push myself up slowly until I'm standing.

I brace myself on the bed until I'm sure I have my balance, then grip the pole that my IV bag is hooked up to and slowly shuffle to the wall with the curtains. Grabbing one, I push it thinking it will be hard, but it slides easily and I have to catch myself from falling because I put too much of my weight into it.

My breath catches at the view. My room seems to be on the side of the house. There are rolling hills with trees that have colorful leaves. So, it must be fall. I'm pretty sure they held me captive for around six months. The night of the party, which is my most recent memory, was in the spring.

I'm rapidly losing the small burst of energy I had, so I attempt to maneuver the chair Phoenix sat in because I want to face the windows, but I quickly realize that isn't happening. So, I lower myself into it and turn awkwardly to look out the window. *If only I had a book to curl up with.*

I wonder how much land Phoenix has. The gardens below are gorgeous. It has a variety of flowers and I'm pretty sure I see apple trees. When I get my strength back, I'm definitely going to explore if I'm actually allowed to. I know Clara said I could, but I'm still skeptical. Especially about leaving the grounds. *Why would he let me do that?*

There's a light knock on the door, so I turn to see who it is. It's Clara and an older lady in a bright pink nurse's uniform with her gray hair pulled up into a bun on top of her head.

"Hi, Miss McKenzie. I'm Millie. I'll be your live-in nurse for a few weeks until we know you're feeling better." I offer her a slight wave as she walks toward me.

"Nice to meet you," I reply.

"It's good that you're out of bed. I need you to start moving more. Dr. Chamberland mentioned you have some bed sores. I'll make sure to keep those treated so they'll heal nicely, but getting out of bed will help." She sits her bag on the side table next to the chair and takes out her stethoscope.

"I'm going to do a quick check up, then I'll unhook your IV so you can take a bath. The needle will need to stay in your arm, though." I nod slightly as she grabs the blood pressure cuff and puts it on my arm that isn't hooked up to the IV. She takes my temperature, listens to my heart, and checks my reflexes.

"You seem to be in decent health, all things considered." She offers me a small smile as she unhooks my IV.

"I'll go start your bath," Clara says and hurries into the bathroom. As Millie writes down her notes, I go back to looking out the window. I'm terrible with small talk. I'd rather have a deep conversation with someone or not talk at all. I'm definitely not going to talk to someone about the weather.

When Millie gets done, she packs all her things. "I think in a few weeks you'll be good as new." *Hardly.* I keep my thoughts to myself, though. My body may heal, but I know it's going to be a long road to healing my mind and emotions.

"Dr. Chamberland says you're also having drug withdrawal symptoms. How are you feeling today?" I push a strand of hair behind my ear as I consider her question.

"I don't feel as anxious as I did yesterday. My stomach is still churning and my throat is on fire. My hands are still shaky, but, like I said, it's not as bad as yesterday. So, we'll see, I guess."

She pats my hand and gives me an encouraging smile. "You've had a rough go of it. I know this isn't easy on you." I scoff and turn my attention back to the view.

"And your employer isn't making it any better." Millie stops what she's doing and turns her eyes to me, but I ignore her. Everyone is acting like me being held prisoner is normal. I don't understand how they're all just going along with this.

Millie doesn't respond. Clara walks back into the bedroom from the bathroom and looks between me and Millie.

"Both of you and Dr. Chamberland act like it's normal that I was rescued from one prison, only to be put into another one. Granted, this one is a lot nicer than my last one."

"Miss McKenzie," Clara says in a placating tone that grates on my nerves. "Mr. Phoenix has his reasons for rescuing you. You'll have to ask him what they are." I slam my hand down on the table, causing them to flinch.

"I want to know what's going on. I deserve to know what's going on." A tear escapes from my eye and I bat it away angrily.

Clara's mouth opens and closes a couple of times before she heaves a sigh. "You'll have to ask Mr. Phoenix."

I want to scream. I want to tear this room apart. I want to run. But I don't do any of those things. I don't have the strength. Instead, I stand with a sigh of defeat.

"I'd like to take my bath now." Slowly walking to the bathroom, I can feel their eyes on me, but I ignore them.

Where is my father? Is he looking for me? Is he worried? Does he care?

Chapter 4

For the next several days, I refused to talk to anyone. Clara brings me broth and adds a croissant to every meal. I'm sure it's her attempt to make me feel better, but I need more than a croissant to feel better. I'm not shaking anymore, so I don't need help to feed myself. Which is good because I'd starve before allowing them to help me again.

I'm angry, sad, and frustrated. That isn't helping my withdrawals. The shaking has stopped, but my body is still craving whatever they were giving me. My emotions are feeding into that craving. It makes me want to claw my skin off.

To make things worse, Phoenix isn't back yet, so I can't ask him the questions running around in my head. My hunger has returned to full force as well. The broth and croissant aren't enough. When Clara comes into my room, I suck up how I'm feeling.

"Clara, could I get something more than the broth and croissant? I'm starving." I finally break my silence, but I refuse to look at her. I know it's not her fault I'm here, but I'm having a hard time disassociating her from this, since she's the person I see the most.

"Of course. I'll go grab you a banana. If you can handle that, I'll get Phillip to make you some mashed potatoes or rice."

"Thank you," I mumble. I close my eyes and sigh. I have to stop blaming her. She's been nothing but kind to me and I've been anything but.

Nurse Millie removed the IV yesterday as long as I drink enough water and there are some supplements Dr. Chamberland told me to take until I'm eating regularly. When Clara comes back with the banana, I have to force myself not to devour it.

She goes into the bathroom to clean and then comes out to dust the furniture. I watch her as I take small bites of the banana.

"Clara?" She turns to me, giving me her attention. "I'm sorry I've snapped at you so much. I've taken out how I've been feeling on you and that's not fair."

She smiles at me before sitting next to me on the bed. Her finger trails along the back of my hand. "I know this hasn't been easy for you, but I'm here if you need me." I lean forward and hug her. It seems to surprise her, but she returns my hug. Pulling back, I offer an embarrassed smile.

"Sorry. I just..." I trail off. She pats my hand and stands to continue her dusting.

"No need to apologize. I'm here if you need hugs, too." I let out a watery laugh before changing the subject.

"Do you know who Phoenix rescued me from?" I hate calling it a rescue when I'm technically still a prisoner. Clara stops dusting for a second before continuing.

"I don't know any details, Miss McKenzie."

I take another bite of my banana as I study her. "But you do know something." She sighs and gives me a pleading look.

"You'll have to ask Mr. Phoenix."

"You said if I needed anything," I remind her.

She gestures to the banana. "I meant if you needed extra snacks, or a hug, or someone to vent to. I can't answer questions I don't know the answers to. So, you'll have to ask Mr. Phoenix."

"He's not here to ask," I mumble. *When will he be back?*

"He had business to attend to."

"When will he be back?"

Clara sighs again. "I don't know. I doubt he'll be gone much longer. But he doesn't tell me his schedule."

Ignoring the frustration that bubbles up in my chest, I stand and wipe my hands down on the leggings I've been provided. There's a closet full of jeans, shirts, leggings, dresses, and shoes in the room they have me in, but I've only taken advantage of the leggings and sweatshirts. I'm never going to be cold again if I can help it.

"I think I'd like you to take me on that tour you've been offering." Clara doesn't try to hide the surprise on her face. Part of me hates to give in, but they chained me to a bed for months and I want to see something that's beyond these four walls. Maybe I can begin planning my escape.

"Of course!" She looks so excited I almost feel guilty for thinking about escaping, but I ignore it. No one else is going to look out for me. I have to look out for myself. She motions for the door and I follow her out into the hallway. I've seen the hallway from my doorway, but that's all.

Clara motions to the room across from mine that always has the door closed. "That's Mr. Phoenix's room." I try to hide my shock. Phoenix is only about one hundred feet from me.

When he's here. Why do I care so much that he's not here? I should be happy.

Both of our rooms are at the end of the hallway. She leads the way to the stairs, but points out things as we go. "That's his upstairs office." I raise my eyebrows at that. *Does that mean he has a downstairs office?* "That's a guest bedroom. It's not normally used, though."

When we get to the end of the hallway, it looks out over the living room and splits with stairs on each side. If we keep going past the stairs, that leads to another hallway, but Clara doesn't take me that way. I stop to look at the artwork along each wall leading down the stairs. It's not the type of artwork I'd picture a man like Phoenix to own, let alone display.

Clara doesn't say anything about it, so I don't mention it. I make my way down the stairs slowly. My energy is returning, but I haven't done anything more than walk to the bathroom.

"Wow! I should have left my room sooner. The living room is beautiful." Clara smirks at me as she leads me through the living room to the kitchen. I pause at the entrance, completely overwhelmed by the grandeur of the kitchen.

I didn't grow up poor. My dad was wealthy, though it was by illegal means, but even we didn't have a kitchen that looked like this. It's white, black, and gray. Running my fingers along the countertops, I'm certain they are white marble with streaks of gray.

One side is the kitchen and the other side is a large dining table in front of a wall full of windows that looks out over a beautiful pool. I always felt like the kitchen was the heart of the home. I spent hours baking with my mom when I was a kid. Sighing, I refuse to allow my thoughts to stay there.

There's a large island with a sink. There are two ovens. I study everything. The stove, the extra ovens, the wine fridge, but I stop when I see the KitchenAid mixer. It's a beautiful shade of green and has a copper bowl.

It seems so out of place because of the color. Glancing at Clara, I motion to it. "Do you think Phoenix would let me use that?"

She smiles widely. "I think he would be okay with that."

"It seems odd to have this color instead of white, black, or even gray, considering that's the color scheme." A look of sadness covers Clara's face so briefly I think I may not have actually seen it.

"Well, there's somewhere else I'd like to show you that I think you'll love." I follow her out of the kitchen and down another hall. There's a closed door, and she points to it. "That's Mr. Phoenix's downstairs office." A few steps down, there's a double door. She opens it and I stare at the shelves and shelves of books.

"This is the library," she says in reverence, which it absolutely deserves. This house has everything I love. The very things I wanted growing up, but wasn't allowed to have. It gives me a different perspective of who Phoenix is, and I'm not sure how I feel about it.

"The sections are divided by genre. There's science fiction, horror, fantasy, romance, non-fiction, and so much more." She guides me down an aisle as I take it all in. Each wall has book shelves that go up to the ceiling. There's a ladder that can be rolled to reach the ones at the top. There are some bookshelves in the middle of the room as well.

She brings me to a window that has a window seat that looks like a cloud. The view shows the lake I can kind of see from my room. Clara grins at me as she leads me further into the room. There's a couch in front of a huge fireplace and in another corner there's a wicker swing. So many places to get lost in other worlds.

"Would you like to stay here while I finish my chores?" I'm sure I don't hide my excitement well from the smirk Clara tries to hide. "There's an intercom at the door. If you need me, just buzz. I'll get Phillip to make you some hot chocolate and bring it to you soon."

"Thank you." She walks out and I begin looking at all the books. This is where I'm going to be spending my days now. If I'm going to be held prisoner here and they aren't going to chain me to a bed, then I'm going to take full advantage of the amenities they offer.

I'm drawn to the fantasy bookshelves and begin scanning them until I find one that catches my eye. I climb onto the swing and pull a fluffy blanket over me as I settle in and get comfortable. Clara brings me a hot chocolate and I sip on it as I get lost in a world with faes. I'm about halfway through the book when my eyes get droopy, so I close it and decide to rest my eyes for a few minutes.

I must have done more than rest my eyes because when I blink them open, it's darker in the library. There's a glow coming from my left, so I glance in that direction to see Phoenix sitting on the couch in front of a lit fireplace. He's reading a book and hasn't noticed I'm awake yet, so it gives me a few minutes to study him.

He's wearing a black button-up shirt with the sleeves rolled up to his elbows and black pants. It contrasts with his ivory skin and dark blonde hair.

Why would he sit in here while I was sleeping? Did he just get home and came in here to check on me?

When we were at the academy together, he didn't pay much attention to me. We were in separate friend groups and many times I felt like he was determined to keep it that way. Although he did wind up in all of my classes. I was always the nerdy bookworm that lived in the library. He did spend time in the library, but he played lacrosse.

I'd go to a game here and there, because one of my best guy friends was on the team as well, but I knew nothing about lacrosse. So, I'd lose interest and wind up with my nose in a book. The only time he'd ever speak to me was to ask me what world I was living in that day.

Sighing, I try to remember anything after the party. Anything at all that would lead him to go out of his way to rescue me from that horrid place, but keep me here. What am I to him? I always thought he wasn't going to go down the same path as his father.

He gave the impression that he hated that lifestyle, but him keeping me prisoner says otherwise.

"You're awake." Phoenix's voice startles me from my thoughts and I focus on him as he turns toward me.

"I didn't mean to fall asleep. How long have you been here?"

He shrugs and places his book beside him. "An hour or so."

I nod slightly and sit up, catching my book before it slips off my lap and onto the floor. I don't know what to say. I've had all these questions running through my mind, but having him here in front of me makes it harder to speak my mind.

He motions to my book. "What world are you living in today?" I swallow and ignore the pang of nostalgia that hits me in the chest.

Glancing down, I lightly run my finger along the book. "A world of faes and fated mates." He adjusts himself on the couch, but I don't look up.

"Do you believe in fated mates?" That question brings my head up so I can search his gaze. His eyes are just as icy as they always are and his face is just as blank.

I shrug. "I always thought my parents were fated to be together, but turns out their love story was more of a tragedy."

His jaw tightens as he glances toward the fire. Everyone knows the story of Isabel and Marcus. When I was a little girl, I thought they were in love. Turns out, he forced her hand. He loved her and wouldn't take no for an answer. Mom always said she loved my father, but I don't know if she was just saying that or if it was true.

I suck in a breath and turn my thoughts off. I refuse to think of that now. "Where were you?" I ask, like I have any right to know. He turns back toward me and runs his left hand through his hair. Light hits the band on his ring finger. My heart drops to my stomach as I lean forward to make sure I'm seeing what I think I'm seeing. *Was that there before and I didn't notice?*

"You're married?" The question comes out without me even thinking about it.

He's married, but he kidnapped me. Why haven't I seen his wife? Where is she? This house is huge, but maybe he has another house. Maybe that's where he was at. This is his secret life and he won't let her come here.

He glances from me to his ring. He balls his hand into a fist and sighs. "I am." I stare at him, waiting for him to explain or give details about his wife, but he just returns my stare.

"How long have you been married?"

His eyes narrow, but he continues to stare at me. "Three and a half years."

My eyes widen in surprise. I wasn't expecting that. He's the same age as me, maybe a couple of months older, so that would mean he's been married since he was twenty.

"Oh." I adjust myself in the swing to give me something to do. "Maybe she's your fated mate." I want to go back to my room. I want to get out of this library. I'll ask him my questions tomorrow, but for now, I don't want to see him anymore. *Why does it bother me that he's married?*

"She is."

I climb off the swing and hold the book to my chest. *If she's his fated mate, why isn't she here with him? Where is she? What is he hiding?* I don't ask any of those things.

"I'm tired. I think I'll go to bed." He lets me leave, and for that I'm grateful.

Chapter 5

I sink down into the tub full of bubbles and allow the heat of the water to relax my muscles.

He's married. Did we go to school with her? Was it an arranged marriage?

One thing I remember from school is him wanting to get as far away from the family business as possible, but it doesn't seem he was successful.

Is she from another crime family that's powerful? Did they come together to become even more powerful? I don't remember seeing that ring before he left. But I was pretty out of it; maybe I missed it. Or was he not wearing it? If he swears she's his fated mate, why would he not wear the ring all the time? It doesn't make sense.

Closing my eyes, I push the thoughts out of my head. It doesn't concern me so I don't need to worry about it. Once I'm rested, I'll ask him my questions tomorrow.

Why am I here? Why did he rescue me only to keep me as his prisoner? What does he plan on doing with me?

I suck in a deep breath and slowly lower my head below the water. It's quiet. I wish quiet meant peace. Hands grab me under my arms and yank me out of the water. I come face to face with icy, angry eyes.

"What the hell are you doing?" I'm too disoriented to cover myself, but the moment his eyes trail along my naked skin I try to curl into myself. His hands tighten around my arms as he shakes me slightly. "Answer me, damn it."

"Let go. You're hurting me." He releases me immediately. Grabbing a towel, he throws it at me, but not before his eyes take in every sliver of skin that's on display. Glaring at him, I cover myself.

"Were you trying to drown yourself?" he accuses.

"No." I huff as I tuck the end of the towel between my breasts. "Jesus. I just wanted to hear nothing and the only time that happens is if I go underwater. I wasn't trying to drown myself." He glances from me to the tub and back at me. The ice in his eyes thaw a little as his gaze wanders down to the cleavage on display. He shouldn't be looking at me like that, but a thrill flows along my nerves.

"Why do you care if I drown myself?"

"McKenzie, I did not bring you here to kill you and I sure as hell don't need you dying on me either."

I roll my eyes. "Why? I'm sure your wife wouldn't want me here." I roll my lips between my teeth at my boldness, but don't take it back. He doesn't respond, simply crosses his arms over his chest and stares at me.

Sighing, I turn away from him and unplug the tub so the water will drain. "Why are you here, anyway?" I ask as I stand to face him again. He stares at me for several seconds before taking a deep breath and leaning against the counter.

"I came up here to see if you were hungry. I know you still can't eat much, but Clara said you were able to keep a banana down, so I asked Phillip to make some mashed potatoes."

"Oh. And you decided to just barge in here to ask that." I wave my hand toward the door and he practically growls at me.

"I knocked. You didn't answer. So here we are." He really looks worried, so I drop it for now. I don't miss how his eyes travel over my towel clad body again, and it takes everything not to say something else. *How would his wife feel if she knew he was ogling his prisoner?*

"I'd like some mashed potatoes, but I need to get dressed. So, if you could?" I motion for the door. He pushes away from the counter, giving me one last look.

"Alright. I'll let him know. Come down when you get dressed." He doesn't give me time to respond before he's out the door. Sighing, I dry myself off and stare at my pajamas. I don't feel like changing into clothes again, so I pull on my sleep shorts and shirt. If he doesn't like it, he doesn't have to look at me.

I'm not sure if he expects me downstairs right away, but I'm taking a few minutes to dry my hair. After spending months dirty, I have enjoyed getting to take luxury baths and showers. I've always loved my hair. It was the one thing about me that the girls back at school couldn't take away from me.

Taking my time blow drying my hair, I enjoy the feeling of the brush gliding through my hair and the heat of the blow dryer. When I'm done, I turn the hair dryer off before I unplug it, wrap the cord, and put it back in its spot. Turning around to head back downstairs, I shriek when I see Phoenix leaning against the door.

"What? Now that you're back, are you going to be around all the time?" I ask, annoyed.

He arches an eyebrow at me. "I came up here to tell you the mashed potatoes are ready. I didn't want to interrupt you."

I rub one of my bare feet with the other, and his eyes drop down my legs. *Maybe wearing pajamas wasn't a good idea.* "Well, lead the way, then."

His eyes snap up to mine and it seems the ice in them has thawed even more. He turns and walks out, and I scoff. Typical.

Why is he looking at me that way? It doesn't make sense after he said his wife is his soulmate.

I follow him out of the bathroom, through the bedroom, and to the hallway. He leads the way to the kitchen. There's a tall man with tawny skin, dark hair, beard, and mustache, stirring something on the stove. He looks up when we walk in and his eyes brighten.

"Miss McKenzie!" he exclaims. "Clara told me you were up and about I hate I missed you earlier. Glad you're beginning to feel better." His enthusiasm catches me off guard, but it brings a smile to my face. He's like a golden retriever. I glance at Phoenix quickly. I'm assuming this is Phillip, but I'm not certain.

"McKenzie, this is Phillip."

Phillip's smile falters a little, but he extends his hand and engulfs mine with his, then he pulls me into a hug. I'm surprised at the tears that burn my eyes. It only lasts for a few seconds, but I needed it. Blinking rapidly, I turn my attention to the pot.

"What are you making?"

"Pho. I think it's something you'll be able to keep down. The essence of the soup is the broth. If you wind up not being able to eat the meat and noodles, you can at least enjoy the broth."

I don't know what to say. I stare at the large pot as he stirs it again. "That's so thoughtful. Thank you."

He offers me a small smile. "It won't be ready until tomorrow. The broth takes some time to make. I'm hoping by the time it's ready, you'll be able to eat the meat. If not, it'll taste just as good with the rice noodles."

He pulls a bowl and a plate out of the oven. "Come on. You need to eat, so you'll keep getting stronger." Phoenix and I sit at the end of the island away from the stove. I take a small bite of the mashed potatoes and hum. They're buttery, creamy, and a piece of heaven.

"So good," I murmur before putting another spoonful in my mouth. Phillip throws a smile over his shoulder as he tends to his soup. I stare at Phoenix's plate with a little envy. He gets mashed potatoes, beef tips, green beans, and bread.

He scoops a small amount of beef tips onto my plate. My head snaps up to meet his gaze. "Just a small bite," he whispers. I don't look away immediately. This man confuses me.

Why is he being so nice to me? I'm scared to trust him. What if this is a ploy to get me to let my defenses down before he breaks me worse than the men where I was being held?

Looking away, I squeeze my eyes shut. At least they kept me drugged, so I wasn't aware of some of the things they were doing to me. I wonder if the drugs caused my memory loss, or I chose to block some of the things out.

Opening my eyes, I spear a piece of beef on to my fork. Bringing it to my mouth, I savor the taste before chewing and swallowing. My stomach hasn't cramped at all in the past day or so, but I've learned to eat slowly. It's a little harder with this meal.

"Will your wife be joining us for dinner?" I ask Phoenix. Phillip drops something, but I focus on Phoenix. His fork hovers in the air before he brings it to his mouth and slowly takes the food off. He stares at me as he chews his food.

"Why are you so interested in my wife, McKenzie?" His jaw ticks as he places his fork on his plate.

"I think it's interesting that I had no idea you were married. I haven't seen her since I've been here. I don't think you would have told me you were married if I didn't see your ring." I scoop up another spoonful of mashed potatoes as I glance at his ring finger.

He sighs and pushes his plate away. "I'm not hungry anymore." He wipes his mouth with a napkin and stands. I turn slightly to face him and grit my teeth at how he's avoiding the question.

"I don't know why you think I owe you any explanation about my life." He steps closer to my chair, making me have to crane my neck to look up at him. "Don't forget your position in this house. You're a prisoner. Nothing more." He turns on his heel and leaves the kitchen, heading down the hall that leads to his office and library.

Turning back around in my seat, I notice Phillip watching me. He has a look of pity. I sigh and return my attention back to my plate. *You're a prisoner. Nothing more.*

Well, this prisoner is going to find a way to escape.

Chapter 6

Dr. Chamberland comes for a visit the next morning. He checks all of my vitals and orders some blood work. All the while, Phoenix hovers watching his every move.

"Nurse Millie will be by later to take your blood."

"Why are you taking blood?" I ask. We're downstairs in the living room. I'm convinced angels crafted every piece of furniture Phoenix owns.

Everything is so soft and comfortable. I don't know why it surprises me so much, but I grew up around a hard man that had a modern style even if it was uncomfortable. Phoenix's home is beautiful and comfortable.

"It will get me a better view of your overall health," Dr. Chamberland answers. I nod, sighing at the idea of needles.

"How's your memory?" He packs his things up and turns to me. "Are you having any flashes or any memories surfacing?" The only flash I continuously have is Phoenix's tattooed hand pushing my hair behind my ear. But he hasn't done that once since I've been here. I don't think he ever did that when we were at school together.

"No. Nothing."

Phoenix is watching me closely, but I have been trying to ignore him and all the questions running through my head since yesterday. I'm beginning to wonder if his wife is sick or hurt or maybe she got kidnapped too and he thought he was rescuing her when, in fact, he rescued me. *Did he see an opportunity when he realized it was me?* I have so many theories, but I don't know if any of them could be possible.

"Well, don't give up. You had a traumatic experience. They may come back all at once or here and there." He looks at Phoenix. "It would be a good idea to let her see Dr. Pearl about her memory."

Phoenix nods slightly, but doesn't comment. I wipe my hands down my thighs and stand. "If that's all, I'd like to go to the library."

Dr. Chamberland chuckles. "One more question. How do you feel after you eat?"

"Like I want more. I'm trying to be careful, but it's hard not to stuff my face." My gaze bounces between him and Phoenix's intense stare. "I went so long without anything but cheese and bread..." I trail off with a shrug.

"And how long was that?"

I squint my eyes. *What does he mean?* "At least six months, right? I'm assuming I was kidnapped at the party, which was during the spring and it's fall now. So." I shrug again.

Dr. Chamberland doesn't respond, he just nods and writes some more notes. I was trying my best to ignore Phoenix, but my attention keeps being drawn back to him. His stare is hard, and his lips are in a thin, straight line.

"What month is it?" I haven't thought to ask until now. I was so focused on taking every day minute by minute I didn't care what month it was.

"October," Phoenix answers. I think back to the party.

"The party was in late March and I've been here for a few weeks, so six months is about right. Right?"

"I wasn't invited to the party you're talking about," Dr. Chamberland states. My eyes turn to Phoenix, but he doesn't respond. *Typical. He refuses to answer any of my questions, and I'm getting sick of it.*

"Well, if that's all?" I mean for it to come out as a statement, but it's more of a question. Dr. Chamberland nods. I give one more glance to Phoenix, but he simply stares. Turning toward the library, I sigh as I walk down the hallway. *Is he hiding something?*

That's the only conclusion I'm coming to because he's so closed off when I ask him questions. I normally keep the door open to the library, but I close it because I need some alone time. I know that won't stop Phoenix. If he wants to come in here, it's his right. This is his house, after all.

I've read a book almost every single day, but even with that pace, I'll never read every book that's in this library. Not that I want to. I like fantasy and I like romance. I think I can make it through all of those books if he keeps me here until the day I die.

Opening the book I was interrupted reading when Dr. Chamberland showed up, I realize about a chapter in that I didn't comprehend anything. I was so angry at Phoenix for leaving days on end, but now I wish he'd leave again. It's like I can feel him, even when he's not in the same room. I hate him for it.

I think back to school and realize it's always been like this with him. I tried my best to take classes I didn't think he'd take, but we always wound up in the same classes. He ignored me, but I have always been hyper aware of him. I hate it. He's married, and this semi-obsession I have with him is unhealthy.

When we were in school, I always felt guilty because I knew he was supposed to be my enemy. I could never find anything to hate him for, though. Unlike my father, there had to be a reason I hated someone. With a sigh, I slam my book shut. Leaving the swing, I walk over to the window seat and gaze out at the lake.

My father hated the Stones because they were "new money" and just getting into the business. They didn't respect him and his territory. So, I tried my best to stay away from Phoenix when I was in school. But I was always watching him. He was different from what I was used to. He was like a problem I needed to solve.

He tried to be who his father wanted him to be, but he also tried to be his own man. I'm sure his father expected him to take over the family business, but I remember him being vocal about never following in his father's footsteps. Considering I'm now his prisoner, I don't think it turned out that way.

"McKenzie?" I jump and turn around, coming face to face with the very person I can't stop thinking about.

"Phoenix," I reply. I have to get out of this house. "Can I go outside?" I ask him before he can say whatever he was going to say. He stares at me for a moment, then nods.

"Yes, but lunch is ready. Let's eat and then we'll go outside." I don't miss how he invited himself, but for now, I ignore it. Nodding once, I follow him out of the library and into the kitchen. I don't want to go outside with him, but beggars can't be choosers, and all that. When we get to the kitchen, Phillip makes our Pho and hands us chopsticks.

"Testing my fine motor skills?" I ask. Phillip winks at me before turning away. Phoenix has the audacity to snort. How very unlike him.

Phillip hands me a fork and a big spoon. "Just in case."

I smile at him before sitting next to Phoenix. My hand isn't shaking at all anymore, so I should be able to do this. I inhale and put the chopsticks between my fingers. I'm able to grab some noodles and meat and bring it to my mouth without dropping anything. It brings a relief I didn't know I needed.

Closing my eyes, I savor the taste. "This is so good, Phillip." I know I shouldn't eat fast, but it's difficult. Even with chopsticks. I'm tempted to bring the bowl to my lips and slurp it up. But I am a lady and that's not how a lady eats.

Sucking in a breath, I force myself to slow down. This is the first time I've been able to have a real meal, and it's probably the best meal in my life.

"I made a few egg rolls, too." Phillip brings over two egg rolls. He hands one to Phoenix and the other to me. "Only one for now, since you're just getting used to eating bigger meals." I stare at them. I know I'm drooling, but I can't help it. Taking a bite of the egg roll, I sigh.

"My goodness, Phillip. This is the best meal I've ever had." He smiles brightly before returning to cleaning up. Glancing at Phoenix, I realize he's watching me with an amused smile on his face. "Wow. I didn't realize you knew how to smile." The smile disappears quickly and I roll my eyes. "I shouldn't have said anything."

"Just because I don't like what you say doesn't mean you shouldn't say it." I pause with my chopsticks in front of my face. Arching an eyebrow, I place the food in my mouth and chew thoughtfully.

"My father would disagree."

"Your father is an asshole."

Turning my head to look at him, I watch his profile as he eats. "I know you don't like my father."

He scoffs. "That's putting it lightly." I think back on anything my father could have done to him. He's a hard man, but he's my father. I shrug and sigh.

"I have mixed feelings about him. I love him, but there have been times I've hated him. So I understand why you feel the way you do."

He shakes his head and pushes his bowl away. "Thanks, Phillip, that was delicious." With that, he turns on his heel and makes his exit.

"You said I could go outside," I call after him.

"I'll send Rex to escort you."

I scowl at his retreating back before turning to face Phillip. "I hate when he does that." Phillip offers a sympathetic smile. "Who's Rex?"

"I'm Phoenix's head of security." I nearly jump out of my seat at the booming voice behind me. Turning, I frown as I study him. He looks like a bulldog. Well, maybe not exactly like a bulldog.

"I'm not a babysitter," he states.

Turning back toward my bowl, I lift one shoulder. "I'm not the one that requested you. So, you need to take that up with your boss. I'm perfectly capable of walking the grounds by myself."

"No," he says in a booming voice, and I jump again.

"Do you have to talk so loud? I'm right here."

Phillips laughs. Rex growls. I huff and turn back to my bowl of soup and finish it. Sitting back after I'm finished, I sigh and wonder briefly how this trip outside is going to turn out.

"Thank you, Phillip. If there are leftovers, can I have that for dinner?" Phillip smiles at my compliment and nods.

"Of course. It's a big pot. It'll last for a couple of days." He turns back to the oven and my gaze lands on the mixer.

"Phillip?" He turns to face me again with a raised eyebrow. "Do you think I could bake some cookies tomorrow?" I gesture toward the mixer.

His eyes brighten at my question. "Of course. What kind would you like to make? I can make sure we have all the ingredients."

"Chocolate chip. I used to bake with my mom and that was always my favorite."

He smiles and rubs his hand over the counter like he's raking up crumbs. "Perfect. I'm sure we already have the ingredients, but I'll double check."

I bring my bowl over to the sink and offer him a grateful smile. Waving at him, I walk toward the doors that lead out to the pool, Rex following after me. Stepping out, I breathe in the fresh air. I wish I could remember the last time I was outside.

Well, the last time I remember was the night of the party. My father and I argued all the way to the party and I couldn't get out of the car fast enough. Stepping off the back dock, I take in the beauty that is the swimming pool.

It's luxurious. It has a zero entry with two lounge chairs you could lay in. The pool gradually gets deeper and leads to a secluded cave with a waterfall. I'd live out here during the summer if this belonged to me.

"The pool is heated," Rex says. I look at him over my shoulder. His hands are clasped in front of him as he watches me. He didn't have to tell me that, but he obviously saw how much I love it.

"Good to know. I'll read out here on warmer days with my feet in the water."

He nods once. "Don't come out here by yourself. Always let Mr. Stone or I know."

Turning to face him, I cross my arms over my chest. "This place is locked down tighter than Fort Knox. I don't need a babysitter."

He arches one eyebrow at me. "You'll have a babysitter as long as Mr. Stone wants you to have one." I slap my hands against my outer thighs in frustration. With a groan, I turn toward the lake and walk away. I know Rex follows, but I ignore him as I take in my surroundings.

The grounds are beautiful. There's a tennis court close to the pool with hydrangeas separating the two. There are hydrangeas everywhere. Stopping at one of the bushes, they're blue, pink, purple, white, and some have a yellowish tint. I fight the urge to pick them to make a bouquet.

Continuing toward the lake, the muscles in my legs begin to ache and I have to focus on my breathing. I am really out of shape and it's a long way to the lake. Finally giving up, I sit down on the grass still a ways from the water. Rex settles next to me, surprising me.

"I can't wait until I start feeling normal again. Whatever that is."

"You will. You just started eating normally. Give it time." Sadness settles in my stomach like a boulder. Pulling my legs into my chest, I rest my chin on my knees. There's a boat out on the water with someone fishing.

"Does someone live close by?" I ask, motioning to the guy in the boat. With how crazy Phoenix is about security, I can't imagine he'd let just anyone near his house, even if it's on the lake.

"That's old man Larry. He's a grumpy asshole," Rex grumbles, but it sounds good natured. Filing that away for later, I can't ignore how low my energy is.

"I think I'm going to take a nap."

Rex stands and offers his hand to me. I take it begrudgingly and let him help me up, dusting off my butt. My steps are slow as we walk back up to the house, but Rex doesn't complain. He keeps his strides short.

Guess I won't be planning my escape until I can walk further than a hundred feet.

Chapter 7

The next morning, I wake up before Clara brings me breakfast. She usually brings me breakfast in my room and I eat while staring out my window. But today I hurriedly throw on some leggings and an oversized T-shirt. My heart beats in excitement as I walk quickly down the stairs. I'd run, but I'm not sure I'm ready to experiment with that.

Pulling my hair up into a messy bun, I enter the kitchen and stop. Phillip and Clara are kissing. I clear my throat, trying to announce my presence. They separate quickly and turn to me. Clara tries to step away from him, but he wraps his arm around her waist and holds her close. A grin spreads over my face as Clara's face turns a bright shade of red.

"You two?" I ask. Clara's eyes flit up toward Phillip and back to me. They both nod and I chuckle. "That's great." Clara sighs, and Phillip kisses the side of her forehead. I squint at them, unable to stop smiling. "I can't believe you didn't tell me."

I lean my elbows against the counter as I wait for an answer. Phillip takes a deep breath. "You've had a rough time, so we've tried to be sensitive to that."

I wave my hand at them. "You deserve to be happy. Don't try to hide that on my account."

Clara's face brightens. "What are you doing up so early?"

"I asked Phillip yesterday if I could bake some cookies today. I was a little excited to get started." Clara chuckles and shakes her head. Phillip turns toward the oven and puts some food on a plate. My mouth waters at the sight of eggs and pancakes.

"Of course, but first you eat." He brings the plate to me. I dance in my seat when I see the bacon.

"Eat slow," Clara reminds me, but grins at my excitement as she places a cup of coffee next to my plate. I can't decide what I want to eat first, so I put a piece of bacon on a pancake and roll it up. Clara places a small bowl of syrup next to my plate. I smile at her in thanks, wondering how she knew what I was about to do. I dip the pancake in it and take a small bite.

The buttery goodness of the pancake mixed with the salty crunch of the bacon is perfection. I bring my fingers to my lips and kiss my fingertips. Phillip chuckles and begins to fill another plate with food. Every time I take a bite of food, I wiggle in my seat like Winnie the Pooh does when he's excited to get his honey.

"Will you be eating in here, sir? Or your office?" Phillip asks. My head whips around to see Phoenix standing in the doorway in pajama pants and no shirt. *Holy shit!* He steps into the kitchen and I swallow the lump that has formed in my throat.

A tattoo covers his right arm from his wrist to his shoulder and on to his right pec. He has a wolf, bear, eagle, and a snake, all in an intricate design. It's so beautiful. Like a story inked onto his skin. On his left pec, there's a compass that turns into an interesting design that reminds me of dragon scales.

"You're staring," Phoenix murmurs as he walks in and sits next to me. I close my mouth and turn, trying my best to ignore him, but it's impossible.

"The last time I saw you, you didn't have that many tattoos." I eat some of my scrambled eggs as Phillip places a plate in front of Phoenix.

He doesn't respond as he begins to eat. I take a sip from the coffee Clara brought me and hum at the delicious, deep, rich taste of it. It feels like I haven't had coffee in ages, so I'm going to enjoy every drop.

"What are you doing down here? I thought you normally take your breakfast in your room?" Phoenix asks. It makes me wonder if he would have gotten dressed if he had known I was going to be down here.

"I asked Phillip yesterday if I could bake some cookies today." I shrug as I take another bite of my eggs. "I was excited," I say around a mouthful of eggs. Not very ladylike, but I don't care. He kidnapped me, so he has to deal with the consequences of his decisions.

He hums as he takes a few more bites of his food. "What kind of cookies are you going to bake?"

I stop in the middle of me rolling another piece of bacon in a pancake and glance at him. *He's interested in what I'll be baking?*

"Nothing fancy. Just chocolate chip cookies." One side of his mouth tips up as he glances at me. I have to force myself not to allow my eyes to drift downward.

"Chocolate chip cookies are my favorite. Especially if they're soft and gooey." I make a mental note of that and turn back toward my plate before I lose the fight with keeping my eyes from taking in his tattoos again.

"Maybe I'll let you have some," I murmur as I take a bite of my rolled up pancake. He scoffs and continues to eat.

We eat in a comfortable silence and after a few seconds, I find it odd how easy this is. It reminds me of the days when we'd find ourselves at the same table in the library because it was so full. I never felt uncomfortable sharing a table with him unless one of his many admirers would try to join.

After another bite, I have to force myself to listen to my body and push my plate away. I want to eat everything. It's so good, but I remind myself I'll be able to have it tomorrow if I want. Phillip is kind hearted and would probably make this exact breakfast for me every day if I wanted him to.

"Had enough?" Phoenix asks.

I nod, looking at my plate longingly. "It's really hard for me to not finish it, though." He chuckles as Clara comes over and grabs my plate.

"Phillip will make it for you tomorrow if you want it again." I give Phoenix a sideways look as he voices my exact thoughts. It shouldn't make my pulse speed up the way it does.

"What are you doing today?" I ask. Like I have any right to know. He raises his eyebrows at my question.

"I have some business I need to attend to in the city." He takes a sip from his coffee. "I'll be gone the majority of the day. Rex will be here, though." I want to ask him what business he has to attend to. Glancing at the ring on his finger, I wonder if he's going to visit his wife. "I'll be back for dinner."

I nod and stand, walking over to the mixer. Disappointment skates across my skin like a spider. *Why do I feel this way?* While he's away, I can check out more of the grounds to see if there's a way for me to get away. I have no idea where we are, though. Turning back toward him, I bite the inside of my cheek before sucking in a breath of courage.

"What city are you going to?" I ask.

He tilts his head and studies me. "Savannah."

I don't know why I'm surprised, but I am. My father's territory is in Savannah. He controls the ports in Savannah. My mom fell in love with Savannah because of its history and southern charm, my father fell in love with it for a completely different reason.

I don't respond, trying to think how far we are from Savannah. We could be fifteen minutes or an hour away for all I know. I turn my attention to Phillip, trying to shake off the unease of why Phoenix would be going to Savannah. *Is he trying to take control of the ports?*

"I'm ready. Can you show me where the ingredients are?"

Phillip smiles brightly at me and leads me to a door at the other end of the kitchen. When he opens it, my eyes widen. It's a huge pantry and is stocked with everything you could possibly need.

"I have everything organized in here, so you should be able to find everything you need. If you ever find you're running low on something, add it to this board here." He points to a white board with a list he's already started. "By running low, I mean if it's the last bag or box of something. I cook breakfast, lunch, dinner, and the occasional party. So, I try not to run out of anything ever."

The occasional party? How occasional is that, exactly? I don't ask because I don't really want to know. At least not right now.

"There's also another refrigerator here." He walks me around a corner and I look from it to him and then back again. It looks like one of those refrigerators you see at a liquor store that holds beer. From the glass door, I can see it's stocked with anything and everything we could possibly need.

"You're going to have to kick me out of your kitchen," I tell him.

He chuckles and shakes his head. "I would never do that. As long as I get to taste test everything you make."

I hold my hand out to him. "Deal." He grins and extends his hand to shake mine. We walk out of the pantry. "Especially since you're making me stronger every day with all the meals you cook." I wish I could express how thankful I am for everything. Even if I am a prisoner, at least I'm not chained to a bed laying in my own filth.

Phoenix isn't in the kitchen any longer. I ignore the twinge in my chest as I take out the ingredients I need for the cookies.

"I'm off to do my chores for the day," Clara says as she walks back into the kitchen carrying an empty bucket filled with cleaning supplies. Phillip meets her halfway and kisses her on the forehead. Something close to feeling homesick hits me in the stomach, and I look away.

I want someone to look at me like that. Has anyone ever looked at me like that? I had one boyfriend at the academy, but he was more of a friend than anything else. He was convenient, but there wasn't passion or anything even close to it. We never even broke up, we just went our separate ways after graduation.

"I'll save you a cookie."

Clara smirks at me. "Just one?"

I return her smile. "Maybe two." I squint my nose at her and she shakes her head at me in amusement. She and Phillip begin doing their daily routine while I measure the ingredients to mix everything. After I'm done, I turn the oven on to begin warming up and take out the cookie sheets.

I don't have a recipe I read from. I know this one from memory. It's the same recipe my mom taught me when I was a little girl and where my love of baking first began. I turn the mixer on after I add the ingredients. I lean against the counter as I watch it.

Arms wrap around my waist and pull me against a strong chest. "Mmmm. My favorite." I place my hands on his hands and chuckle.

"The cookies or me?"

His lips latch on to the sensitive spot on my shoulder. "I think I need to taste both to make that decision."

A flight of a thousand hummingbirds takes off in my stomach as he licks my neck and pulls my earlobe between his teeth.

"McKenzie!" My eyes fly open and I look up at the voice. *How did I end up on the floor?* Rex kneels down in front of me, his eyes assessing me.

"What happened?" His voice is rough, but not booming like it did yesterday. I open my mouth and close it again. I don't know what happened. *Did I just have a memory?* I try to bring it back, but it evades me like a cloud of smoke.

"McKenzie? I need to know you're alright." I focus on Rex and realize he has a phone to his ear.

"Is she alright?" Phoenix barks. Rex puts his phone on speaker.

"I'm… I'm alright." I swallow, trying to get rid of the dryness in my mouth. "I think I had a memory." Rex goes perfectly still, and Phoenix is silent for several seconds.

"What was the memory?" Phoenix asks. I close my eyes, still remembering the feeling of strong arms wrapped around me and the swoop of my stomach, knowing I was about to feel amazing. "McKenzie?" Phoenix's voice is strained.

"I was baking cookies." Opening my eyes, I study Rex to see what his reaction will be.

"You were baking cookies?" Phoenix asks. I run my hand through my hair, but my fingers get tangled in the messy bun I put it in earlier. Yanking the hair band out, I take a deep breath. The passion I was just wondering about, have I experienced that? *Who was it with?*

"Yes. Someone was with me, but I don't know who it was. I know I knew them, though." There's another long stretch of silence.

"That's good," Phoenix finally says. "We'll tell Dr. Chamberland when he checks on you in a few days." There's a slight pause. "I'll call Dr. Pearl today to schedule an appointment with her." I put my hand on the floor and push myself up. That feeling of being homesick hits me again.

"Will you be back today?" I ask Phoenix. I blink my eyes quickly. *Why do I feel this way?*

"Yes. I'll be home in time for dinner." I think he already told me that, but I guess I needed to hear it again.

"Okay," I whisper. "I guess I'll save you some chocolate chip cookies for dessert."

He chuckles. "My second favorite dessert." There's someone talking in the background. "I have to go. I'll see you tonight." He hangs up before I can respond. *I wonder what his first favorite dessert is?* Rex pockets his phone and looks from me to the mixer that's still going. I turn around and cut it off.

"I'll save you some too, Rex."

"That's very kind of you, Miss McKenzie."

I arch an eyebrow at him over my shoulder. "Don't be nice to me just because I had an episode."

His eyes narrow. "You didn't have an episode. You had a memory. And I can be nice to you when I want to. It's my prerogative." He sounds so offended, I smirk.

"Sorry. Didn't mean to offend you." I suck in a breath. I'm letting my guard down with everyone in this house. I need to stop. Ignoring Rex, I grab a spatula and make sure the cookie batter mixed well before I begin scooping it out onto the cookie sheet.

Placing the cookie sheet in the oven, I set the timer and walk to the library to grab a book to read while they're baking. I grab the book I've been reading and walk out, noticing Phoenix's office door is cracked open.

Glancing down the hallway, I listen to see if I hear anyone. Taking a deep breath to try to calm my racing heart, I slip into his office. I've only been in here once. He told me I could come in anytime I'd like, but I don't know if that meant only if he was here or not.

I probably know the answer to that, but ignore it for now. Now that I'm in here, I'm not sure what to do. *Should I try to look for clues about how he found me or even why he took me?* Tiptoeing to his desk, I try to open one of the drawers, but it's locked. I try the other drawers, but they're all locked, too.

He's never left his office door open before. Was he in a hurry to leave? It doesn't seem like something he'd forget to do.

Turning around to look at the bookshelves behind his desk, I look at the titles to see what all he has in here. Maybe one of them will give me a clue. I don't touch anything, so I don't put anything out of place. I know I only have a few more minutes before the cookies will be done, so I scan my eyes quickly. I stop on a book that isn't flush with the other books. Glancing behind me to make sure I haven't been caught, I slowly slide it out.

It's a journal. Flipping through it, I stop when I see a photo stuck in it like a bookmark. Glancing over my shoulder one more time, I take it out and my heart stops.

The picture is folded in half longways. It's of me and Anna, my best friend from the academy. We're in our uniforms laughing at something. It was folded with Anna facing forward. I haven't talked to her in years. We drifted apart, just like I did with everyone else at school.

Is Anna Phoenix's wife? I want to pocket the picture, but I know better than to leave any evidence behind that I was in here. Looking at the photo one more time, I take a deep breath and put everything back where I found it. I even leave the book out a little. Quickly grabbing the book I got from the library, I walk to the door and peek out.

No one is in the hallway, so I leave Phoenix's door cracked a little and walk back to the kitchen. It wouldn't surprise me if Anna married Phoenix. She always had a crush on him, just like our other friend Timothy and every other girl in our class, and some of the guys, too. I make it to the oven just as the timer goes off. Sitting my book on the counter, I grab an oven mitt and take the cookies out.

Did Anna get kidnapped too? Maybe I need to figure out what happened to me and how I ended up in that godforsaken place before I try to escape. Obviously, I won't get any answers from anyone else.

Chapter 8

Every day I bake something different. I've baked chocolate chip cookies, chocolate lava cake, blueberry muffins, and today I'm making red velvet cupcakes. Phoenix has been really busy this week and has been gone almost every day before I wake up. He always makes it home to eat dinner, though.

Home? Is that what this place is becoming to me? I haven't had another memory. Dr. Chamberland came to check on me yesterday, along with Dr. Pearl. She told me it would be a good idea to write the memories as they come and as soon as it happens so I don't forget. I'm not ready to begin talking about anything, so she said she'll check in on me once a month until I'm ready.

Last night at dinner, Phoenix gave me the journal that I leafed through in his office. Was it a coincidence? I'm not sure, but I kept my face neutral as he handed it to me. When we were done eating, I went to my room and wrote down the memory I had a few days ago.

I wish I could remember more. The sound of the man's voice is fuzzy, and I never looked at him. Sighing, I stop the mixer and begin scooping cake batter into the cupcake liner.

"Red velvet cake?" Phoenix asks and I nearly drop the spoon. Turning to face him, he raises his eyebrows at me.

"What are you doing here? I thought you were gone," I ask as I turn my focus back to the cupcakes. He walks over and leans his hip against the counter, crossing his tattooed arms over his chest. I ignore how his T-shirt clings to his biceps. He's normally dressed in black slacks and a button-up shirt, but today he's in sweats and a T-shirt.

I'm in sweats and a T-shirt too, but I look frumpy while he looks like a dream. He sticks his finger out to scrape out some of the batter, but I slap his hand. My eyes widen at my reaction, but I'm in it now, so I go with it.

"Wait until they're done," I scold. Glancing at him out of the corner of my eye to gauge his reaction, I'm surprised by the small smile on his lips. I wish he'd step closer to me. I wish he'd hang out with me all day. I force myself to look at his wedding band and remind myself he's taken.

Clearing my throat, I continue to scoop batter into the cupcake pan. "Umm... I was wondering. Where is your wife?" He tenses next to me and pushes away from the counter. *Why did I say anything? He was at ease.* It's for the best, though. I needed a reminder of where I stand with him. *I'm his prisoner, nothing more.*

"She's gone," he answers. I pause, surprised he answered my question. After the last one is filled, I take the pan to the oven, put it in, and set the timer. Turning my attention to him, I study him for a moment as he leans back against the kitchen island.

"Where did she go?" A look of pain crosses his face.

Did she leave him, or is she dead? She's gone could mean a lot of different things.

"She was kidnapped," he answers. *Oh god. He was looking for her and he found me instead.* I want to ask if Anna is his wife, but then he'll know I was snooping in his office.

"I'm sorry," I whisper. He doesn't respond, not that I expected him to. I'm at a loss for words when Phillip walks into the kitchen.

"Mr. Stone. Miss McKenzie," he greets us.

I tip my lips up in a small smile. "Hi Phillip."

He glances back and forth between the two of us. "I'm grabbing my list to go grocery shopping. I'll be back in time to cook lunch."

"Don't rush Phillip. I'm sure we can manage if you're not back in time," Phoenix tells him. *So, he will be here all day.* Phillip thinks about it for a few seconds before nodding.

"Okay. I think I'll stop by the restaurant and give them my newest recipe." Phoenix nods and Phillip walks to the pantry to grab his list.

"Restaurant?" I ask. Phoenix runs his hand over his head and crosses his feet.

"I own a few restaurants in Savannah. Phillip creates recipes for them and trains the chefs." My mouth forms a small O.

"I'd like to go to one of them." Phoenix stiffens. And that's my answer. I wave my hand at him. "It's okay. I didn't think when I said that." Disappointment settles in my stomach like acid. *I really am his prisoner.*

"We can go."

I tilt my head at him. "What?" I can't hide the surprise in my voice.

"If we go, we will have security. More than what you have here. Understand?" I nod eagerly. Getting out of this house, away from this place, I didn't realize how much I needed it.

"We'll go tonight. Be ready by six." I break out into a big smile, and Phoenix shakes his head at me.

"All I have are leggings and T-shirts," I tell him.

"Have you gone into your closet at all?" he asks. I have, but I've refused to look at everything. Plus, what's the point of wearing nice clothes when all I do is bake, read, and occasionally go for walks with Rex? I wonder if Phoenix will go for a walk with me today instead. Shaking my head, I push that thought away quickly.

"I'll go look. Is there a dress code?"

He shakes his head. "No. You could go in leggings and a T-shirt and it would be fine."

I huff and roll my eyes. "What are you going to wear?"

"What—"

"Let me guess, slacks and a button-up shirt?" I interrupt him, and he narrows his eyes at me. I laugh at his expression, and he pushes away from the island and walks toward me. My breath catches in my throat as I take a step back and run into the counter.

"Are you making fun of me?" he asks. His hands land on either side of me, caging me in. I swallow and lift my head to look up at him.

"I'd never make fun of you." My voice comes out breathy, but I can't find it in me to care.

"I'll make sure I roll up my sleeves." I want to crawl into a cabinet and hide. He's noticed me staring at his arms. He's hard not to stare at when he's in a room. "As long as you wear your hair down."

He lifts his hand and pulls at the hair tie around my messy bun, releasing it so my hair falls around my shoulders. I can't seem to find my voice, so I simply nod. *He likes my hair?* It is the one unique thing about me.

"Good girl." He turns and walks out of the kitchen. My knees give out and I slide down the counter to the floor.

I am so screwed. I can't have these feelings. Whatever these feelings are. Lust? Like? Definitely lust. When's the last time I had sex? Have I had sex? I can't remember. Maybe in college?

I take several deep breaths and push myself off the floor. My heart is racing, but I ignore it as I finish adding the batter to the rest of the cupcake liners. Leaning back against the kitchen island to wait for the first batch to finish, I put the hair tie on my wrist and snap it a couple of times.

My wrists healed nicely. I have a couple of scars, but it's not as bad as I thought it would be. I'm still a little self conscious about the track marks on the inside of my arm. Those have healed too, but there were a lot of them and they're noticeable. I refused to wear short sleeves the first couple of weeks, but I forced myself to get over that. Dr. Chamberland said they would heal too, but I might have a couple of scars.

I'm not letting whoever kidnapped me control me. Phoenix walks back into the kitchen. His eyes trail over me and my stomach flips.

"Not reading?" I shake my head. He grabs a glass and fills it with water. "How long before the cupcakes are done?"

The timer goes off just as he says it. "This batch is done," I answer as I take them out and put the second batch in, setting the timer again and leaning against the counter. "This one will take about fifteen minutes. They'll have to cool before I can put icing on them." He takes a sip from his glass and I watch as his Adam's apple bobs. Every part of this man is finely tuned.

Pushing away from the kitchen island, I grab the bowl out of the mixer and begin to wash it. I need my hands to be busy and my eyes focused on something else besides him. After I wash the bowl, I grab the icing out of the fridge.

"I made the icing yesterday, but I need to mix it to soften it," I ramble. A finger dips into the icing and I turn in time to see him sticking it in his mouth. My jaw drops. "I can't believe you did that."

He pops his finger out of his mouth. *Oh god. What the hell is happening to me?* My body temperature is rising and there's nothing I can do about it. *Unless...* I stop that thought in its tracks and turn around.

Why is he here? He needs to go away. Why did I want him to stay earlier?

"I'm not sure I'm ready to go out," I murmur.

"You are." Tilting my head to look at him. His arms are crossed over his chest again. I swear he's doing that on purpose. Running my fingers through my hair, I grimace. I'll need to wash my hands before I ice the cupcakes.

"What makes you so sure?" I ask as I attach the bowl to the mixer to soften the icing.

"You were excited about it earlier. Go with your first instinct. You've been cooped up in this house for two months." I'm thankful he doesn't mention the months I was chained up.

"You didn't seem too thrilled about me asking."

He doesn't respond, instead taking a step toward me and leveling his eyes with mine. "This isn't about me." I pull my bottom lip between my teeth and his eyes drop to my mouth quickly before he takes a step back. "I'm going to watch a movie. Come watch it with me once the other cupcakes are done."

He heads down the hallway with the library and his office. Further down that hall is the theater. He didn't wait for me to answer. *What if I choose not to go? Will he make me?*

He wouldn't. I've never had alone time with him. Not like this. He's intruded on my reading time. I've woken up and seen him sitting in the chair in my room, and he does eat dinner with me most nights. But somehow this is different.

Mixing the icing, I place a paper towel over it when I'm done and wait for the timer to go off for the others. Checking the cupcakes I've already taken out to see if they're cooled enough. I go ahead and pipe icing on them and place them on the cupcake stand Phillip found me earlier.

When the timer for the second batch goes off, I take them out so they can cool and turn off the oven. Taking a deep breath, I turn toward the hallway Phoenix disappeared down and put one foot in front of the other. I had every intention of going to the library, but here I am, staring at the back of Phoenix's head. He's sitting in the middle of the theater.

There are five rows, six seats in each row. The seats look like they might recline, but I can't be too sure. "Come on," he says without turning around. *How did he know I was here?*

I huff and walk down the aisle until I'm at the end of the row he's sitting in. "I won't bite."

I'm not so sure about that. I lick my lips and get up the courage to take the seat next to him. "What are we watching?"

"The first *Fast and Furious.*"

"Aren't there like a thousand of those?" I put my foot on the chair and fold it under me as I sit.

"That's why I said it's the first." I chuckle and settle in as he starts the movie. I watch in disbelief. I've seen this movie, but it's been ages.

"That is so unrealistic," I gripe as I motion to the screen.

"How do you know?"

I make a face at him. "When's the last time you drove under an eighteen wheeler?"

"Yesterday."

I stare at him, trying to decide if he's joking or not. "How low is your car?"

His tongue snakes out and licks his lips before he turns to face me. He leans over the armrest and it takes everything I have not to lean away. "Which one?"

I roll my eyes. "That is not the flex you think it is."

He throws his head back in laughter. I grin as I admire him. His guard is down. He doesn't have that stoic look on his face. I like this Phoenix. His eyes sparkle as he focuses on me.

"There are a lot of things I can do with my car." He smirks at me before turning his attention back to the screen. "And in it."

Did all the air get sucked out of the room? I'm hot. Standing quickly, I turn to walk away, then turn back, then away.

"What are you doing?" There's humor in his voice.

"I think the rest of the cupcakes are cool. I'm going to go put the frosting on." Before he can respond, I hightail it out of there. *Please don't follow me. Please don't follow me.* It's a mantra in my head. When I get to the kitchen and he doesn't show up, I breathe a sigh of relief.

After frosting the rest of the cupcakes, I grab one and walk back to the theater. He's still in there watching the movie. His lips tip up in a small smile when I hand him the cupcake.

"Thanks." Everything in me wants to stay, but I can't. He affects me too much and I can't let that happen. I'm his prisoner. He made that clear from the first night he brought me here.

"You're welcome. I'm going to go get ready." He doesn't call me out on the fact that I still have hours. He simply nods and takes a bite of his cupcake. I stare for another second before turning and heading to my room.

Why is he keeping me here? What does he want with me? I need to focus on the fact that I am his prisoner. Even if he treats me better than my last kidnappers. Maybe I can use this outing as an opportunity to look for ways to escape. I have to get out of here before I become too comfortable.

Chapter 9

Sinking down into the hot suds, I sigh as the heat relaxes my muscles. There's this feeling I have right behind my belly button I can't quite place. It's sadness, mixed with what feels like being homesick and also like I'm forgetting something.

I snort and lean my head against the lip of the tub. Of course I'm forgetting something. I can't remember the six months before I was kidnapped. I play the night of the party over in my head.

How is it I can remember up until the crunch of the rocks under the tires of our car and not anything after? Was I kidnapped at the party? Would Phoenix know the answer to that?

I haven't asked a lot of questions because I didn't think he'd answer them, but I'm beginning to wonder if that's all in my head. He's surprised me with how kind he has been. He doesn't treat me like I'm his enemy or his prisoner.

Closing my eyes, I take a deep breath and sink under the water. The quiet doesn't bring the peace I crave, but it helps drown out the constant barrage of thoughts so I can focus.

"I don't understand why I need to wear this." Father forced me to put on this skin tight black dress with a slit that reaches the top of my thigh. He also gave me a necklace that looks like a ribbon, it's red, tight, and uncomfortable.

"You've been begging for years to go to one of these parties. You must dress the part." I'm hugging the door on the other side of the backseat. Unease slithers up my spine. He's not telling me something, but I don't know what it is. He's right, I've always wanted to go to one of these parties and I was always told the same thing. One day, when I'm old enough.

I just turned twenty-three. I guess that's old enough. Ivan, our driver, turns down a road that's lined with rocks and pebbles. The sound of them under the tires makes the hair on the back of my neck stand on end.

"You are to stay with me the entire time. You don't speak to anyone unless spoken to." I don't know how to respond. Why did I want to go to this party? It doesn't seem like it's going to be much fun. "Do you understand?" Father asks impatiently.

I nod, unable to speak. Breathe in. One. Two. Three. Breathe out. Three. Two. One. My heart stops racing just as Ivan pulls up to the front door, where the valet is waiting.

"Here." Father thrusts a mask at me. It's red and matches the necklace he told me I had to wear. He pulls on a white mask. "Put it

on now." His voice doesn't leave room for argument. I slide the mask into place and swallow. The valet opens my door and extends his hand to help me out of the car.

Placing my hand in his, my fingers shaking slightly, I allow him to help me out of the car. Stepping onto the cobblestones, I wait for my father to take my arm and lead the way. Why do I feel like I'm walking the plank with hundreds of sharks swimming under my feet, ready to eat me alive?

Pushing myself out of the water, I gasp for breath and rub at the sting in my eyes from the suds. "Oh my god." Standing, I grab the towel I placed on the floor next to the tub and wrap it around me, not bothering to dry off. Racing out of the bathroom and bedroom, I run straight into a hard chest. Phoenix's hands come up and grasp my upper arms, steadying me.

"McKenzie? Are you alright?" I'm dripping all over his floors, but he doesn't seem to care. His eyes rake over me, his pupils dilating slightly. Maybe I should have taken the time to put on more than a towel.

"What did my father do?" I ask.

The grip he has on my arms tightens slightly before he releases me. "Did you have a memory?"

I begin pacing as I clutch the towel between my breasts so it doesn't fall. "Oh my god," I whisper it over and over again.

I remembered the party, or at least I thought I had. I thought I had argued with my father over me wanting to wear the dress, but he forced me to wear that dress. Because at one time I didn't feel comfortable wearing clothes like that. After college, though, I did want to break out of my shell, but the way he acted that night made me uncomfortable. So, I didn't want to wear it. Not with the way he was acting.

"My father made me go to that party." I run my hand through my sopping wet hair. I'm making such a mess, but I don't care. When Phoenix doesn't speak, I finally stop and stare at him. "Why? Why did he make me go to that party?"

Phoenix closes his eyes and sucks in a breath through his nose. "You don't want to know, McKenzie."

I glare at him. "Tell me, Phoenix. I deserve to know."

He runs his hand up his jaw. "He made you go to sell you."

My heart breaks into a thousand little pieces. Like a vase that's been thrown against a wall in anger. My father sold me. The man who used to push me on the swing in our backyard. The man who would sneak me a cookie when my mother said no.

My mouth opens, but no sound comes out. My face and chest are hot with so many emotions. "So, I wasn't kidnapped. I was bought?"

Phoenix exhales, his hands balling into fists. I stare at him, pleading with my eyes that he tells me the truth.

"You were kidnapped, but not from the auction," he says. His voice is devoid of all emotion. *Auction?*

"I... What?"

I don't understand. He will come for me. He always comes for me. He's *not my father. Who is* he? *So, if I wasn't kidnapped from the party... auction. It was an auction. I was bought.*

"You bought me." The truth is clear in the way he squares his shoulders. The way there's a brief flash of regret. Maybe?

"Yes, your father sold you to me. You were kidnapped from me."

I stare at him, my already broken heart stutters. This man I had a crush on for years bought me at an auction I didn't know I was going to. *Why?* "You bought me," I say again. He doesn't say anything. Simply watches me as I process the information he just told me.

"I was kidnapped from you? By who?" His fists get so tight his knuckles turn white. I'm obviously asking questions he doesn't want to answer. And he doesn't; he simply stares at me. I step up to him, tilting my head back to glare at him. "I deserve to know the truth." I swallow the lump in my throat. "Please. I need answers."

"Your father kidnapped you. He didn't like that his enemy bought his daughter." My chest heaves as I take all of this in. My father sold me and he kidnapped me. A tear slips down my cheek and I swipe at it angrily.

"I'm alone. No one is going to come rescue me."

Phoenix took me back from my father because he bought me. Why did he have to be so nice? Why did he let me bake and form a relationship with Phillip and Clara? Why did he say we could go to his restaurant? Why don't I remember him buying me?

"I think I'll stay in my room tonight. I don't want to go out after all." Turning, I walk back to my room and he doesn't try to stop me. I yank the towel away and pull on an oversized shirt. After I quickly dry my hair, I sit in the oversized chair and look out onto the property.

When the sun begins to set, Phoenix steps out the front door and climbs onto a motorcycle. I've seen him come and go a few times. I've never seen him on a motorcycle. He's wearing dark pants, a white shirt, and a black leather jacket.

His head tilts up toward my room and I swear our eyes connect. I stare at him. Maybe he can see me. At this point, I don't really care. I feel numb. No one is coming for me. After several more minutes of us just staring at each other, he pulls his helmet on, starts the motorcycle, and drives off.

Pulling my feet up, I bend my knees and rest my chin between them. "My name is McKenzie. I'm twenty-three years old. I've been kidnapped. No one is coming for me. No one."

The next day I stay in bed, so Clara brings me breakfast and lunch, but I barely eat. I switch between watching TV and reading. It's a welcome escape.

"Will you be going downstairs to eat dinner?" Clara asks. She places the book I asked for on the table next to the chair I've taken up residence in.

"Not tonight. Can I eat in here?" I don't look at her because I don't want to see the look of pity in her eyes. Phoenix must have told her what happened, or at least part of it. She's treated me like a fragile china doll all day.

"I'm fine Clara, just don't feel good today." I assure her for the hundredth time. She knows I'm lying because even on the days I wasn't feeling my best, I still went to the library. But nowhere is safe. I don't think Phoenix left the house today, so I was afraid I'd run into him.

And I'm not ready to face him. He bought me. My father sold me. I hug my knees even tighter to my chest. The boulder in my stomach doubles in size. This was the wake up call I needed. The feelings that were beginning to arise needed to be dealt with. This solves that problem.

"Clara?" I don't look at her, but I can feel her gaze on me just the same.

"Yes?"

"Did you and Phillip meet here?" She sighs. The kind of sigh of a woman in love.

"No." That catches my attention, so I face her. She has a small smile on her lips. "My mother was really sick, and we were starving. We were squatting in a house that hadn't been lived in for years. So, one night I waited in the alley of one of Mr. Phoenix's restaurants. I was determined to get food for my mom and I one way or another."

She pauses as she gets a faraway look in her eyes, like she's remembering that night.

"Phillip came out with food he was throwing away. So, I jumped out of my hiding spot and scared him so bad he dropped all the food." She chuckles as she sits on the edge of my bed.

She shrugs. "I would have still eaten it. I was desperate. He said absolutely not, led me into the kitchen of the restaurant, and proceeded to make me a meal for my mom and me. He told me to come by the next day for more food. When I did, he introduced me to Mr. Phoenix. He hired me on the spot. Then he took me to pick up my mom and got her checked out by Dr. Chamberland. He gave us an apartment in his building and made sure my mom got the help she needed."

She has a goofy grin on her face. "Once I started working here and spending more time with Phillip, things progressed. He lives with my mom and I now."

I thought hearing her story would give me hope, but it just caused the crack in my chest to get bigger. The Phoenix she describes in her story is the one I remember from school.

How did that man wind up buying me? And why? Why did he buy me?

Clara stands from the bed with a sad smile on her face. "I'll bring you your dinner." I nod as she leaves the room. I spot Phoenix in the hallway.

He gazes in like he wants to speak, but I turn back around and stare out the window. It's not like I can stop him from coming in;

this is his house after all. And apparently, I'm not just his prisoner. I'm his property.

Chapter 10

I avoid Phoenix for the next week. The only time I'm forced to be in the same room as him is when Dr. Chamberland and Dr. Pearl come to check on me. I think I might be ready to begin talking to Dr. Pearl, but for now I've written the couple of memories I've had. I've also been writing in it every night about my day, hoping it will help jog something or at least help me work through all the emotions I'm currently feeling.

"Have you been writing in your journal?" Dr. Pearl asks.

"Yes." Phoenix hasn't taken his eyes off me since I came down to the living room. I try to ignore him, but he's like a magnet my eyes keep getting drawn back to. He's dressed up today. More than he usually is. I wonder why.

He's wearing dark gray slacks, a white button-up shirt, and he has suspenders. *Who would have thought suspenders could look so sexy?* I growl inwardly at how he draws me in, no matter how angry and hurt I am.

"That's good. I recommend reading the memories regularly; it might help spark other memories." I huff. I don't know if I want to spark any other memories. I'm still reeling from the last memory I had.

Dr. Chamberland does a quick checkup. After he's done, I have this need to flee. I can't be in the same room with Phoenix anymore. He affects me too much and I don't know what to do about it.

"Are we done? Can I go?" I rub my hands down my thighs.

"You're coming with me today," Phoenix says matter-of-factly.

"What? No, I'm not." I stand and glare at him.

"You are." His voice leaves no room for argument. I slap my hands against my thighs as my blood pressure rises.

"Are you done, Dr. Chamberland?" Phoenix asks calmly.

"I am," he replies, unphased by this turn of events.

"Dr. Pearl?" Phoenix asks her. She nods as she puts her notepad in the bag she brought in. Of course. They're on Phoenix's payroll.

Before they leave, Dr. Pearl turns to me. "Do you think you're ready to talk to me?" I swallow. "It can be somewhere you're comfortable. The library. Or your room." I glance from her to Phoenix to Dr. Chamberland.

"Maybe," I finally reply.

"Okay. I'll schedule an appointment with Phoenix for next week and if you choose not to talk, we can have tea or coffee together. Whatever you're comfortable with." Her voice is soft and soothing and it eases some of the anxiety I'm feeling with all three of them in the room.

"It's also a good idea to try walking every day," Dr. Chamberland suggests. Rex walks in just as he says that.

"I've been taking short walks with Rex almost every day." Rex nods in confirmation as he stops by Phoenix, whispering something in his ear. My eyes narrow at their interaction, trying to figure out what's going on.

"That's good. Try to go further each day to increase your stamina. I can tell you're getting stronger, but it will help a lot."

"Okay." I'm ready to run out of here. I wonder if Rex will go walking with me now so I can get away, but just as I'm thinking it, Rex walks out of the house. Guess that's a no.

"I'll make sure she begins walking more," Phoenix says. Dr. Chamberland nods and he and Dr. Pearl leave. I turn on Phoenix.

"Yeah. Got to make sure your property doesn't up and die on you." I spit the words at him. His eyes narrow and he stalks toward me. I force my feet to stay rooted where I am. He will not intimidate me.

"I am sick of your attitude. You will go upstairs, you will get dressed, and you will come with me." He towers over me, making me crane my neck to look up at him. Bastard. I dig my fingernails into my palms. I breathe out a huff of air as anger settles in my chest like a hot iron.

"You're sick of my attitude? Is that an inconvenience to you?" I mock. "You poor thing. I'm not like other property you own." Motioning to his couch, I continue. "Your couch, your TV, your fucking motorcycle. No! This property has feelings. But if that's too inconvenient for you, then please let me go back to ignoring you for days. I quite liked it that way." I take a step toward him, leaving barely any room between him and I. His eyes narrow and his breathing comes out in sharp pants.

"Because whether you like it or not, my feelings are valid. Ass-hole." I turn on my heel so I can walk away, but he grabs the back of my neck and forces me back around, his lips ghosting over mine.

My eyes widen and for the first time since I woke up in this house, I'm afraid. His grip on my neck isn't painful, though. He pulls me close enough so he can rest his forehead against mine, his icy eyes staring into mine. My hands hang awkwardly at my side as I stare back.

"If I hadn't bought you, someone else would have." The words sound like they're being ripped out of his chest. "The people that go to those auctions are bad people."

"Yet you were there," I whisper. He lets out a breath that ghosts over my lips. Just a centimeter and his lips would touch mine. I swallow.

"I was." It's the only reply he gives me. "And your father hated it so much that he took you from me and kept you chained in that hole." I close my eyes and try to block out the pain those words bring.

His grip on my neck loosens, and he cards his fingers through my hair. "Go get ready, McKenzie. Or I'll take you in your pajamas."

My muscles loosen in defeat, or maybe it's surrender. "Where are we going?"

"I have business to attend to, and then we're going out to eat." I nod once. He takes a step back, dropping his hands, giving me the chance to escape.

Forty-five minutes later, I'm seated in the back of a black SUV I'm pretty sure is armored. The tint on the windows is so dark I know it can't be legal. Rex is in the driver's seat, and Phoenix is sitting too close to me.

It's freezing outside. So, I'm wearing black leather pants that fit me like a glove. How he guessed my size I'll never know, with an ivory cashmere sweater and some black ankle boots. I flat ironed my hair, put on some makeup, and finished it off with some red lipstick.

I stare out the window and watch as the scenery changes. Rex pulls out onto the highway and heads toward downtown Savannah. I try to pay attention to the turns, but lose track after a while. Even if I didn't, from his house to the main road it has to be at least two miles. *How many acres does he have?*

If I were speaking to him, which I'm not, I'd ask. The entire ride to River Street Phoenix is either texting or taking phone calls. It's convenient for me. It's giving me time to think about what he said earlier.

Why was he at that party? Or auction… whatever it was. And why did he buy me? The way he made it sound, it was like he was trying to save me from a worse fate.

I lean my head against the headrest and take a deep breath.

Why would my father sell me? Was he in debt? Did he get into trouble? I'm sure he's been to these parties several times because I was always forbidden to go.

My whole world has been flipped upside down this past week. I was convinced the *he* in my mantra was my father. Now, I have no idea if *he* even exists.

And what about Phoenix's wife? Where was she during all of this? A thought hits me square in the gut. *How long ago was his wife kidnapped? Did he think someone kidnapped her, and she was going to be sold at the auction? Maybe he was there to rescue her, but he wound up with me.*

Turning my head in his direction, I study him as he types away on his phone. "Your thoughts are very loud over there," he says without looking up from his phone.

"I'm just trying to figure you out."

He finishes his message, then pockets his phone, turning his attention to me. "Good luck with that."

I shake my head and take a deep breath. I don't know what to say to him. *Thank you for buying me, so I didn't wind up with someone worse? Thank you for saving me again when I was kidnapped? Thank you for saving me from my father?*

"How are you feeling?" he asks, interrupting my thoughts. I shake my head and lift my shoulders with a hard sigh.

"Like I have whiplash." I gather my courage, then let all of my thoughts out. "I wish you had told me. I wish you had been up front with me about why I was in your house. Instead of making me believe I was your prisoner. Why did you do that? Why didn't you tell me?"

He raises his hand and rubs his knuckle along my cheekbone before dropping it again.

"How do you think that would have gone? You remembered the party, but you couldn't remember why you were there. I could tell you didn't know what your father did, and I didn't want to disrupt your world completely again. You had just come out of some horrid conditions, and I was trying to make you feel as comfortable as possible." He runs his hand along his jaw. "I wasn't trying to hide things from you."

"You were trying to protect me. Again." I clear my throat and run my hands down the smooth leather on my legs. "I'm grateful and angry at the same time," I admit.

He chuckles and taps his pointer finger and middle finger on my thigh. "I can live with that."

"Of course you can." I decide to table this discussion for now. I'm still not 100% happy, but I feel better than I have this past week. "You know you handle my anger well."

He smirks at me and arches an eyebrow. "Is that a compliment?"

"It's just, growing up, especially when I became a teenager, I was not allowed to disagree with my father in any way. Yes, I remember the father from my childhood that was doting. But as I got older, he changed." I pull my bottom lip between my teeth. "I didn't realize he'd sell me, though."

"Is that why you went home less and less during breaks when we were at the academy?"

I nod. "He changed when my mother got sick. It was hard being around him. She brought a softness to him that completely vanished when she died." A huff of laughter leaves me. "I didn't even realize what my father did until I went to the academy. I was so naïve."

I give him a sad smile and he tilts his head at me. "Yeah, I tried my best to stay out of this life. I hated that my dad loved it and turned out to be good at it," he admits.

"What changed? How did you get into this life?" I ask. He inhales and turns his head to look out the window.

"Something happened the summer before my freshman year. It changed my path." It's all he says. He doesn't explain further. I realize he's not going to, so I don't ask anything further.

Rex pulls down onto River Street and into a parking garage of a hotel. He stops at an entrance. Phoenix sits up and taps me on the nose.

"Stay with Rex. I'll meet you two in just a few minutes." Before I can respond, he's out of the car and walking toward the entrance. Unease prickles in my stomach.

What is he going to do? Is he in danger? Why doesn't he have security with him? He said last week when we were going out to eat there, would be more security. Was that just for last week?

"He's going to be fine, Miss McKenzie." I meet Rex's eyes in the rearview mirror and nod slightly.

"Shouldn't you be with him?"

"I'm with you. That's more important." I disagree and I'm sure it's written all over my face from the look I get from Rex. "He has men with him."

I scrunch up my eyebrows. "What? I didn't see anyone."

Rex chuckles as he continues to climb up the parking garage. "That means they're doing their job well."

Huh. So, we do have security, I just don't know who they are. That's a relief and creepy at the same time.

Rex brings his phone to his ear. "Yes, sir," he answers, and I know it's Phoenix. "Alright, we'll be there soon."

Rex hangs up and heads up what I'm assuming is the last ramp to the top of the parking garage. He pulls into a parking spot closest to a stairwell. Once he's parked, he exits the vehicle and comes to my door to let me out.

"Where are we going?" I ask. Despite the fact I was given no choice but to be here, excitement simmers in my veins. It's been a long time since I've worn anything else besides sweats or pajamas. And I get to do something besides sit at home.

"I'm taking you to Mr. Stone. You two are having dinner at his rooftop restaurant."

Chapter 11

I step out of the elevator, Rex following behind me. The restaurant is busy, but not overcrowded. And it's beautiful. There are wooden beams with glass covered in garland, and lights covering the tables. Each table has a round chandelier hanging over it and there are red bows decorating each one.

"It's close to Christmas," I say as the realization hits me.

"It is," Rex confirms. I haven't kept up with the days or months since Phoenix rescued me. I did ask him a while ago what month it was, but I haven't kept up with it since then.

"What about Thanksgiving?" I ask. Thanksgiving was always my favorite. Especially the baking. I'd make as many desserts as I could, even if they didn't all get eaten. The cooking part, not so much.

"Thanksgiving is in five days."

I stop in my tracks and Rex almost runs into me. "What?"

Before he can respond, Phoenix is sliding up next to us. Rex walks away to watch us from somewhere in the restaurant with the other security that I haven't seen yet.

"What?" he asks. I turn to him with my hands on my hips. He arches an eyebrow. "What did I do now?"

I scowl at him. "Thanksgiving is in five days?"

He places his hands in his pockets and nods. I can tell from his expression he knows he messed up. "It is."

"So, that gives me just a few days to bake desserts? I can't believe you didn't tell me."

He takes a step closer to me, invading my space. "When exactly was I supposed to tell you? You've been avoiding me all week." *He has me there.*

"You could have told Phillip to tell me. Or Clara." He rolls his eyes as he takes his hands out of his pockets and wraps an arm around my shoulders, guiding me to a table that is reserved for us. Goosebumps breakout over my arms at the contact.

"You know I need to plan for these things. I can't believe you didn't give me some kind of warning." I huff as he pulls my chair out for me. I sit down and wait for him to walk over to his side of the table, but he doesn't move. I lean my head back to look up at him, and he's staring at me with this strange look in his eyes. "Phoenix? What's wrong?"

He squats down next to my chair and places his hand over mine. "How do you know I know you need to prepare for these things?"

I stare at him in confusion. "Huh?"

He lifts his hand and pushes a piece of my hair behind my ear. I suck in a breath and hold it. He's done that before. That wasn't a fantasy, it was a memory.

"You said, 'you know I need to plan for these things.' How do you know I know that?" he asks.

I have to force my brain to keep up with him. It's still stuck on him pushing my hair behind my ear. "I… uh…" I try to think. *How would he know that? Why did I know he would know that?* "I don't know," I admit.

Disappointment flashes in his eyes, but he hides it quickly. He rubs his knuckles along my jaw. "You will." He says it with such conviction I can't help but believe him.

He stands and walks to the other side of the table. I don't move though. I still can't get past the fact that I wasn't fantasizing about him, but it was a memory. How I know I'm not sure, but I know it is.

Turning in my seat to face him, I force a smile and try to relax the muscles in my shoulder and neck. I want to feel normal. I want to be normal.

The server stops at our table. "Good evening, Mr. Stone. What can I get you to drink tonight?"

Phoenix watches me for a few more seconds before turning his attention to the server. "We'd like a bottle of Merlot and water." The server nods and walks away.

"Are you okay?" Phoenix asks. I open my mouth, then close it again. *What do I say? How do I tell him?* He slides his hand across the table and rubs his thumb along my wrist. "Kenz?"

"I…" My eyebrows cave in. "Were we in a relationship?" He turns to stone, which is fitting, considering that's his last name.

"Why do you ask that?"

"You're evading my question with a question," I say, calling him out. He doesn't deny it, but he doesn't say anything else. He's not going to tell me until I answer his question.

"Just now when you pushed my hair behind my ear. I've had this recurring visual of you doing that." I suck in a breath through my teeth. "I thought it was me fantasizing about it." My face heats up at the admission, but I power through. "But when you did it just now, I realized it wasn't. It was a memory. So, you've done it before."

He brings his thumb up to his lip and rubs it a few times. "Yes. I have," he finally says. He doesn't say we were in a relationship, just that he's done it before.

"Oh." It's the only reply I can come up with. Before either of us can say anything else, the server comes up again, setting the water down and pouring us wine, then placing the rest of the bottle on the table.

"Have you decided what you'd like to eat?" he asks. I haven't even looked at the menu.

"You can choose for me. I'm pretty sure you know what I like."

He stares at me for a moment before turning his attention to the server. "She'll have the lobster ravioli with a baked potato and caesar salad. I'll have the filet, medium rare, with mac and cheese and a garden salad, ranch dressing."

The server grabs our menu. "Yes sir. I'll bring you some bread and your food will be out soon."

"Thank you," Phoenix replies, and he faces me again. The power of his gaze causes heat to stir in my stomach. I have so many questions, but I don't know if I want to know the answers to them.

I rub my hands along the white tablecloth and gaze out over the river. "Wow. This view is beautiful." I can see across the river to the hotel that's there. There are ships floating down the river to drop off their cargo.

"This is the best table in the restaurant," Phoenix replies. The server brings the basket of bread and our salads. I feel Phoenix's eyes on me, but I keep my focus on the river.

"You know, I've always wanted to do a riverboat cruise." I grab my glass of wine and take a sip from it. I stare at him over the rim of my glass.

"Then we'll go." He takes a sip from his glass, like going on a riverboat cruise isn't a big deal. Maybe to him it isn't, but to me it is.

"Okay," I whisper. "Could we maybe make a day of it? Go to Tybee Island, do the riverboat cruise, and walk River Street?" I don't know if I'm pressing my luck, but it's worth asking. One side of his mouth tips up and he nods.

"Let's do it next weekend. We can watch the Christmas Parade too."

I smile at his response and nod. "Clara told me you'd let me out of the house, but I didn't quite believe her."

He leans back in his chair and chuckles. "Because you don't trust me?"

I think about it for a few seconds before shaking my head. "No. I guess because of my previous circumstances." I take a sip from my glass of wine again before sitting it down and grabbing a piece of bread from the basket. "Maybe I didn't trust you a little."

He smiles at me and takes a sip from his wineglass. We eat our salads as I think about how much fun next weekend will be. The server arrives at our table, dropping off our food, and we don't talk for a few minutes as we dig in. I keep eyeing his steak, but eat my lobster ravioli. He cuts a piece and holds it up on a fork toward me.

"Want a bite?" he asks. I glance from him to the steak and back again. He's very observant.

"Yes."

He extends his arm further across the table, so I lean forward, keeping my eyes on him as I place my teeth around the tines of the fork and he pulls it away slowly. Heat settles in my stomach as I keep my eyes on him. I chew slowly, unable to look away.

Why does this feel so intimate? What would he do if I were to give into the white hot lust vibrating through my veins?

I hum at how good the steak tastes. I close my eyes to savor it and to break the connection with him. It's too much; I can't handle it anymore. I shouldn't want him. I shouldn't be thinking of him in that way at all, but the boy I knew in school is not the same man that's sitting in front of me.

Swallowing the steak and taking a sip of wine, I turn my attention back to him. "I remember you from school, but that's the last time I remember seeing you," I admit.

He pauses in cutting his steak as he stares at me for a few seconds. His expression doesn't give him away.

Does that upset him? That I don't remember him buying me at the auction. What has happened since then? It's the end of November. How soon after he bought me was I kidnapped? He said he bought me, and my father couldn't stand it, so he kidnapped me. Would he have kidnapped me if anyone else had bought me? Or is it because Phoenix bought me? The son of his enemy.

"Do you know why my father sold me?" I ask as I move food around on my plate.

He sighs as he puts his fork and knife down. "I don't think you want to know the answer to that." He lifts the napkin from his lap and wipes his mouth.

"I do." Dread settles in my stomach. I know I'm not going to like the answer, but I have to know. I need to know.

"Do you remember Mr. Reynolds?"

I squint my eyes at his answer. "The dean of the academy?"

He leans forward, placing his elbows on the table. "Yes."

I lean forward, mimicking his posture. He slides his hand across the table and intertwines our fingers. "He wanted you."

It takes me a couple of minutes to comprehend what he was telling me. "He wanted me?" I remember my father and Mr. Reynolds had a relationship. From what I remember, I think he was the only friend my father had.

Phoenix rubs his thumb over my knuckles. It calms me a little. "Yes, and your father planned on selling you to him at that auction."

Where did the man go that used to push me on the swing when I was little? Has he completely lost his way since my mother died? I didn't think my heart could break anymore, but knowing my father had planned it; that he had set it in motion? The little trust I had left in him vanishes.

"Why didn't that happen?" I squeeze Phoenix's hand, thinking he might pull away, but he leans forward.

"Because I outbid him."

"How much did you bid?" I don't know why I want to know this or even why I need to know, but I do.

"Six million dollars." He makes it sound like it's not a big deal, but that is an astronomical amount. "It's the most anyone has ever bid at one of those auctions, so they didn't try to outbid me because they knew it would look suspicious."

I wish I could remember. I close my eyes tightly, trying to force my brain to recall that memory. Sighing in frustration, I open them to stare into Phoenix's eyes.

"You'll remember," he says, reading my mind. "I know you will."

My tongue darts out to lick my dry lips. I turn to face the bar across from us. I stare blankly at one of the televisions showing a news station. I'm about to turn away when the date at the bottom of the screen catches my eye.

Pulling my hand from Phoenix's hand, I stand and walk to the bar. *Oh my god. Oh my god. Oh my god.*

The bartender walks over to me. "Can I help you?" she asks. Phoenix calls my name, but it sounds like he's far away.

I point to the television. "The date." She turns and looks at the television I'm pointing at. "Is that right?"

Her eyebrows furrow and she slowly nods. "Yes."

I try to swallow, but my throat doesn't seem to be working. Heat rises up my neck and my heart pounds. Hands grip my shoulders and rub down my arms.

"McKenzie?" Phoenix's voice is full of concern.

I squeeze my eyes shut. "I'm not twenty-three, am I?" I ask.

He turns me around in his arms and looks at me with concern. I beg him with my eyes to tell me the truth.

"No, no, you're not," he replies.

I'm twenty-six. I lost three years of my life.

"That auction. It happened three years ago?"

One of Phoenix's hands slides up my arm, over my shoulder, and to my neck. He cups the back of my neck, massaging the sore tendons there.

"Three and a half."

Chapter 12

"I want to go home." My voice is hoarse. I'm trying to keep it together. We're in a public place, a restaurant Phoenix owns. I don't want to embarrass myself or Phoenix.

"Can you tell Luke we had to leave?" Phoenix asks the bartender.

"Of course, Mr. Stone."

He places two one hundred-dollar bills down on the counter. "One for you and the other for him."

Before she can respond, he's wrapping his arm around me and guiding me toward the elevator. I'm vaguely aware of Rex following us. Somehow we wind up in the SUV headed home.

Phoenix's arm and thigh are pressed against me like he's trying to provide support the best way he knows how. I pull my lips between my teeth before releasing a long breath.

"Why didn't you tell me?" I ask. Phoenix wraps his arm around my shoulders and turns, so his lips press against my hair.

"I wanted to," he murmurs against my head. "The first night when you said that mantra of yours, but..." He trails off as he sucks in a breath. "I was trying to be careful. I wasn't sure if you were willing to hear it or if you'd accept it. I've been contemplating telling you for the past couple of weeks. I'm sorry you had to find out that way."

I want to be angry with him, but at the same time, I understand. "It seems like you're always trying to protect me," I whisper. He hums, but doesn't say anything. I want to ask about his wife, but I'm enjoying this bubble we're in right now.

"How long did you have me before I was kidnapped?" I ask.

He goes completely still at my question. "When I rescued you, you had been kidnapped three months prior," he replies.

A whimper escapes from my chest. "How is it that in three months I forgot three years of my life?" I ask.

"I wish I knew, Kenz."

I rest my head on his shoulder and close my eyes. He cards his fingers through my hair the rest of the ride home.

When we get home, I tell Phoenix I'm going to take a shower and go to bed. He says he has some work he needs to take care of. Once in my room, I undress and head into the bathroom. Turning the shower on to warm up, I stare in the mirror and try to will myself to remember.

There has to be a way to jog my memory. Stepping into the shower, I let the hot water wash over me and hide the tears I can no longer keep at bay. I've had to process so much information in the past week.

My father tried to sell me, Phoenix bought me, and I've forgotten three years of my life. I'm twenty-six, not twenty-three. How did I not notice that? How could I not tell?

Rubbing my hands over my face, I try to bring my emotions under control. Thinking back over the last few months, I try to recall any clues. I remember Dr. Chamberland asking me when the last time I saw Phoenix was. At the time, I thought it was a strange question, but it was probably his way of seeing what I remembered last.

The last time I remember having seen Phoenix was at graduation. He invited me to a party that night, but I declined because my father and I were flying out right after the ceremony. It was the first time Phoenix had paid any attention to me when we were in school.

After I'm done in the shower, I put on pajamas and head to Phoenix's office down the hall from our rooms. His door is open, so I step in and wait for him to notice me.

It doesn't take long. He's on the phone with someone, but his eyes find mine immediately and he gestures for me to come in. He's still in his dress pants and button-up shirt, but he has removed the suspenders. His shirt is unbuttoned down to the middle of his chest, so I have to force myself not to stare.

It takes him a few minutes to end the conversation, but when he does, he rounds his desk and leans against it, gesturing for me to come to him. I take in a deep breath, trying to calm my racing heart. Putting one foot in front of the other, I stop in front of him and tilt my head so I can look at him. I want him to wrap his arms around me and make me feel better. There's a hole in the middle of my chest and I need something, anything, to fill it and make me feel better.

"What do you need, McKenzie?"

I stare at him for a few seconds before shrugging. "I don't know. I feel..." I stop, not sure how to explain what I'm feeling or even why I'm comfortable telling him. "What do you do?" I ask instead.

He tilts his head and crosses his arms over his chest as he studies me. "What do you mean?"

I gesture to his office. "What kind of business do you run? Is it legal? Are you in the mafia? What do you do?"

I slap my hands against my thighs. I want to know everything about him. I'm not sure if he'll tell me, but he hasn't berated me yet about all the questions I ask. So, I'll keep asking them until he tells me to stop. Even then, I'm not sure I'll stop.

He doesn't answer right away. He turns his head to look out the window. "The majority of what I do is legal. But there are parts of it that aren't. I own several hotels, like the one we went to tonight. It's a hotel with the rooftop restaurant. I own a few other restaurants and I own several bars. All of those are legal."

I wait to see if he's going to expand, but he doesn't. "So, what do you do that's illegal?" I might be walking a very thin line with this line of questioning, but I need to know he's not like my father.

I found out my father imported fentanyl and other drugs through the ports in Savannah and distributed them to other cities, like Atlanta, Charlotte, Memphis, and probably other cities I didn't know about. He's responsible for thousands, maybe millions of drug-related deaths.

Right after I found out, he shipped me off to the academy, and I didn't see him again until graduation. I went to college and didn't see him for a few years during that time. I tried my best to avoid my father as much as possible. I know he shipped me off to the academy because he didn't want to deal with the knowledge I had just gained. Or the grief I was dealing with from my mother's death.

When I graduated college, the plan was to come home for a few weeks, then move up north. I wanted to be as far away from him as possible. When he told me I could go to the party, I had been excited. I wanted to believe it was his olive branch. I take a deep breath. How naïve I had been.

"I have some underground fight clubs and a lot happens at those fights." He's being vague on purpose. I press my lips together as I think about what he could mean.

"A lot happens at those fights?" I ask.

He runs his hand along his jaw and grabs the back of his neck as he narrows his eyes at me. "There are women that offer services at those fights."

My heart drops to my stomach and I take a step back. "After my father tried to sell me to a man that was going to do who knows what to me you do that sort of thing?" I ask.

"They do it willingly. They're not forced. I don't allow pimps in. These women run their own business and it's because they want to." I have a hard time believing that. *Why would they want to do that?*

"You're sure? They're not stuck in this lifestyle because they feel like there's not another way out?"

"I have made it very clear to each one if they want out or they don't want to do it, I have enough legit businesses I will happily hire them at." I shake my head and turn away. I begin to pace as I try to comprehend what he's telling me.

"I'll have to see it to believe it."

He pushes away from his desk and steps in front of me as I turn to continue my pacing. He grabs my arms and rubs his hands up and down my biceps.

"I'm not ready to introduce you to that world. For a lot of reasons, but the top one is I have to make sure you're safe. Until you remember certain things, you won't be safe."

"Why?" I ask.

"Because these people know who you are and you won't remember them. They don't know why you haven't been around. I kept your kidnapping very hush hush. The only people who know are people on my payroll."

"What can I do to help me remember?"

"I'll call Dr. Chamberland tomorrow and ask him to stop by."

I take a deep breath, stepping back until the back of my knees hits one of the chairs in front of his desk and sit down. He was just here today and he'll be by next week for his weekly visit.

"Okay. I know Thanksgiving is coming up, so if he can't come until next week—"

Phoenix interrupts me. "He'll come tomorrow." He steps forward and kneels down in front of me. "You're his most important patient right now. So, he'll make you a priority."

I tilt my head. "Rex said the same thing."

"He said what?"

"Well, he said I was more important. So, maybe not exactly the same thing." Phoenix still has a confused look on his face. "When he dropped you off and stayed with me. I asked him why he wasn't going and he said I was more important."

Phoenix's face transforms when he lifts his lips into a soft smile. "You are." He trails his fingers up my arm to my shoulder, leaving goosebumps in their wake. His large hand grips the side of my neck and he rubs his thumb along my jaw.

I stop breathing as I stare into his eyes. I could get lost in them. My tongue darts out to wet my lips. His eyes dart down to my mouth and linger there before he raises them again to look at me.

"Phoenix," I whisper. *I want to kiss him. I want him to kiss me.* Without thinking, I shift forward. Phoenix's grip on the side of my neck tightens before he drags his hand to grip the back of my neck.

Anticipation builds in my stomach as my heart begins to beat at the speed of a hummingbird's wings. I lower my eyes to his mouth. This man. He's a beautiful specimen, with his ice-blue eyes, long eyelashes, and full lips. He leans forward. I lower my eyelids.

"Mr. Stone!" Clara's voice cries out. My entire body slumps in the seat as Phoenix stands just as Clara enters his office.

"They found her!"

Chapter 13

I look between Clara and Phoenix, wondering who Clara is talking about. Rex enters a few seconds after Clara. Phoenix walks back to his desk pulling open a drawer. He grabs a gun and shoves it in the small of his back. My eyes widen at the sight.

What the hell is going on? Why does he need a gun?

"Where?" Phoenix barks as he grabs an extra gun magazine and puts it in his pocket.

"A shipping container at the port," Rex answers.

I stand slowly from my chair as I try to piece together what they're saying. *Who did they find?* "What's going on?" I ask.

Phoenix stops in front of me on his way to follow Rex, who has already left. "I have to go. I might be gone for a few days, maybe longer."

He kisses me on top of my head before walking out the door. Clara walks over to me and wraps her arm around my waist, rubbing her other hand up and down my arm.

"Who did they find?" I ask her.

"Her name is Anna. I believe the two of you graduated with her."

I open my mouth, but close it again.

I knew she was his wife. I knew it. And here I was, two seconds from kissing him. Oh god. And it seemed like he was going to kiss me, too. Why would he do that? The way he ran out of here, she obviously means a lot to him. Maybe he's lonely. If he bought me three years ago...

"Come on. I'll make you some chamomile tea. It'll help calm you so you can get some sleep tonight." I mindlessly follow behind her to the kitchen. Sitting at the island, I watch as she makes the tea.

"Clara?"

"Hmmm?" She hums as she puts a kettle on the stove and turns it on.

"Why would Phoenix buy me if he was married to Anna? Or maybe they got married after he bought me?"

Clara turns to me with a look of shock on her face. Maybe she didn't know Phoenix bought me. "Mr. Stone told you he bought you?" Or she's surprised I know that at all.

"I had a memory that led to him telling me."

She nods and wipes down the counter. "And you thought he was married to Anna when he did that?"

"He said his wife was kidnapped." I twist my lips, deciding if I should confess to snooping in his office. "Then one day I was looking around in his office and I saw a picture of Anna in there."

"Oh. You'll need to ask Mr. Stone why he bought you."

"He said it was because if he didn't, then someone else with bad intentions would."

The kettle begins to whistle, so she turns to take it off the heat and turn the stove off. "He does that."

I stare at the back of her head, ready for her to expand further, but she doesn't. "He's done that before?" She still doesn't reply. "Clara, I need answers. How often does he go to these auctions?"

She puts a tea bag in a teacup and pours the water over it. "I can only tell you what Phillip has shared and even he hasn't shared a lot. But it seems like he goes to every single one since he's found out about them. But he didn't go to the last one because he had just found you."

"How often do these auctions happen? Do you know?" I ask.

"Every quarter," she answers.

Placing my cold hands around the cup, I let it warm them. "I wish I could remember more," I whisper as I bring the cup to my mouth and blow on it.

Clara sits across from me and offers me a sympathetic smile. "I know this has to be hard. I can't imagine." Taking a cautious sip, I hum. My mind drifts to Phoenix and wondering how long he'll be gone and when he returns if he'll have Anna.

"How long have Phoenix and Anna been married?" I hate myself for needing to know. I need to know more so I can get this obsession I have with him out of my mind.

"Miss McKenzie, Mr. Phoenix isn't..." She shakes her head as she trails off. Phoenix isn't what? "When he gets home, ask him these questions," she encourages. "I'm sure he'll answer the majority of them. He may have been trying to be careful because he didn't want to upset you since you didn't remember a lot. But you are remembering things and he might be able to give you some more information."

Placing the cup in front of me, I think of all the questions I want to ask. "If it's alright, I'm going to take this up to my room and write in my journal."

"Of course. I'll be staying here tonight just in case you need anything."

Walking around the island, I wrap my arms around Clara in a hug. "Thank you, Clara. For being so kind, for taking care of me, for so many things."

Clara returns my hug. "Of course Miss McKenzie. Anytime you need me, just let me know." I lean back and offer her a small smile.

"You can call me Kenzie." Her eyes widen. I know I told her when I first woke up not to, but I've felt guilty ever since. "I'm sorry I was such a hag that first day we met. Or, well... The first day I remember us meeting."

She smiles at me and pushes my hair over my shoulder. "Thank you, and you don't have to apologize. I know that was a lot." I give her one more hug before grabbing my cup and walking to my room.

I grab a fluffy blanket and my journal, then curl up in the chair overlooking the grounds. I wonder who's on security if Rex went with Phoenix. I've seen a few guys around, but haven't met any of them. I wonder if that's been on purpose.

Opening my journal, I take a sip from the tea and read the entry from the first memory I had. It was when I had baked chocolate chip cookies. The arms wrapped around me, did they have tattoos? The voice, was it soft but rough around the edges? The lips, were they full and inviting?

I swallow as I imagine all the things I'd like Phoenix to do to me. In school all the girls were so boy crazy, but I had a different outlook. I knew how cruel my father and the men he surrounded himself with could be. I had decided then I'd rather die alone than be with someone like that.

Flipping to a blank page in my journal, I grab the pen I keep on the table. It hovers above the paper as I try to think of what day it is. It's not like I'm on any type of schedule or anything. Putting my pen to paper, I begin to write.

I wish I could remember more. I wish I knew what they did to me to make me forget. Is it a trauma response? Or is it from the drugs they gave me? Or was I abused? Dr. Chamberland did check for any out of the ordinary injuries and didn't find any head injuries. I'm supposed to meet with Dr. Pearl soon. Will she be able to help me remember?

I had bruises and sores all over my body, though. Is that because they beat me? Or something else? I know how cruel my father can be, but I still want to think of him as the man from when I was a little girl. Was that man real? How could he go from pushing me in the swing to selling me?

I stop writing and gaze out the window as I drink the rest of my tea. Either the tea is doing the trick or I'm just exhausted because my eyes are growing heavy. Pulling the curtains shut, I turn the lights off and climb into bed. I hope when I wake up in the morning Phoenix will be back.

"It's time to wake up, Mrs. Stone." I try to hide my smile and pretend like I'm still asleep. He's on his side and his chest is pressing into my side. He runs his nose along my jaw before tracing the same path with his tongue.

I'm fighting a losing battle trying to keep my breathing even. "I know you're awake, love." He nips at my chin before covering my mouth with his. I give up all pretense and wrap my arms around his broad shoulders as he climbs on top of me and deepens the kiss.

My breath hitches as he rocks his hard cock against me. I can't believe I'm married to this man.

I sit up in bed as my heart pounds against my chest a mile a minute. Running my fingers through my hair, I turn to climb out of bed so I can grab my journal, but stop at the sight of Phoenix. He's laid back in the chair next to my bed, his long legs sprawled out in front of him. It's been three days since he and Rex left and here he is, safe and sound. The knot that's been in my stomach for days begins to loosen at the sight of him.

Tiptoeing closer, my fingers itch to run over his closed eyelids. This man is beautiful awake, but asleep? His guard is down, so I can study him. He's in pajama pants and no shirt. My eyes trail along his tattoos, down to his abs and tapered waist, to the V that disappears into the waistband of his pajamas.

I want to drop to my knees and see what I find there. I'm reminded of the dream—no, it wasn't a dream. That was a memory. Glancing down at his left hand, his ring shines like a beacon to me. I run the tip of my finger over my left ring finger.

Phoenix is my husband. I'm his wife. How did that happen? When did it happen? Where's my ring?

Stepping closer to him, I give into temptation and rub my finger over his wedding band. Phoenix shifts, so I lift my eyes to his face again and catch him staring up at me with hooded eyes. My breath catches in my throat, but he doesn't say anything, simply watches me.

He looks exhausted. I wonder what time he got in. Licking my lips, his eyes drop to my mouth and heat begins to simmer in my belly. On instinct, I step between his spread legs; he sits up slightly, extending his hands to touch the back of my thighs. He doesn't do anything else, simply keeps his hands there, letting me decide what will happen next.

Taking a deep breath, I put one knee on the chair and bring my other knee to the other side of him, straddling his lap. He scoots up further and slides his hands to my ass. This time he squeezes once, but that's all he does.

I sit on his upper thighs and we stare at each other. "Are you my husband?" I whisper.

Relief washes over his face, and his shoulders relax a little. Like he's been carrying a weight that was too heavy for him.

"I am." His voice is rough with emotion. I lean forward and place my forehead against his.

"I had a memory. It was short, but you called me Mrs. Stone." One hand slides from my ass up my spine, leaving goosebumps along the way, and ends up holding the back of my head. His hand grips some of my hair, then his other hand pushes me so I'm flush against him.

I gasp, my breath washing over his lips. "I'm Mrs. Stone," I say in disbelief.

"You are." Phoenix leans up and captures my mouth with his. He nips at my bottom lip, then runs his tongue over it, soothing the bite. He sits up completely, wrapping his arms around me and pulling me as close as physically possible without him being inside me.

I open my mouth in an invitation, and he doesn't hesitate. His tongue flicks against mine, staking his claim, as his strokes become more demanding; all-consuming. One hand in my hair, the other slips under my nightshirt, rubbing along my spine and holding me even tighter. The spark I've felt for weeks now catches fire and becomes an inferno.

I rock against him, needing friction. His erection rubs against my pussy, and I moan into his mouth. He spreads his hand out along my back, his fingers wrapping slightly around my side, just a breath away from the side of my breast.

Need, desire, lust gather in my stomach and an insistent ache begins in my core. I wrap my arms around his neck, running my fingers through the back of his hair, trying to get closer.

His hand trails back down my spine, to my ass, and grips my thigh. He stands in one fluent motion and I wrap my legs around him tightly as he walks us to the bed and lays me down on it gently. My pulse pounds in my ears as he climbs on top of me.

I have so many questions, but they flew out of my brain the moment his hands landed on my ass. He rocks against me and a whimper escapes me.

"McKenzie." His voice is like sandpaper as he reaches behind him to where my feet are still linked behind him. He grasps one of my ankles lightly and rubs the palm of his hand up my calf, to my thigh. He grips it tightly and rocks against me again.

"Phoenix." His name is ripped out of my chest. I could come just from this. He places his left hand on the bed beside my head and rubs his cloth covered dick against my covered pussy.

His mouth lands on mine again, kissing me deep, his tongue stroking mine and causing a deep shudder of need to rip through my body. I claw at his back as he moves his mouth from mine and peppers my jaw with kisses, followed closely by flicks of his tongue.

I arch against him as the need in me crescendos to an ache so deep; I know if he doesn't do something soon, I may combust. There's a knock on the bedroom door, making me want to scream. He doesn't move right away. In fact, his lips find my ear and he nips at it before his lips find a sensitive spot on my throat I wasn't aware existed, but he probably knows my body.

And he's proving it as he latches on to that spot. I cling to him, hoping whoever is at the door will take a hint and go away.

There's another knock on the door, and this time I groan in frustration. "Mr. Stone, she's awake." I freeze at that sentence.

Phoenix stops his assault on my throat as he lifts his head slowly. I let my legs fall from his waist to the bed and push myself back into the mattress so I can get a better look at his face.

"Who's awake?" I ask. He sighs deeply.

"Anna."

Chapter 14

Phoenix climbs off the bed slowly, adjusting his erection and walks to the door, swinging it open. I scramble to a sitting position, horrified that I must look completely debauched. And Phoenix isn't doing anything to hide the outline of his cock against his pajama pants.

Rex looks from Phoenix to me, then back to Phoenix. Worry is etched all over his face, the two wrinkles between his eyebrows more pronounced than they usually are. "Sorry to disturb you, but you told me to let you know when she's awake."

Phoenix runs his hand over his jaw. "You don't have to apologize." He motions for me. "Come on."

I get up slowly, grabbing the robe off the back of the door and putting it on. We walk out into the hallway and Rex is already at the stairs. Phoenix goes into his room and comes out pulling on a T-shirt.

I bite my lip as his skin slowly disappears. Grabbing my hand, he pulls me toward the stairs. As we descend, my thoughts turn to Anna. *She's here in his house. Our house?* We walk through the living room, to the kitchen, through the kitchen to another hallway I'm sure Clara showed me on the tour she took me on all those months ago.

Clara stands at an open door I'm assuming is Anna's room.

What am I going to see when I walk into that room? Is she going to be a shadow of herself? I know I was. Was she drugged, too? Will she have her memory? Breathe McKenzie.

I count as I inhale, then exhale. Phoenix stops at the door and turns to me. He places his hands on my biceps, a look of concern on his face.

"Are you going to be okay?"

I huff. "She's the one we should be worried about."

"I am. But I'm worried about you, too. If you don't want to go in there, I understand."

I swallow and look from him to the open doorway and back to him. "I want to go. It'll be hard, but I want to be there for her." He nods once, kissing me on the forehead. He glances at Rex, who is standing outside the door, giving him a slight nod. A look I don't understand passes between them; then he leads the way into the room.

Her room isn't as nice as mine, but it's still beautiful. The walls are a light blue. There's a dresser against the wall where the door is. On the other wall, there's a window looking out over the other side of the house. It's dark out, so I'm not sure what the view is like. The bed is against the wall, it's covered with a navy blanket, and Anna is sitting up looking dazed, leaning against the headboard.

She has her knees drawn up against her chest, her arms wrapped around her knees. She's biting her chapped lips as her eyes flit around the room. Her chest heaving like she's trying to not have a panic attack.

I try to swallow past the lump in my throat. She's pale, her blonde hair hangs limply around her shoulders. There are such dark circles under her eyes, it looks like she's been beaten up. Maybe she was.

Her eyes land on me, and she gasps, bringing her hands to her mouth. "McKenzie?" she croaks. I take a deep breath and try to give an encouraging smile, but I'm sure it looks more like a grimace.

"Hey, Anna," I whisper. She places her head in her hands and begins to cry. I don't hesitate. I cross the room, sit next to her, and wrap my arms around her. She wraps her arms around me and clings to me with what little strength she has.

"You're okay," I promise her. "You're going to be okay." I blink, trying to dispel the tears, but they fall anyway. *Why did this happen? To me? To her?* I think she tries to speak, but nothing comes out. Sitting back slightly, I study her.

"Water?" I ask. She nods. Before I can move, Clara is handing me a glass of water. Anna reaches out with shaky hands, tears falling down her cheeks. "Let me help you."

She looks from the glass to her hands to me. Anna nods and I lift the glass to her mouth. She takes a few sips, humming. Probably at how good it feels. "It's been days since I've had water." Her voice is still scratchy. I want to find the people who did this to her and make them pay.

"I promise you'll be taken care of here."

She gazes at me. "Where is here, exactly?" Her voice is barely a whisper.

"Do you remember Phoenix?" Her eyes light up with recognition and she nods. "You're at his house." She doesn't seem taken aback by that.

"What are you doing here?" she asks.

I glance over my shoulder at Phoenix. "Phoenix saved me, too." She glances over my shoulder.

"A doctor will be here soon to check you over," Phoenix tells her. She doesn't respond, simply stares at him for a few seconds.

"They drugged me. They chained me up and did awful things to me." She sucks in a breath like she's remembering. Then she breaks into a coughing fit. I grab the glass of water and lift it to her lips again so she can take a few sips. She begins to cry again and my heart breaks for her.

Rex steps into the room. "Anna." I turn toward him, my eyebrows caving in. Anna goes completely still as she takes him in.

"Oh my god," she whispers. I glance back at her in complete confusion and back at Rex.

He steps forward. "I'm so sorry, Banana."

My mouth drops open. He's always been so rough around the edges for him to call her banana. I look toward Phoenix, but he's not giving anything away. *How does Rex know Anna?*

"Tobias." *Tobias?* I scramble off the bed to give room for Rex to take my spot. He sits gingerly on the edge of the bed. Grabbing her under her arms, he gently pulls her into his lap.

He wraps his arms around her. "I have looked everywhere. I promise. I never stopped looking."

The sincerity in his voice brings tears to my eyes. I glance up at Phoenix, but his face is still stoic.

Anna remembers. She remembers Rex or Tobias. I'll have to find out about that later. But, I don't remember. Why? I wonder how that makes Phoenix feel. I didn't remember him. I still don't remember our lives together.

An ache begins to form in the middle of my chest. Bringing my hand up, I rub the ache, hoping it will disappear, but it only increases the more I think. Rex is whispering to Anna, and she's crying softly.

Unable to take it anymore, I walk out of the room and to the kitchen. Frustration boils in my veins. *Why can't I remember? I want to remember.*

"Kenz?"

Turning to Phoenix, I shake my head. "I'm sorry I can't remember. I wish I could remember."

Phoenix crosses the kitchen to stand in front of me. His hands grasp both sides of my neck and his thumbs rub along my jaw. "You do not need to be sorry about that."

"Why can she remember and I can't?"

He chuckles, but stops when I glare at him. "She wasn't kidnapped by your father." He says that like I should know what he means.

"Does my father hate me that much?" I wrap my arms around my stomach. He steps closer and pulls me into his body, wrapping me in his arms, his warmth, his scent. It calms me in a way I didn't know was possible.

"He hates *me* that much," he corrects.

"I have no idea what that means." I wrap my arms around his waist, snaking my hands under his t-shirt to feel his toned skin.

"I have wanted to tell you so much since the day you woke up." I rub my hands up his spine. I have thought about doing this for weeks now.

He leans down and runs his lips along my earlobe. "Kenz." It sounds like a warning and a promise.

"Do you have a cute nickname for me like Banana?"

He chuckles as he replaces his lips with his tongue. I let out a shaky exhale. "I call you McFeisty."

"What?" I don't know whether to laugh or be offended.

"Usually it leads to an argument, then the best sex of my life." He kisses me right below my ear as I try to comprehend what he just said to me.

"So, we've..." I don't finish my sentence.

He leans back and looks me in the eye. "We're married, love. And I'm not built to be celibate, so yes, we've Dot. Dot. Dot."

I roll my eyes, but inside I'm on fire. *I want to dot dot dot, now preferably.*

"Now that you know, you'll sleep in our room tonight. I'm sick of sleeping in that fucking chair," he says.

Fear, maybe anxiety, settles in the pit of my stomach. *What if I fart when I'm sleeping? Or talk? Or snore?* I know technically he's my husband. But I still remember him as the boy I had a crush on in high school. "Where's my ring?"

He freezes, and I'm not sure if that's a good or bad sign. "Do you want it?" he asks.

"Of course I do." I look out over the backyard. "I may not remember being married to you, but when we were at the academy, I fantasized about it enough," I admit. I don't know if I ever confessed that to him or not.

He smirks at me. Leaning down, he places his forehead against mine. "Now I can kiss you whenever I want." His mouth lands on mine. I gasp, giving him free access to slip his tongue in. He doesn't hesitate as he strokes my tongue with his.

He grasps the back of my neck, pulling me in even closer as I feel him grow hard against my stomach. His other hand snakes down over my ass to the back of my thigh and he encourages me to jump. He grips my thighs, turns and places me on the kitchen island.

"You definitely taste better than chocolate chip cookies." I can't say anything before his mouth is devouring mine again.

I tighten my legs around him, bucking against him needing some friction. He scoots me to the edge of the counter and gives me exactly what I need. He thrusts against me slow and hard, touching every sensitive spot I have. I swear I feel every ridge of him.

"Nix, please," I moan. He pauses and gazes at me. He has an unreadable expression, but before I can ask him about it, he unties my robe and grabs the band of my pajama shorts. I don't hesitate; I put all my weight on my hands and lift my hips. He pulls my shorts and panties down my legs. Dropping to his knees, he spreads my legs.

I expect him to dive in, instead he stares. Leaning up, I look to see what he's doing. When he continues to stare, I try to shift and close my legs.

"Did I say you could move?" His eyes don't leave my pussy. I open my mouth to talk, but I don't know what to say, so I close it. He places his lips on the inside of my knee, kissing it gently before he moves higher up my thigh.

Anyone could find us. Clara or Rex could walk out here, but I don't care. He pulls me closer to the edge. I think I might fall off. When I'm where he wants me, he spreads my legs until my knees hit the island. I lean back, catching myself on my hands as his lips touch the crease of the inside of my thigh.

"Oh god," I moan. I want to beg him to do more, but I'm still not sure where this is headed, so I wait.

"No, love. I want you to say my name." One hand comes to his head and I card my fingers through his hair as I look down at him. He winks at me before he turns his attention to my pussy and licks me from my center to my clit.

My head falls back as I focus on the wicked things his tongue is doing to me. The pressure, the speed, everything. It's so good. He changes from licking me to thrusting his tongue. I rock against him as my arms lose strength and I sink down onto the island. I need more. I'm not sure what I need more of. But when he thrusts two fingers inside of me, I realize that's exactly what I needed.

He knows my body so well; it's amazing and creepy at the same time. I'm sure he's done this hundreds of times before. He knows exactly what will get me off. He crooks his finger rubbing against my g-spot as he circles his tongue around my clit.

"Nix," I moan. I'm on the edge of the cliff and I want, no need, him to push me over. He pumps his fingers and flattens his tongue to give stronger licks. The pressure reaches a precipice and I have to focus on breathing so I don't pass out. "Please. please. please."

He sucks my clit and swirls his tongue around me. I grip the edge of the island when my legs tighten and shake as I explode. Trying to control how loud I am so everyone in the house doesn't hear, I pry one of my hands from the island and cover my mouth as I ride out the orgasm.

A shaky breath escapes me as I try to recover, but I still feel the tremors going through every muscle in my body. He stands slowly, gazing down at me with a haughty grin on his face. "I love the sounds you make when you come."

Chapter 15

I'm still trying to catch my breath as I look up at him. "I want to do that again." He chuckles and grabs my hand, helping me to a sitting position.

"I'd love to do that again. It's one of my favorite things." He grabs me under my arms and lifts me, so I wrap my arms and legs around him as he walks quickly to his room. *Our room.*

I lay my head on his shoulder and face his neck. His tattoo calls out to me. Leaning closer, I run my tongue along the outline. His grip on my ass tightens, but he doesn't stop me.

Attaching my lips to his neck, I kiss and lick. I wonder if I could give him a hickey. *Have I ever done that before?*

"Done what?" he asks as he lays me down. *Guess I said that out loud.*

"Given you a hickey." He smirks as he grabs the back of his T-shirt and pulls it over his head, revealing the beauty underneath it.

"You have." He climbs onto the bed and lays next to me on his side. Wrapping his arm around my waist, he gets so close to me his chest touches my side. It reminds me of the memory I had. "It's kind of your thing."

I turn to face him and begin tracing the tattoos on his arm. "My thing?" I ask.

He leans back and pulls his pajama pants down slightly. Right on the edge of his V is a tattoo of lips. "That was the first spot you gave me a hickey, so I memorialized it with that tattoo."

"Huh." I stare at the spot as my face heats up for something I don't remember. Apparently, things don't change even with memory loss. I want to touch the tattoo, but I control myself. He releases the band on his pajamas, covering the tattoo. I ball my hands into fists so I don't reach out and pull it back down.

Sucking in a breath, I roll onto my back trying to get my wits about me. Taking in my surroundings, I'm astounded at how beautiful Phoenix's home is.

I thought my room was pretty, but this one. It is beautiful. On one side there's a wall of windows, similar to mine. Except here the windows are separate with arches and the middle one has a window seat to look out over the gardens below.

The moonlight streams in. It brings a peace I'm not used to. Turning my attention to the rest of the room, I notice how it's almost double the size of the one I've been staying in. I'm sure there's a walk-in closet and a bathroom.

There's a fireplace in this room as well, with an empty spot above it. I lean up on my elbows, tilting my head, trying to figure out why it feels like something is missing.

"You don't have a TV in here?" I ask. Phoenix rolls over onto his back, placing his hands behind his head.

"No." He doesn't expand further as I continue to stare at the spot above the fireplace.

"Is something missing from above the fireplace?" I finally ask. He sighs deeply, as if he's contemplating whether he should tell me or not. Turning to look at him, I arch an eyebrow. "Phoenix?"

"A canvas used to be above it."

"What aren't you telling me?" I ask.

He sighs again and faces me. "We did a boudoir shoot before the wedding. It was a picture from that session." I wasn't expecting him to say that.

"Can I see it?"

He rolls away from me, grabbing his phone off the nightstand. "I'm going to call Dr. Chamberland and have him come see you after he's done with Anna." He pulls up Dr. Chamberland's contact information and presses the call button.

"Okaaayyy."

"Can you stop by McKenzie's bedroom when you're done?" I push myself up into a sitting position. *He said my bedroom, not his.*

"Why is he coming to my room and not here? And why does he have to see me?" I rub my hand along the silky comforter. If I could remember, maybe it would be different.

Phoenix sits up next to me. "No one is allowed in our room. This is the only place where it's just you and me." Relief flows through my veins. I don't know why I needed to hear that so badly, but everything is so up in the air. I have no idea how I wound up here.

How did it come to be that I married Phoenix? Why did he buy me? Then risk his life again to save me? Why did my father sell me? Why did he kidnap me?

I have so many unanswered questions. And they could all be answered if I could just remember.

"I'm having him come up so I can get some clarification on what I can share with you. In the beginning, he told me to be careful, but now that you're beginning to remember some things, I don't see why I can't answer some of your questions."

I crawl off the bed and walk to my room. Phoenix follows me. Sitting down in what I'm assuming is his favorite chair, he grabs me around the waist and pulls me onto his lap. The tension that's built up in my muscles in the past few minutes releases as I curl into his chest and lay my head on his shoulder.

"The memory I had I think it was from our honeymoon, or maybe the day after our wedding. The bed we were in didn't look like the bed in your room."

He pulls me tighter against him. "Our room," he corrects. "And if it was from early on, it wouldn't have been that bed. We had this place built and moved in a year ago."

"Oh. How long have we been married?"

His thumb runs up and down my spine. "I told you this when you asked me how long I've been married." I purse my lips, thinking back.

"Three and a half years?" I ask. He nods. "Wasn't the auction three and a half years ago?"

"It's been a little longer. Let's wait until Dr. Chamberland gets up here and we'll talk about that further." I nod slowly, lots of thoughts running through my mind.

"Okay. Well, back to the memory I had. You were telling me it was time to wake up, and I was pretending to be asleep. You called me Mrs. Stone; that's how I realized we were married. Or maybe it was just knowing. I'm not sure." I pause, picturing the memory in my mind. It's still a little fuzzy around the edges.

Phoenix doesn't interrupt. He begins rubbing his thumb along my spine. "You were flirting with me. Kissing me. Rocking against me. I'm sure it led to sex, but I woke up and there you were, sitting in this chair."

"How did you feel? Knowing you were married to me?" he asks.

I huff. "Relieved. I thought you were married to Anna. I was so jealous."

He pushes me back slightly so he can look at me. "Why would you think that?" I wince, realizing I have to come clean.

"I was sneaking around in your downstairs office one day trying to find something, anything, to give me clues about why I was here. I found a picture of Anna and me from the academy. It was folded in half." I shrug. "I just assumed you were keeping it hidden so I wouldn't find it, but you wanted it close so you could look at it whenever you wanted."

He shakes his head at me, leaning up to kiss me on my forehead. "Kenz, do you know how much I've wanted you since the first day I saw you?"

I make a face at him. "Obviously not."

He shakes his head and chuckles. "So smart, yet so oblivious." A sense of déjà vu happens, like we've had this conversation. Before I can respond, Dr. Chamberland knocks on the open door announcing his arrival.

"You wanted me to come up here? Is everything alright?" He looks between Phoenix and me, his eyebrows rising slightly.

"Yes. McKenzie had a memory." Dr. Chamberland looks surprised, but he grins. I think. He looks caught off guard a little. I wonder if Phoenix has him do house calls like this a lot. I'm sure he's probably exhausted.

"She remembered we're married, but that's all. Do you think it's safe if I begin sharing some of our life with her? Maybe it'll trigger more memories?"

Dr. Chamberland nods before Phoenix finishes talking. "Perhaps." He runs his hand through his black hair. "What were you doing when you had this memory?"

"I was sleeping. It woke me up. But before I went to sleep, I was writing in my journal." I pick up my journal off the table and leaf through it.

"I don't see any harm in sharing things with her, Mr. Stone. But be aware it might cause anxiety or a panic attack. Some memories may be hard, even if they're good memories."

Phoenix nods as he runs his fingers through my hair absentmindedly. "Okay. Thank you, Dr. Chamberland. Sorry to call you out so late."

He shakes his head. "Happy to help. I'll be by in a few days to check in. Nurse Millie will be by tomorrow to check on Anna.

And I'm sure Dr. Pearl will be happy to hear you've had another memory." He walks out and I curl even deeper into Phoenix's chest. I'm exhausted.

The next day Phoenix has business to attend to, so he leaves right after breakfast. Phillip is in the kitchen prepping for Thanksgiving, and I watch him as I sip on another cup of coffee.

"Phillip?" He turns toward me, giving me his full attention. "Would I be in your way if I made a few desserts for Thanksgiving?" I ask.

He walks to me with an encouraging smile and pats me on the hand. "I love having you in the kitchen."

"You do?"

He nods as he goes back to the bread he's making from scratch. "Yes. We always had so much fun in the kitchen." I smile at him, glad that he's sharing this with me.

"Really?"

He turns back toward me. "Yes. When you showed interest in baking, I went out right away and bought you the KitchenAid mixer." My eyes fall on the mixer I've been using for the past several weeks.

"That's mine?" I ask.

Phillip chuckles as he places a damp paper towel over the bowl and pushes it aside. "It is, and the day Clara took you on the tour and you noticed it right away, she was practically giddy. She was convinced your amnesia wouldn't be permanent. That your memories are just suppressed."

I nod slightly as I stand and walk to the refrigerator to take out some eggs and butter so they can be at room temperature when I need them. "I'm beginning to feel more hopeful, too."

"We're all glad you remembered you're married to Mr. Stone. That was the hardest thing not to acknowledge after he rescued you." He takes cornmeal and flour out of the cupboard. I'm assuming he's making cornbread next. "It's been a while since we've seen him smile." He pats my hand again. "Just in time for the holidays."

He puts his finger up, letting me know he'll be right back as he walks into the pantry to get other ingredients he needs. When he returns, he begins to prepare the batter for the cornbread.

"Who all comes over for Thanksgiving?" I haven't met anyone outside of Rex, Clara, Phillip, Nurse Millie, and Dr. Chamberland. There are other staff here, but they don't really talk to me. It seems like they avoid me. I wonder if they were instructed to ignore me.

"I think it's just going to be us this year. We've had a lot of guests in the past, but Mr. Stone doesn't want to overwhelm you or Anna." I want to protest, but I remember what it was like the first few weeks after I was rescued. Anna needs time to recover.

"I think I'm going to go for a walk real quick. I'll be back in just a few minutes to begin baking."

"I'll call Clara to go with you." He grabs his cell phone out of his pocket and I shake my head.

"No, it's alright. I know she's busy trying to get everything prepared." He hesitates, but reluctantly nods as he puts his phone back in his pocket.

"Don't go too far."

I wave my hand at him in an attempt to tell him not to worry. Grabbing my coat, I put it on and walk out the patio doors. Staring at the pool longingly, I continue past it toward the lake. I've tried a couple of times to get to the lake, but I still haven't made it all the way down the hill.

I could probably make it down the hill, it's getting back up it that I'm worried about. Maybe I can try later when Phoenix gets back. He can help me if I need it.

I get further, but finally give up about halfway. I rest on a bench that blends in well with the surroundings and pull my jacket around me tighter as the breeze picks up. It looks like it may be cold this Thanksgiving.

I watch two birds in a tree chirp at each other. It kind of sounds like they're having an argument. I can only imagine what they're communicating. One of the birds looks at me. It's a little eerie how he's watching me. "Why is she mad at you? Did you forget to put the toilet seat down?"

I snort at my dumb joke and the birds fly off. This land is so beautiful. Another breeze blows across the hill, it causes a chill to race across my spine. Something at the edge of my brain tingles, kind of like déjà vu. Like I've been in this exact same spot, resting, trying to gain some sense of control.

Why would I have felt that way? I understand why I feel that way now; I lost my memories. But what could have happened in the past that made me feel that way?

Standing, I walk a few more steps down the hill and fear overwhelms my senses. Similar to the fear I felt when I was chained up, but worse. *Why?* I turn slowly in a circle, taking in my surroundings again.

"If you don't come with me, I'll kill you, but first I'll kill Phoenix and I'll make you watch."

Chapter 16

I run up the hill. And by run, I mean walking at a very fast pace. When I make it to the kitchen, Phillip and Clara are laughing about something. I'm trying desperately to catch my breath as they turn their attention to me with looks of concern.

Clara walks over to me, pushing my hair off my face. "Miss Kenzie? Are you okay?"

I shake my head. "I need to talk to Phoenix. Now." Phillip is already taking his phone out and dialing Phoenix as he brings it to me.

I place the phone against my ear. "Hey Phillip. Everything okay?" Phoenix answers on the second ring.

"It's me."

"Kenz? What's wrong?" His voice is full of concern. Phillip and Clara continue to stare at me with concern in their eyes. *Am I overreacting? That was a memory.*

I hold my finger up to Phillip and Clara, letting them know I'll be right back and walk toward the library. "I remembered the day I was kidnapped."

"You did? What did you remember? Are you okay?" I sit down at the window seat and look out over the lake.

"I only remember someone saying, *'If you don't come with me, I'll kill you, but first I'll kill Phoenix and I'll make you watch.'* And I'm pretty sure it happened on the hill going down to the lake."

There's a long pause. "Switch to video call." We switch and seeing his face, knowing he's safe, brings me peace.

"I'll be home soon, but I needed to see your face." He's in the back of an SUV, maybe the same one we took for our date the other night.

"I'm okay. Just remembering that. Hearing that voice threaten you, even if it was a memory, it freaked me out." I pull the blanket over my lap as a chill skates down my spine.

"Did the voice sound familiar?" he asks. I purse my lips as I try to think.

"It did, but it also sounded altered. Like they were hiding who they really were." A text message pops up, reminding me I'm using Phillip's phone. "By the way, do I have a phone? I want to be able to call you without having to use someone else's."

He chuckles. "I had a feeling this conversation would be happening soon, so I actually got you one today. The one you had..." He trails off. "Well, it was discarded." I'm assuming he means by my father. I think back to the voice.

"Nix, I don't think my father kidnapped me. That did not sound like his voice. I mean, the voice was distorted, but I think I'd recognize it if it was his."

He's quiet for a few seconds. A look passes over his face like he's trying to decide what to say next. I can tell the minute he makes the decision. "Kenz, they didn't kidnap you from the house. We wouldn't still be living there if you had been."

My eyebrows draw down in confusion. I was so sure. "How was I kidnapped?"

Phoenix shakes his head. "I don't think it's a good idea for me to tell you that. Not yet. That's one of those memories I wouldn't be mad about not returning." I nod in understanding. I want to know, but it's not on the top of my list either.

"Can you tell me where I was kidnapped?" I push.

"Not over the phone. We'll talk about it when I get home. Okay?" I agree and we hang up. Returning to the kitchen, Phillip is cooking, while Clara is wiping down the glass on the patio doors. They both turn to me when I walk in. I can tell they've been waiting for me to return.

"Sorry if I made you worry. I had a memory I needed to tell Phoenix about." They both give me sympathetic looks and I sigh. I hand Phillip his phone back. "How many employees does Phoenix have?" I ask as I gather the ingredients I need to make the chocolate chip cookies. I know that's not a normal Thanksgiving dessert, but they're Phoenix's favorite.

"Well, there's me, Phillip, Rex, Nurse Millie, and Dr. Chamberland. That's who you've met," Clara says as she sprays another window to clean. "He has four other bodyguards. Jeremy, Ryan, Shrek, and Donkey."

Phillip snorts, and I stare at her in surprise. "Shrek and Donkey?"

Clara's lips lift in a mischievous smile. "That's what I call people when I can't remember their names." A huff of laughter escapes before I'm out right laughing. Phillip and Clara laugh with me. It takes me a few minutes to control my laughter.

Phillip puts a pot of something on the stove. "Their names are Clyde and Louis."

"Too bad one of their names isn't Bonnie. That's a missed opportunity." I walk into the pantry to grab a few more ingredients I'll need. I'm surprised he has so many bodyguards. Not that I should be, especially after what happened to me. *Has he always had that many?*

Walking back into the kitchen, I place everything on the counter. "Is Rex the lead?" I ask.

Phillip nods. "Yes, Mr. Stone met Rex after he graduated from high school. I don't know the whole story, so you'd need to ask them. But Rex saved Mr. Stone's life and ever since then, Rex has been Mr. Stone's right-hand man."

I make note of that so I can ask Phoenix about it later. I briefly wonder how Rex is doing. *Is he with Anna, or is he driving Phoenix?* I'm going to visit Anna at some point today when I can build up enough nerve. I know she needs a friend.

Her experience is different from mine. She didn't lose her memory, but I'm sure she still needs someone other than Rex. Or maybe she doesn't.

"Then you have the gardeners," Clara brings my attention back to the question I asked. "There's a pool guy that comes by once a month during the off season and then almost every day during the summer. And there's the guy at the gate. He's considered security."

I notice she doesn't say their names either. "Are they Shrek and Donkey too?" She chuckles and nods. Although I'm grateful she doesn't tell me everyone's names, because I wouldn't remember either. "I can't believe I haven't noticed any of those other people."

I measure out the ingredients, putting the butter and eggs in the blender first. Phillip clears his throat. "I think Mr. Stone told everyone to keep their distance." I tilt my head at Phillip. *Guess I was right about that one.*

"I'm going to finish the living room. Let me know if you need anything," Clara says before walking out of the kitchen.

"I'm glad Phoenix didn't tell you or Clara to keep your distance," I tell Phillip. He shakes his head with a smirk.

"He knew better. There was no way he'd keep us from you. He considered hiring someone to help you instead of letting Clara. Clara threw a huge fit, so he changed his mind." Learning that she fought to stay around me makes me smile. Sadness tries to creep in at the thought of me not being able to remember them, but I'm holding out hope that my memory will return. Hopefully soon.

Phillip has finished doing his prepping for today, so he's left me to my baking. I'm pulling the last batch of cookies from the oven when Phoenix walks in. I can't hide my smile or my eyes as I take him in.

He's wearing his usual dark pants and white button-up shirt with the sleeves rolled up to his elbows.

I'm wearing leggings and an oversized T-shirt with my hair in a braid to keep it out of my face while I'm baking. *He looks like a snack. I look...* That thought trails off when Phoenix walks to me, his eyes never leaving me. I place the cookies down just as he reaches me.

He wraps his arm around my waist, pulling me as close to him as physically possible, and wraps his hand around my braid, pulling my head back gently. His mouth is centimeters from mine, but he stops. I lick my lips as I stare up at him, waiting to see what he's going to do.

When he looks at me like that, it makes me forget all my insecurities. "Hello, wife," he murmurs before his mouth touches mine.

Him calling me wife, his mouth on mine, and my hair wrapped around his hand is causing a chain reaction in my body. His mouth fits against mine perfectly as his tongue licks my bottom lip. I gasp and he takes advantage of the opening as his tongue begins to massage mine.

I wrap my arms around him, holding him tight against me. The hand not in my hair travels down my spine and I arch even further into him. I'm on fire. The heat from my body could burn the cookies I just took out of the oven.

He lifts me, making my feet dangle, but I pull them up and wrap them around his waist. He adjusts me as he turns and places me on the counter, away from the hot cookie sheet. I run my fingers through his hair, loving the feel of it against the palm of my hands.

He pulls away, giving me the opportunity to suck in a much needed breath as his mouth drifts down to my jaw, to the sensitive spot on my throat I didn't realize I had, but he seems to know all too well. I tilt my head, giving him better access.

"Are you telling me I've been missing out on this type of greeting for the past several months?" I ask. He chuckles as he runs his tongue along my collarbone, up to my shoulder, and then back to my neck.

"If I lick it, it's mine." I swallow and he tightens his hand around my throat more. I can still breathe, but I can't move. "Your tears belong to me and I promise I'll be taking a lot of them."

Phoenix pulls back to look at me, sensing the difference in how I was responding to him. He lets go of my hair before cupping my jaw. "What's wrong?" he asks. His eyes search mine.

"I had a memory." He stands to his full height as he continues to study me, almost like he wishes he could read my mind so he knew what I remembered.

He was upset. I was upset. Did he make me cry a lot?

"What was it?" I can tell by the hesitation in his voice he's worried. He doesn't know if it's going to be a good memory or a bad memory. I'm conflicted with how I want to respond. Part of me wants to pull away, another part wants him to assure me.

"I think I was laying in bed and you were hovering over me with your hand around my throat." His eyes widen and he steps back slightly. "You said, 'If I lick it, it's mine. Your tears belong to me and I promise I'll be taking a lot of them.'" He stares at me, his expression not giving anything away. "Did we not get along? Did you not like me? Did I not like you?"

He exhales slowly before stepping closer to me. "We had a love-hate relationship after the auction. We tried our best to resist each other and one of my ways was to keep you at arm's length." He wraps his arms around me, pulling me closer to him. "Obviously I didn't succeed."

He shows me his ring. I rub my thumb over my ring finger, wondering where my ring is. It reminds me he never answered my question about when we got married.

"How long after the auction did we get married?"

His hands trail up my arms slowly, leaving goosebumps along the way. "Three months." My mouth opens slightly. I wasn't expecting it to be so soon. One arm wraps around my waist while his other hand wraps around the side of my neck, his thumb brushing over my jaw. "Like I said last night, I've wanted you since the moment I laid eyes on you."

I rub my hands from his abs, up his chest, over his shoulders, and back down to his chest. I play with the top button of his shirt, slipping it out of the hole to show a slither of tattooed skin. "Our hate..." He trails off.

"It eventually turned to love?" I ask. One side of his mouth tips up as he leans forward and brushes his lips over my cheek to my ear. He hums in agreement.

Another button slips from his shirt, so I rub my fingers over the part of the tattoo I see. His hand flexes at my lower back.

"You came to an auction with me and saw how I was trying to save some of the girls that didn't want to be there." He kisses me right below my ear. "Then when you found out about Anna—"

I lean back. "Anna?"

"Yes. You found out she was one of the girls I was trying to rescue. Rex used to be Anna's security. She got sold. Not too long after that, he saved my life. So, I hired him to be my security, and I vowed I'd find her."

My eyes widen at this piece of information. "What? When did she get sold?"

"Three months before you were. The auctions happen every three months. Rex tried to stop it, but he found out too late and didn't get there in time."

My head is spinning with all of this information. "Rex was Anna's security." That makes sense. Her father is a senator, who I think was on the path to running for president, eventually. "Did she get kidnapped to be sold at the auction?"

He stares at me for several seconds before responding. "No, she came home for winter break from college and her dad took her to the auction." He pauses for a brief moment. "She thought it was a party, too."

I'm speechless. I only met Anna's father a few times when he'd come to the academy for parent's weekend, but it's hard to imagine he'd do that to her. I think about my father. It's hard to imagine he'd do that as well.

"Are there more girls who have been sold?" I don't want to know the answer.

"Yes, several."

Chapter 17

I don't know what to say. He steps back and crosses his arms over his chest, making the opening in his shirt wider and giving me a better look at his tattooed skin underneath. Swallowing, I focus on what he just said.

Several girls were sold. "Did all the girls who were sold go to Brighton?"

"The majority." He surprises me when he answers. I don't know why. So far, anytime I've asked him a question outright, he's answered. And as far as I know, he's been honest. My mind begins to whirl. *What could that mean?*

"Were they all sold against their will?"

"Those who were sold from Brighton, yes."

I bring my hand up to my mouth. "What does that even mean?"

He sighs and leans against the counter. "There are some people who are sold at these auctions that do it willingly." I open my mouth, but close it again.

I need to stop keeping my head in the sand and begin doing research. I've been avoiding this because I don't want to know why my father would sell me. Or why the principal would want to buy me. *Who bought Anna?* I rub my hands up and down my arms before jumping off the counter.

"I'm going to check on Anna." Phoenix doesn't respond, but he doesn't try to stop me either. I want him to tell me everything, but at the same time I don't.

Walking down the hall, I stop at Anna's door. It's cracked slightly, so I glance through and see her laying on her side facing the windows. I'm not sure if she's asleep or not, so I knock lightly. She turns toward me and the haunted look in her eyes makes me want to kill whoever did this to her.

"Hey Anna," I whisper because I remember how loud everything seemed when I first got here.

"Hey," she whispers back. Her voice cracks and she grimaces. There's a pitcher of water on her nightstand, so I walk over and pour her a glass. She struggles to sit up. I want to help her, but the determination in her eyes tells me it wouldn't be appreciated. When she's situated, I sit next to her and hand her the water.

Her hands shake as she brings the glass to her lips. I keep my hands under the glass just in case it falls, but allow her to do it on her own. She almost drops it, so I grab it and help her take a few more sips. Releasing a frustrated sigh, she leans her head back and closes her eyes.

I sit the glass back on the nightstand. "I hate this," she whispers. Her voice sounds different than what I remember.

"I know. It will get easier," I promise her.

She turns her head to look at me. "Tobias says you've lost your memories." I have to remind myself Tobias is Rex.

"Yes. I don't remember the past three years of my life."

She turns away and looks out the windows again. "You're lucky. I wish I could forget."

I don't know how to respond to that. I understand where she's coming from and my heart hurts for her, but I wish I could remember. At least the parts where I've forgotten Phoenix and my life with him.

"I always knew you and Phoenix would wind up together." One side of her mouth lifts into a small smile. She changes the subject, probably in an attempt to not talk about herself.

"How did you know that? I always thought you had a crush on him."

She chuckles as her gaze finds mine. "I did. Everyone did, but he only had eyes for you." My eyes widen. She shakes her head. "And you were completely oblivious."

I shrug as I play with a loose thread on my shirt. "I was just trying to make it through so I could get out." I sigh. "I don't even know why I was ready to get out. It seems, for the most part, my life was better while I was there." I was so angry at my father for sending me to Brighton right after my mother died.

I hadn't even had time to mourn before he was shipping me off. Everyone in that school had connections to the mafia, or government, or world leaders. I don't even think they accepted anyone that didn't have high connections.

"I'm so sorry your father sold you," I whisper.

How could he do that to her? Especially when he has high ambitions for his career. Isn't he afraid of getting found out?

She sniffs and pulls her knees up to her chest. "I'm sorry your father sold you," she replies. "Who would have thought our first loves could do something like that to us?" A lump forms in my throat. I know my father isn't a good man, but until my mother died, he wasn't horrible. He was a hard man, but I never thought he was capable of something like this.

"Did you know who bought you?"

She pulls her bottom lip between her teeth and shakes her head. "I didn't know him like you knew Phoenix. I knew of him. He was one of my father's colleagues. I was with him for almost a year before I was kidnapped."

My mouth drops open. "What?" That can't be a coincidence that we were both kidnapped from the people who bought us.

She nods. "I think his wife planned it. She was jealous, even though I never asked for his attention." I have so many questions, but I don't want to upset her.

"Did he..." I trail off. She picks at the blanket.

"No, he never did. Well, except..." She shakes her head and trails off. *Except what?* I want to ask her, but she clearly doesn't want to talk about it, so I leave it. "The only thing he ever wanted me to do with him was read while he was working in his home office. Or join him for dinner. His wife was never home. I think he was lonely. She didn't care about any of that, though. It's when he started buying me nice things that she got jealous and upset."

She pauses, sighing deeply. "Now the people who kidnapped me..." She trails off again and my heart breaks for her. I'm okay with that part of my memory never returning.

"How do you know Rex?" I ask, changing the subject. I already know what Phoenix told me, but I want to hear it from Anna. A genuine smile lights up her face. She releases the tension in her muscles and sighs.

"He was my bodyguard before my dad sold me." *I knew Rex was older, but how much older is he?* "He didn't know anything about the auction. He knew my dad went to these secret meetings, but that's all he knew."

She pulls her hair over her shoulder, running her fingers through it a few times before leaning against the headboard. I can tell she's beginning to get tired. "The first day I met him was the day I came home after graduation. I fell fast. I was eighteen, he was twenty-eight, so I knew he'd never want me. But we got close. He became my best friend." I tilt my head at her. From the other night, it seemed like there was something between them, but maybe I was reading into something that wasn't there.

"He even went to college with me. Dad got me an apartment and Rex stayed there with me." She laughs. "Of course, that blocked me from having a love life."

"My father took me to that auction without telling him. I had no idea it was an auction. I thought it was a masquerade party. He gave me a mask to wear and told me I couldn't take it off the entire night. I listened until I went to the restroom. I took it off so I could touch up my makeup."

She sucks in a breath and swallows hard. "Another girl came out of a stall. When she saw me, she took her mask off too. I recognized her from Brighton, but I think she graduated the year before us. Her mask was red and black, though. Mine was just red. She told me I needed to find a way out, then she put her mask back on and left."

She shakes her head and covers her face with her hands. I lean close and wrap my arms around her. "You don't have to tell me anymore." I'm surprised she's told me this much.

"That part is the easy part, but after. I don't know if I'll ever be able to talk about that." *After? After what? She was kidnapped?* There's a soft knock on the door. We both look over and see Clara coming in with a tray. Rex walks in behind her and I can feel the relief that washes over Anna. I stand, giving Rex a small smile.

"I have lunch for you, Miss Anna." Clara says with a smile. "Your lunch is ready in the kitchen, Miss Kenzie."

"Thank you, Clara." I walk out with one more glimpse over my shoulder. Rex sits on the bed and pulls Anna onto his lap like he did last night. I smile at their interaction. *Is he doing that to comfort her or is there more?* I turn and walk back to the kitchen. Maybe it's a good thing I don't remember everything, but everything in me wishes I could remember my relationship with Phoenix.

He and Anna are right. I was oblivious to how Phoenix felt about me. But I was not oblivious to him. I loved that he'd come to the library and sit at the same table as me while I was studying, or that he always ended up in the same classes as me. Even if I did try to pick classes I didn't think he'd choose. Mainly because he made me nervous.

Walking into the kitchen, I watch Phoenix as he grabs two glasses and pours iced tea into them. Phillip is back in the kitchen preparing for Thanksgiving, but Phoenix doesn't expect him to do everything.

I love that. I rub my thumb and forefinger over my ring finger on my left hand.

I want my ring. Even if I can't remember marrying him, I still want it. Phoenix turns to me, his eyes assessing me to see if my mood is a little better from when I walked out of the kitchen.

He approaches me slowly. Phillip walks into the pantry and I can't help but wonder if it's to give us some privacy. "You okay, love?" He stops in front of me and tugs on my braid lightly.

I step closer to him, my hands rubbing from his abs, which contract at my touch, to his chest and around his neck. I'm standing on my tiptoes so I can reach him. He wraps his arms around me and supports me so I don't fall.

"I want my ring."

He brings his forehead down to mine and brushes his lips over mine. "Okay."

He releases me slowly. Grabbing my hand, he leads me through the kitchen, living room, and up the stairs to his—no, our—bedroom. I stop at the entrance as he walks to the closet door and opens it. I follow him and stop at the beauty of the walk-in closet.

I haven't been in here yet, but it is breathtaking. There's a chandelier in the middle of the spacious room. It's almost like a separate room that's been made into a closet. On the far end is a vanity, with a white and gold armchair.

On the right are lines of his shirts and pants, with racks for his shoes. On the left are my clothes that I didn't even know were in here. He turns to me as he leans against the dresser in the middle of the closet. "I didn't put all of your clothes in the other room. I've already asked Clara to begin moving those clothes in here."

I step further into the closet as I gaze around. "This is gorgeous," I whisper.

He walks toward me, stopping when his toes touch mine. "You designed it."

I suck in a breath. "What?"

His hand comes up to cup my neck, his thumb running over my jaw. "You practically designed this entire house. We had an architect, but you helped with every single room." I'm so surprised I don't know what to say.

That has to be why everything is so comfortable, because I hated how sterile my house was growing up. Nothing was comfortable, so I practically lived in my bedroom because it was the only place I was allowed to make comfortable. I had always promised myself when I grew up and moved out I would have comfort and beauty.

"Thank you," I whisper. He tilts his head at me. The lines next to his eyes crinkle as he gazes at me.

"For what?"

"For letting me be comfortable." His eyes flare with understanding and familiarity. I wonder if we've had this conversation before. I sigh, trying to ignore the disappointment that comes at that thought.

He turns and goes to one of the drawers on his side. Opening it, he lifts out a small black box. I lick my lips as my heart begins to beat in my ears.

Turning, he walks to me. I expect him to hand me the box, but instead he drops to his knee and opens it. I cover my mouth with my hands as I look from him to the box he's opened.

"Will you be my wife?" he asks. Technically we're already married, so he can't ask me if I'll marry him. Instead, he's asking me to be his wife. He's giving me a choice.

"Yes," I whisper. He smiles and stands, taking the engagement ring and wedding band out of the box before placing them on my finger.

I'm going to marry Phoenix, who is my father's enemy. I never expected my life to turn out like this.

Chapter 18

The flash of memory confuses me for a moment, but my attention is quickly brought back to the present as Phoenix finishes placing the rings on my finger. His fingers cup mine and he brings my hand up to his mouth, kissing it softly as he stands. His eyes connect with mine and my stomach swarms with butterflies at the desire there.

He flips my hand so my palm is facing up. He kisses the middle of my palm before rubbing his lips up to the pulse of my wrist. My breathing picks up as his tongue flicks out and licks the sensitive spot on the inside of my wrist. Goosebumps break out on my skin.

He knows all these spots on me that respond to him so well. I need to figure out which spots on him elicits a response. His mouth travels further up my forearm to the crook of my elbow, his eyes never leaving mine.

His pupils are dilated. I can only see a sliver of his icy blue eyes. I can't look away as his lips continue up my bicep to my shoulder, then to the crook of my neck. A sigh, that sounds a lot like a moan, escapes as he licks the column of my neck.

I tilt my head, giving him better access as I clutch at his shirt. His other hand wraps around my waist and pulls me against him so I can feel every hard ridge of his body against mine. I fumble, trying to find the buttons of his shirt as he assaults my senses.

The need to have him right now is all-consuming. I can't think past wanting to have his skin against mine. His hand on my waist rubs up my spine as his lips run along my jaw to my chin. I can't control the pants of breath leaving me. His hand cups the back of my neck as he guides my mouth to his.

The moment his soft lips touch mine, I open for him and he doesn't hesitate. His tongue invades my mouth as I release the last button of his shirt and push it off his shoulders. He yanks it off, gripping the hem of my shirt and pulling it over my head.

Our mouths part for the briefest moment to allow it clearance. His mouth devours mine as he lifts me and I wrap myself around him. I expect him to sit me on the cabinet in the middle of the closet; instead, he turns and walks back into our bedroom.

He places me on the bed and walks over to the door, closing it and locking it. I lean up on my elbows as I watch him prowl toward me, like a predator that's about to devour its prey. He stops at the edge of the bed and looks down at me.

The bulge in his pants is proof of what he wants to do next. I take in everything about him. His scuffed up hair, the quickening pulse at his neck and his sharp breathing. The definition of his abs and the V that leads to exactly what I need.

"Tell me to stop and I'll walk out of this room," Phoenix says. "But I need you to tell me now, because the moment I climb on this bed, I plan on doing everything I've been fantasizing about since I found you." His hands ball into fists like he's having to force himself to stay exactly where he's at.

I push myself up and get on my knees, kneeling before him on the bed in my leggings and bralette. I place my hands on his chest and slowly rub down his abs until I get to the button of his pants. "I don't want to stop."

He doesn't move as I unbutton his pants and pull his zipper down. But when I cup him with my hand, everything happens at once. He moves my hands aside and pushes his pants down over his hips so he's standing in front of me in black boxer briefs.

I seek out the tattoo he showed me the other day from when I gave him a hickey. A moment in time I don't remember, but I'd like to repeat. He grabs me under my arms and lifts me, tossing me gently further back on the bed. He crawls up the bed laying between my legs and rocks his hard cock against my covered pussy.

I clutch his shoulders as I meet him. "Oh, god," I moan just as his mouth comes down on mine. He kisses me with such fervor I think I might pass out from how good it is.

He rubs his large palms along my sides to my bralette. I force myself to remove my hands from his muscular back and lift them over my head as he pulls the bralette over my head. He leans back, looking down at my body, taking in my breasts and rosy nipples. Leaning down, he pulls one into his mouth. I arch against him as he rubs his hard cock against me again.

"Nix, please," I whisper as his fingers pinch the nipple on my other breast. He sucks my breast into his mouth and I claw at his back. He lifts his head slightly, kissing the top of my breasts.

"Fuck, I love it when you do that," he moans as my nails scrape down his spine. My stomach sinks. We've done this before and I don't remember, but I push that away for now and take note that he likes it.

His mouth nips at my other breast as he sucks, bites, and kisses it. I think he might be marking me, but I'm not sure. When he lifts his head to inspect what he just did, I know he did, in fact, mark me. I run my fingers through his hair.

"Guess I'm not the only one who marks their territory."

His eyes collide with mine. He smirks as he leans down and runs his nose along mine. "Let's see who has the most by the time we get done."

I lick my dry lips at the challenge. Wrapping my legs around him, I turn quickly so he flips over on his back. He grins up at me, his hands coming to my breasts, and I know he let me do that. If he still wanted me on my back, I'd be there.

Leaning down, I kiss him lightly, but before he can turn it into more, I kiss up his jaw to his ear and pull it between my teeth. He hisses as his hands cup my ass. I rock against his hard cock and we both moan. My panties are sticking to me; I'm so wet.

Licking down his neck, I stop when I get to the skin that connects his neck and shoulder. He sucks in a breath and I know I've found another sensitive spot. *This is fun*. Sucking the skin between my lips, I rely on instinct as I'm determined to mark him like he marked me.

As far as I can remember, I've never done this before. But according to him, it's my thing. And I can understand why. It's addicting having someone react this way when you touch them. His hands grip my ass as I mark him.

When I'm done, I lean back to inspect my work, smiling in satisfaction. He flips us again so I'm on my back and grips the band of my leggings, pulling them down along with my panties. My heart lodges in my throat as I become completely exposed to him.

He sits back and gazes at me, longing and desire evident in his eyes. I love the way he looks at me. Almost like he's in a battle with himself, like he wants to savor and devour me at the same time. He lays down between my legs, throwing one over his shoulder. I stare at him as his eyes catch mine and he swipes his tongue from my pussy up to my clit.

I arch up at the suddenness of it, but I don't stop him. I want more. I need more. He winks and smirks at me before his mouth covers my clit and he pulls it between his lips.

Digging my heel into his back, I try to get closer as he sucks then flicks it with the tip of his tongue. His hands rub up my shins to my thighs and push me down as he spreads me wider. I buck against him, wanting to fuck his tongue, but he controls my movements as he removes his lips from my clit and spears me with his tongue.

I grab the back of his head and hold on as he fucks me with his tongue. "Nix," I moan. "Fuck, Nix." He spreads my pussy with his fingers as he licks from my pussy to my clit over and over. All I can do is hold on as I climb higher and higher.

Every muscle in my body is drawn tight as he strums my sensitive nerves. "Please," I whisper. He inserts one finger, then two, as he crooks them just so and rubs against my sensitive wall. I grip his hair as I ride his tongue and fingers.

My legs shake when he sucks my clit into his mouth again, holding me on the edge before he bites gently and flicks me over and over while rubbing my walls with his fingers. I shatter into a million pieces, calling out his name.

He doesn't wait for me to come down from my high as he pushes his boxers off, then climbs up my body. Grabbing my thigh, he pulls my leg over his hip. He holds himself up with his hand and gazes down at me. His cock teases my entrance. My eyes widen at the sensation. *He's pierced. Holy shit.* I moan, knowing the stretch is going to be so good.

"You ready?" he asks. His hand sneaks between us, and grabs his cock before rubbing the head up and down my pussy lips.

I shudder at how good it feels. "When did you...?" I ask as I nod frantically letting him know I'm ready. "Yes, please. Yes."

He can tell me later when he did that. His forehead lands on mine as he slowly enters me. I suck in breath after breath until he's completely sheathed by me. *Oh god, it feels so good.* He wraps his arm around my lower back, lifting me slightly, making him go in deeper.

"Fuck, you feel so good," he moans against my throat. He pulls out and thrusts back in. My nails dig into his shoulders as he does it again and again. I'm sure the entire house can hear us, but I don't care. The weight of him on top of me, how he feels thrusting in and out of me. His piercing. It's all perfect.

He pulls out, but before I can protest, he wraps his hands around my waist and flips me so I'm on all fours. He lifts my hips and thrusts into me from behind. At this angle, he's deeper and his piercing is rubbing me just right. I lay my cheek on the sheet and grip the sheets in my hands. I push back against him as he holds me tight.

He touches every spot in me as I try to hold on. He wraps his arm around my waist as his thrusts become more erratic. His hand snakes between my legs and he strums my clit with his middle finger.

"Fuck," I whisper as he swirls his finger around me.

"Come on, love. I know you can give me one more." I push back against him, chasing the orgasm that's cresting. My walls flutter and he moans as he thrusts harder and faster.

"Nix." He pinches my clit between his thumb and forefinger and I scream out my release. My walls clench around him as he thrusts four more times and comes with a long, drawn-out moan. He falls on top of me, catching himself before he completely squishes me.

I drag in breath after breath, my heart beating out of my chest. He pushes my hair out of my face and kisses me just below my ear. Pulling out of me, he rolls to the side and pulls me back to his chest. Wrapping an arm around my waist, his lips brush over my shoulder.

"I've missed you, love."

I take a deep breath, still trying to control my breathing, and roll over so I'm facing him. His cum drips out of me and I try not to think of the possible consequences at the moment as I stare at him. I wish I could tell him I've missed him, but I can't remember what I've been missing. I do know this is something I've wanted since I was at Brighton, and I don't regret a single moment.

Chapter 19

I need to finish my baking for Thanksgiving, and I'm sure Phoenix has things he needs to do. Instead, we're lying here facing each other. His hand is cupping the back of my head while I trace his tattoos with my finger.

"Did you know I had a thing for you the entire time I was at Brighton?" I ask him.

He chuckles as he combs his fingers through my hair. "Yes, but only because you've already told me." I stop tracing his tattoo for a few seconds before continuing.

"Right." I've had so many conversations with him I don't remember, and I hate it. The closer I get to him, the more it bothers me.

He leans forward and brushes his lips over my cheek. "To be fair, I had a thing for you, too."

I lean up and kiss him before continuing my exploration of his tattoos. "When did you get the piercing?"

He chuckles. "That's new. I got it when you were kidnapped this last time. The pain, it helped." I hum in understanding. At least that's something I can say we experienced together for the first time.

"Anna told me something today that made me start thinking. At the auction she was bought at she wore a red mask and she ran into another girl that may have graduated a year ahead of us in the bathroom. She was wearing a red and black mask. Do the different color masks mean different things?"

Phoenix doesn't answer right away. *Is he trying to choose his words carefully?* "Yes, they do," he finally replies, but he doesn't expand.

"Okay, what do they mean?" I ask. He sighs and rolls over onto his back. He places his hands behind his head as he stares up at the ceiling.

"The white ones mean they're selling, the black ones mean they're buying. The red ones mean they're for sale, the black and red ones mean they're taken, but willing to share." He takes a deep breath. "Silver means they've been purchased and not up to sharing. Gold means they are an owner and aren't buying."

My finger pauses in tracing his tattoo as I digest this. "Why would they bring those who have been purchased but don't want to share?"

Phoenix breathes in deep and lets it out slowly. "Some people like to watch." I freeze at this revelation.

"So, after the auction, is there a sex party?" I don't know what to call it.

He nods slowly. "Yes, and those who have been bought have to have sex before they're allowed to leave."

I sit up and pull the sheet up to cover myself. "So, you bought me and had sex with me at this party? Did people watch to confirm this actually happened?" He sits up, watching me closely. I know immediately this is what happened. I scramble out of the bed. "How..."

I squeeze my eyes, trying to recall the night, but there's nothing. "How did that go?"

"Kenz—"

"Tell me. I need to know." Wrapping the sheet around me, I stare at him and wait. He doesn't answer, though. It's the first time he hasn't answered one of my questions.

"Phoenix—"

"I'm not talking about that night."

I blink back the tears that want to fall. "Was it that bad?"

He sits up and runs a hand through his hair. "It wasn't." He doesn't elaborate. I choke on a whimper. I know I was a virgin up until that night.

"You took my virginity," I state.

His eyes are full of... Regret? "I did."

"I... I need to go finish baking." He lets me pull on my clothes and leave.

Oh god, all those years at Brighton, I wanted him. I wanted him to be my first. But not like that. People were watching us? Why did we have to prove we had sex?

When I walk into the kitchen, I stop and try to take in everything Phoenix just revealed. Thinking back to the conversation Anna and I had earlier, I wonder if that's what she meant about what came after she was bought. *Did the man who bought her have to have sex with her in front of everyone, too?*

I wonder if Rex is still with her or if she's taking a nap. I pull myself together as quickly as I can and walk towards her room. Her door is open, so I stop just inside and see she's sitting in a chair overlooking the grounds.

"Anna?" I whisper, so I don't startle her. Rex isn't here, so he must have only stayed for a little while. She turns to me with a small smile.

"Two visits in one day."

I return her smile and walk into the room, sitting next to her in the other chair. "There's a library here. I can bring you some books if you'd like." Her eyes light up and she nods. That's how we became friends. She was popular. I wasn't. But we bonded over reading.

"I'd love that," she replies.

"There's every book imaginable, but if it's not there, I'm sure Phoenix won't mind ordering it." I wonder if he'll take me to a library this weekend when we go on our date. *Have I already forgiven him for the bomb he just dropped on me?* "I'll grab some I think you'll like and when you begin feeling better, you can join me in the library to read. It's the best room in the house."

She nods enthusiastically and I almost don't want to bring up what I'm about to ask her.

"I have a question, but if you don't want to answer it or talk about it, I'll understand."

She tilts her head at me, her crease between her eyebrows becoming more pronounced. "What is it?"

I look outside, trying to gather my thoughts and wits about me. "When you were talking earlier about being bought at the auction..." I take a deep breath. "Did the man who bought you have to have sex with you in front of people?" I force myself to look at her. She takes in a shuddering breath and licks her lips. She doesn't answer right away and after another few seconds of silence, I almost tell her to forget about it.

"He did," she finally answers. "I wasn't a virgin, so it didn't hurt. He tried to make it good for me, but I wanted it over as quickly as possible. So, that's what he did. He made it quick so we could get out of there."

I lean forward and cover her hand with mine. "I'm sorry for asking and making you talk about it. I should have—"

"No, you're my best friend. Well, you were in high school. But even after we graduated, I always thought about you. I wanted to contact you, but I wasn't allowed. My phone and everything was taken when I started living with the Kirbys."

My eyes widen. "The Kirbys?" She sighs and nods. "As in Vice President Joel Kirby?" She nods again.

"I think my dad sold me to him to get an in somehow. I mean, people have to vote for him, so it's never a guarantee, but..." She shrugs. "Who knows?"

"But didn't he have to win?" I think back to conversations Phoenix and I have had. He said he bid so much on me so the person my father had arranged to buy me didn't win. If only Anna had had a Phoenix.

"He did win. He bought me for two million dollars. I was the highest bid of the night." Two million. Phoenix bought me for six. He really did pay a lot if Anna's was the highest bid at her auction.

"Why are you asking all of this?" she asks. I run my fingers through my hair and gaze out the window for a few seconds before turning back to her.

"Phoenix told me about having to have sex in front of a bunch of people. I don't remember that. My memories from that part of the night haven't returned."

She grabs my hand and holds it tight. "Oh, Kenz. I'm so sorry."

My lower lip trembles slightly. Finding out this information, having her here, I'm a little overwhelmed. "I was a virgin, Anna. I don't even remember my first time. For all I know, my first time was thirty minutes ago."

"What?!?" She grips my hand tighter, the palm of her hand digging into the ring Phoenix just gave back to me. She pulls her hand back and stares down at my finger. "You're married?" I laugh and she looks at me like I've grown another head. But I can't stop. The absurdity of it all is catching up with me. She simply stares at me while I try to get myself under control. Taking a deep breath, I force myself to stop.

"I thought he was married to you."

She leans back in her chair as she tries to process everything. "You thought Phoenix was married to me?" I nod and lean back in my chair as well.

"I don't remember anything, Anna. I remember my father taking me to the auction that I thought was a party. And the only reason I realized we were married was because I had a small memory where he called me Mrs. Stone. And until this past weekend, I thought the auction had happened a few months ago. I lost three years of my life." Now I feel like I might cry. My emotions are on a rollercoaster today.

She gives me a crooked smile. "We'll get through this. Together." She doesn't ask anymore questions. We simply sit and stare out the window together. This side of the house is just as beautiful as the other side. I can see the tennis court and I think there's a gazebo beyond a beautiful flower garden.

Glancing over at Anna, I see she's dozed off. So, I grab a blanket from the foot of the bed and place it over her. I'll check on her later when I bring her some books. Taking a deep breath, I walk out into the kitchen. My shoulders loosen when I realize it's empty. I just need a few minutes to myself. I'm still reeling a little from everything.

Putting the cookies in the cookie jar, I clean up quickly before going to the pantry to grab the ingredients for the apple pie I'll be making. Closing the door, I lean against it, thinking about this crazy day.

I got my ring. Phoenix and I had sex, and it was the best sex I've ever had. As far as I know, it's the only sex I've ever had.

I chuckle softly and think about how well Phoenix knows my body. My skin flushes as I replay the past few hours in my head. Everything is so complicated. The more I learn about him buying me at the fucking auction, the more I want to crawl in a hole. *What did he mean when he said it wasn't bad? He saved me, but there was a price.*

"I'm sorry, McKenzie," Phoenix whispers in my ear. I try to ignore the crowd that has gathered in the room they've led us to. This is going to happen. The guy I've had a crush on since Brighton is going to have sex with me in front of all these people.

"Phoenix," I whisper. My stomach is in knots as more and more people enter the room we've been escorted to.

"Have you done this before?" he asks as he moves to the bed on the other side of the room. At least people can only stand behind us.

"This? No."

"I mean, have you ever had sex before?"

"Oh." He's asking if I'm a virgin. Everything is happening so fast. My knees hit the bed and his chest hits my back. If this were anywhere else at any other time, I might be excited. But the fact that we have to do this in front of all these people, excitement is the last thing I'm feeling right now.

I try to look around, but Phoenix's body is blocking the view. I shake my head. "No, I haven't."

"That explains why your bid was so high," he murmurs. I don't know how to feel about that. I'm still in shock that I'm here. How could my father do this? I squeeze my eyes shut, trying to distance myself from the breaking of my heart.

My breathing becomes erratic. All I can feel is the bed in front of me and Phoenix behind me. He wraps an arm around my waist. I glance down at his tattooed forearm, blinking away the tears.

"Dig your nails into my arm," he instructs. I don't move. Why would he want me to do that? Does he get off on that? How many girls has he purchased? How many girls has he done this with?

"I'm going to be sick," I murmur. My stomach rolls and acid works its way up to my throat.

"Breathe McKenzie." He pushes my hair away from my neck and blows on it. Goosebumps breakout over my skin as he tries his best to cool me down.

"Why did you buy me? Why are you here?"

"We don't have time for those questions right now. They're going to expect something soon." I try to look around Phoenix again, but he blocks my view. Again.

"Don't look for them. Pretend like they're not here." I want to snatch the mask off I'm wearing. The red one I was wearing has been replaced with a silver one Phoenix gave me when he met me in a separate room. The black one he was wearing has been replaced with a gold one.

My father was pissed he bought me. Why put me up for sale if you're not willing to give me to the highest bidder?

"I can't do this, Phoenix." He takes my hand and guides it to his arm. I dig my fingernails into his forearm like he instructed me to, and it does offer some comfort. Almost like it's grounding me.

"We don't have a choice, pet." I recoil at the nickname.

"I'm not your pet." I seethe. He moves his hand I'm clinging to up my stomach, between my breasts and to my neck. He tilts my head to the side, unphased I'm drawing blood.

"You are here." It's a warning. A whimper escapes. I want to be strong. I want to pretend like this won't affect me. But it will. It's something he'll never be able to take back.

"I can make you feel good," he whispers against my neck. I shake my head slightly, but his hand is still wrapped around my throat.

"Just get it over with." Defeat is evident in my tone. Are we going to be expected to do this a lot? Will we have to come back? I don't think I can do this over and over. I'll kill myself before I allow that to happen.

There's grumbling coming from behind us and I know without Phoenix saying anything they're becoming impatient. Is my father here? I hope so. I hope he has to watch his enemy take his virgin daughter.

I'm going to make him pay. Make him suffer for doing this to me. And I know without a shadow of a doubt Phoenix will help me. His lips caress my ear. "Kenz, they're getting impatient."

I nod. "Is my father in here?" I ask. He pauses as he shifts. Maybe he's looking.

"Yes, he is."

I take a deep breath. "Make me feel good. Make him regret doing this." He chuckles against the skin of my neck.

"It will be my pleasure, pet."

Chapter 20

"Kenz?" I open my eyes slowly. I'm sitting on the floor in the pantry, leaning against the wall, my knees drawn up to my chest. Phoenix is sitting facing me, his eyebrows are drawn in as he studies me.

I push away from the wall and climb into his lap. He wraps his arms around me and holds me tight. "I remembered the night of the auction," I whisper.

Phoenix's muscles tighten and he holds me tighter. He doesn't say anything, so I continue. "I don't remember everything," I admit. "I don't remember the auction itself. I remember you winning and I remember us having to go into that room. People were watching us."

I stop talking and turn so I can put my nose in the crook of his neck. His scent calms my racing heart.

He runs his fingers through my hair. "Are you angry?" he asks.

"No. You went out of your way to protect me. From what I could tell. I don't remember us actually having sex. But I do remember telling you to make my father regret it."

He huffs. "I knew at that moment that I loved you." My heart jumps into my throat at his proclamation.

Leaning back, I look into his beautiful eyes. "You love me?"

He cups my jaw and smiles. "Of course I do. You're my wife."

"I love you too." Something flashes in his eyes before he kisses me softly before leaning back. "Why didn't you want to talk about it?" I ask.

He sighs and pats my hip. "Let's go for a walk while we talk."

I stand and he follows, opening the door of the pantry and leading the way to the patio. He grabs me a sweater and I pull it on before stepping outside. Instead of walking toward the lake, Phoenix walks in the opposite direction. I haven't explored over here before. I've been so determined to make it to the lake, I didn't think about walking this way.

"What's over here?" I ask, wondering if I'll see the gazebo and garden I saw from Anna's room. He links his fingers with mine as he walks at my pace.

"The tennis courts are over here, but there's also a garden and a gazebo." He confirms my thoughts. "You liked to come out here and read when the weather was nice." I smile at the thought.

"Would you come out here with me?" He chuckles and nods. I wonder if he's remembering something I can't remember. Sighing at the disappointment that swirls in my stomach, I shake my head, trying to dislodge my thoughts. "So, why didn't you want to talk about it?" His hand tightens around mine.

"Because what I had to do..." He trails off. "Taking your virginity in front of thirty men isn't something I ever thought I'd do. But every one of those men has suffered in some way since that night." I stop in my tracks. He turns to face me, not a sliver of guilt evident on his face.

"What?"

He steps closer to me. "They will all suffer for what they did to you until the day they die." It's a promise. A declaration. I've never seen this side of Phoenix. At least, not that I can remember. "You and I..." He takes a deep breath. "We had a plan. We were doing it together and then you were gone." He interlocks his fingers and places them on top of his head.

"I searched everywhere for you. And now I'll make sure those who took you suffer just like those who watched us that night. But I won't show any mercy this time."

I step toward him, putting my hand over his heart. It's beating as wild as mine. "Is this the first time they took me?" I ask. His hands grip my biceps and he shakes his head.

I'm not surprised. When I say my mantra, it's always *he will come for me, he always comes for me.*

"Can you tell me about the other times?" He starts walking again, but doesn't speak. I let it go for now and take in the beauty of the garden we're approaching. I can understand why this would be a place I'd like to read in. He walks into the gazebo and sits on the swing.

I feel him pulling away from me, so I sit sideways, draping my legs across his lap. He wraps his arm around my shoulder, so I lean my head on his bicep. He's changed into sweats and a white fitted T-shirt. I can't stop myself from rubbing my hand along his bicep and his chest. He tilts his head to look down at me, a smile playing on his lips.

"You're very irresistible," I murmur as my hand drifts down to his abs. They contract beneath my hand and his cock jumps against my leg. I lick my lips.

He runs his fingers through my hair and his other hand lands on my ankle as he rubs it up my shin to my thigh and back. "You're irresistible too, love." My breathing picks up. As badly as I want to give into this, I need answers.

"Are you going to talk to me?" I ask as my hands continue to explore. His hand continues to explore as well, but he turns his head so he's looking out over the garden.

"You were only taken once. We went back to the auctions together. You were taken at one. I was able to get you back immediately. I learned from that mistake and never let you out of my sight. But then you were taken again." He looks at me again. "This last time. You were missing for three months."

He takes a deep breath and shakes his head like he's trying to get rid of the memories. I begin tracing the outlines of his abs through his T-shirt.

"I wish I could remember more. I don't necessarily want to remember what happened to me when I was taken, but everything else," I whisper. He grips my chin with his thumb and forefinger, lifting my gaze to meet his.

"You will. You've had several memories over the past week. At least at this rate, you're able to digest it before you're assaulted with all those memories at once."

He's right. I know he is, but having these huge gaps in my life hurts my head. He leans forward and slots his mouth against mine. He pulls my bottom lip between his and sucks. I sit up and straddle him. His hands find my ass and he rocks me against his hardening cock.

"Want to know my favorite memory that happened in this gazebo?" he whispers against my lips. I run my fingers through his hair and nod. He spreads his fingers as they cover my ass completely, his middle fingers teasing me slightly.

"You were reading one of your naughty books and you texted me and told me you needed my big, juicy dick right now." I laugh and lean back to look at him.

"Really?" That doesn't sound anything like me, but I'm gathering being with Phoenix brought me out of my shell.

"Yes, really. It has been my pleasure watching you explore all the things you like. Especially since you have explored it with me." He moves so his fingers are even closer to my pussy. I rock against him and move back slightly, so they brush over my opening.

Tilting my head back, he leans forward and licks up the column of my neck. "I love when you do that," I moan. He grips me harder and pushes me against his cock again, hard and slow. Glancing down, the head of his cock peeks out of his sweats, glistening with pre-cum, his piercing beckoning me.

"What kind of piercing is it called?" I ask as I continue to stare.

"Frenum piercing," he answers.

I lick my lips and scramble off his lap. The swing rocks with my abrupt movement, but Phoenix stops it with his feet. "What are you doing, love?" I answer him by dropping to my knees. The wood of the gazebo digs into my knees.

I pull on the waistband of his sweats. He doesn't stop me; instead he lifts his hips slightly, allowing me to pull them further down. His cock jumps again as I stare at him. Leaning forward, I kiss his piercing and look up at him.

His eyes are dark with desire. "Come on, love. Suck it." My mouth curves into a smile as he fists my hair. Keeping my eyes on his, I lean forward and lick him, teasing him. His Adam's apple bobs, but he doesn't try to control my movements.

Sucking his tip into my mouth, I swirl my tongue around him, paying attention to the piercing. A growl vibrates his chest and escapes his mouth just as I drop down on him.

"Fuck," he whispers. I'm surprised I don't gag when he touches the back of my throat. Maybe my body is used to this even if I can't remember. I thought doing this with him being pierced would be hard, but it isn't.

I suck and pull up his length slowly, wrapping a hand around him as the skin is exposed. He's soft, velvety, and so hard. When I get to his tip again, I swirl my tongue around him and lick off his salty taste. Dropping back down on him, his abs shake as I start the process all over again.

"Jesus Christ, Kenz." His hips buck slightly. My knees are beginning to ache, but I push it out of my mind as I pop off him and lick from his base to his head over and over. I'm about to drop down on him again, but he sits up, grabbing me under my arms and lifts me to my feet.

He kisses me hard before turning me around and walking me to the banister. He pushes on my back so I lay across the banister, my arms supporting me. Pulling my leggings down, he kicks my feet apart. I suck in a breath just as his cock teases my entrance. He grabs my hips as he pushes forward.

We both groan. I just had him a couple of hours ago, but it wasn't enough. Laying my forehead against my arm, I rock back against him.

"That's it, love. Fuck my cock." My walls flutter and my stomach flips. He leans forward slightly, running his palms up my stomach to cup my breasts, plucking my nipples with his fingers.

The pressure is building and pleasure tingles across my skin like I've been electrocuted. "Harder," I groan as I continue to ride his dick. He removes his hands from my breasts and grips my hips so hard, I'm sure there will be bruises that look like his fingerprints. But I don't care. The bite of pain adds to the pleasure. The sound of him entering me over and over again is obscene. But god is it making me wetter.

"Nix. Yes!" He's touching that spot in me over and over again, and I know I'm minutes from imploding. His hand skates around my waist and travels down to my clit, brushing his fingers over me lightly. And those minutes turn into seconds.

He kicks my legs further apart, his fingers parting my pussy lips. I swallow, trying to wet my dry mouth. He leans forward slightly, giving him better access. When his middle finger touches where he's entering me, I gasp so hard it scratches my throat.

He applies pressure and I'm coming so hard and so long he has to hold me up as he thrusts into me chasing his own orgasm. He moans his release and collapses on my back.

"I fucking missed this so much," he murmurs against my neck. I'm still trying to catch my breath, so I breathe in through my nose and out my mouth a few times before I attempt to speak. He pulls out of me and I miss him immediately. He helps pull my leggings up and turns me around, wrapping me in his arms.

So much for getting any baking done. Phoenix is proving to be a very big distraction.

"Is it always like this?" I ask. His hand stills on my back.

"Always."

Chapter 21

Phoenix promises to let me be for the rest of the afternoon as I bake some pumpkin spice cupcakes, an apple pie, and a red velvet cake. I had to bribe him with the chocolate chip cookies I made, but they were his anyway.

Grabbing a jar of peanut butter out of the pantry, I dip a spoon in it and lick it as I wait for the red velvet cake to finish cooling so I can put icing on it. Dr. Chamberland and Dr. Pearl walk in, followed by Rex and Phoenix.

They both greet me. "I'm going to do a quick checkup," Dr. Chamberland says.

Dr. Pearl offers me a small smile as I sit so Dr. Chamberland can take my blood pressure. Once he's done, Dr. Pearl speaks.

"Hi Miss McKenzie. Mr. Stone tells me you've had another memory."

I nod as I sip on a cup of milk, trying to wash the peanut butter down. "Yes." I don't want to give details. That was something very personal.

Phoenix walks over and runs his fingers through my hair. "You don't have to tell them details."

Taking a deep breath, I gather my courage. "I remembered the night of the auction. The night Phoenix bought me."

Dr. Chamberland's eyes crinkle at the side as he takes in this information and Dr. Pearl nods as she grabs a notebook out of her bag and begins writing. "That's good. Did something happen to trigger these memories?" she asks.

"Phoenix and I were talking earlier about some things related to the auction."

She nods. "Ahh, yes. Many times someone who may be dealing with trauma induced amnesia can regain memories from simple conversations." She begins talking about another case she had years ago with similar symptoms and how talking about things helped her recall memories.

"So, you think my amnesia is trauma induced?" I ask.

Dr. Pearl looks up from her notebook. "It could be."

"When we first met, I thought you said it could have been from the drugs they gave me?" I ask Dr. Chamberland.

He glances from me to Phoenix back to me. "It could have been both." Dr. Pearl nods in agreement.

I huff. "Okay." I don't know what else to say or how to respond. *Why don't they know for sure? Am I expecting too much?*

"I'm going to check on Miss Anna." Dr. Chamberland gathers his things and follows Rex down the hallway to her room.

"Are we still going to meet next week?" Dr. Pearl asks. I nod, still unsure if I want to talk about anything, but I promised I'd try. "See you then. Have a happy Thanksgiving." She leaves and I walk into Phoenix's arms. I notice the look of concern on his face.

"I'm so desperate for my memories to come back. Do you think it's becoming an unhealthy obsession?"

He sits on the chair in front of the island and pulls me between his legs. "I think it's completely normal."

"But..." I wave my hand at him, knowing there's a but.

"I think it will come back when it comes back and nothing you try to do will make it come back any faster."

"But—" He holds his hand up, stopping me.

"We can continue to talk about things as they come up, and I will try my best to answer your questions. But it's hard for me too, Kenz. There are certain things I don't want to talk about."

My heart lodges in my throat at his confession. "I've been selfish, haven't I?"

He cups my face and kisses me gently. "No, love, you haven't. This is hard and when I first rescued you, I wasn't going to tell you anything, but I see now how unhealthy that was. And the more I open up and talk, the more your memories come to the surface." He takes a deep breath, pulling me into his embrace. "But I'm not going to lie. There are some things I hope you never remember."

I pause at that confession.

Why? Is it because he's traumatized from those memories or is it because there are things he doesn't want me to find out? He doesn't seem like someone who would hide things from me, but maybe I'm wrong.

Turning, I grab the icing and begin putting it on the cake. He sticks his finger in the icing and puts it in his mouth before I'm able to stop him.

"Mmmm. My favorite."

I turn and place my hands on my hips. "What? I thought the chocolate chip cookies were your favorite."

He walks toward me slowly, an evil glint in his eyes. "Anything you make is my favorite, but..." He dips his finger into the icing again and continues his trek toward me. I put my hands up, knowing exactly what he's about to do, but he's quicker than I am.

He grabs me around my waist and wipes the icing down my cheek and jaw. "It tastes better when I'm licking it off you," he murmurs before he does exactly that. I squeal as his licks turn from teasing to more. He grabs my thigh and lifts it so he can rock against me.

"Nix, you promised," I protest half-heartedly.

"Like I said earlier, you're irresistible." His mouth lands on mine and I give in, like I wasn't going to, anyway. I'll never get enough. To think this man is mine. He grips the back of my head as he deepens the kiss.

The brush catches on a tangle as I pull it through my hair. I can't believe I'm graduating today. The past four years have been interesting. As much as I hated being sent here, I think I really found myself here.

"You ready?" Anna asks as she walks in. A vision in white, her blonde hair pulled up into a high ponytail, and her makeup perfect. I'm going to miss her. She lives near Chicago, close to fourteen hours away from Savannah. This might be the last time I see her.

She pulls out a tube of lipstick and walks toward me. "Here. I got this for you." She takes the top off, showing the bright red.

"No. Anna."

She smiles as she walks closer to me. "Trust me. It's perfect for your skin tone and hair color."

I stare at the lipstick with uncertainty. Lifting my hands, I give in. "What the hell?"

Anna's face lights up. "Perfect."

I let her apply the lipstick, and then she takes it further when she decides to do the rest of my makeup. It's her dream come true. After she's done, we put on our graduation gowns and make our way down to the courtyard to meet our families. I'm still not sure if my father will show or not. We pass the headmaster, but he stops us.

"Girls, you're looking lovely as ever." His gaze sweeps over us in such a way it makes me feel like I'm naked. "I have snacks in my office if you two would like to join." He offers.

"No, thanks," I reply immediately. "We need to get to the courtyard to take pictures."

His eyes narrow and his mouth curves into a hard smile, but he nods. Anna grabs my hand and pulls me along.

"He is such a creep," she whispers. I nod in agreement as we make it to the courtyard. There's so many people, but my gaze is drawn to Phoenix like he's a beacon that calls out to me.

"Go talk to him." She pushes me toward him.

"What? No." I shake my head frantically.

"He's headed this way." I try to control my breathing as he gets closer. "Hey Phoenix."

He nods to her in greeting. "Anna." Then he turns those eyes in my direction. I swear they're so crystal blue I can see my reflection in them. "McKenzie, can you go for a walk?" My mouth opens in surprise as I look between him and Anna.

"Sure... sure." I reply. He links his arm with mine and I swear my knees nearly give out. What. The. Hell. We walk out of the courtyard toward the lacrosse field. I fidget with my gown as I look around, trying to find my father.

"Are your parents here?" I ask, trying to fill the uncomfortable silence.

"My father is." He doesn't say anything about his mother, so I leave it.

"What about siblings?" All these years we've gone to school together and I don't even know if he has any brothers or sisters.

"No," he replies. I don't know if he means no, he doesn't have any siblings or if his siblings aren't here. I don't ask anymore questions. He stops when we get to the bleachers. I look under them and wonder briefly if he'll take me under them.

Apparently, he's done that a few times. I hated hearing about it, but always wanted to be on the receiving end of his attention. Sighing, I turn to him.

"So, did you want to talk about something?" If my father does show up and sees me talking to him, I'll be in so much trouble.

"Your father doesn't like me," he states, like he can read my mind.

"No. He doesn't like your father either." There's no point in hiding it. Anytime there was a parents' weekend that he actually attended, he and Phoenix's father always wound up in a screaming match of some

kind. I'm shocked they haven't killed each other yet. "Do you know why?"

I clear my throat and shift from foot to foot. "I've learned some things in the years since I've been here," I reply. I used to be so naïve, but I'm not so much anymore. "It seems your father is encroaching on my father's business."

Phoenix snorts as he puts his hands in his pockets. "Not in the way you think, though."

I purse my lips as I wait for him to explain further, but he doesn't. "What do you mean?"

He runs his hand through his hair. "I mean, when you realize what an awful man your father is. I'll be there to rescue you. I promise."

I sit straight up in bed. *Holy shit.* I touch the place next to me, but come up empty. Phoenix isn't in bed.

How had I forgotten that? Is it something I pushed out of my brain because it has to do with what my father did to me? Did he know then that my father would sell me eventually?

Crawling out of bed, I head into the hallway. Looking toward his upstairs office, I don't see a light, so I walk downstairs and to the kitchen. I grab a glass of water before walking toward Phoenix's downstairs office. Light is coming from under the door.

Stopping at the door, I raise my hand to knock when I hear his voice. He's talking to someone. The door is cracked slightly, so I push it to open a few more inches.

"She's not ready." His voice holds no room for argument. My eyebrows draw down over my eyes as I try to figure out what he's talking about. He runs a hand through his hair as he stares out the window.

"You don't understand. She hasn't been well, and she's not ready." His words are ripped out of his chest. I'm sure he's talking about me. *What am I not ready for?*

"Well, we'll have to skip it this year." Skip what? "I know, goddammit!" I flinch at the anger in his voice.

"Fine. I'll have Phillip plan for it. But she will not be in attendance." His hands ball into fists and the muscles along his back are strung so tight his veins are popping out. He hangs his head in defeat.

"Jesus Christ. Okay. She'll be there." He finally gives in. Dread drops in my stomach like a boulder. *What is he agreeing to on my behalf that he's so pissed about it?* He hangs up and slams the phone on his desk.

I step back slightly, so I'm not caught. "I know you're there. You can come in." His head lifts slowly, his gaze finding mine.

"Phoenix? What's wrong?" The angst in his eyes makes the boulder in my stomach flip.

"We're hosting an auction at our home in downtown Savannah this weekend and you're expected to attend."

Chapter 22

A bark of laughter erupts from my mouth, but he's not smiling. He's being serious. Closing my mouth, I grab on to the door so I don't sink to the floor.

"Why would I do that?" My voice comes out calmer than I'm feeling. His face is the perfect picture of stone. It reminds me of when I first woke up and he didn't show any emotion. Like he's pushing it away, so he doesn't have to feel.

"It's part of our roles."

I take a step forward. "I know you don't like to give details without me asking you specifically, but I need you to elaborate."

He sucks in a breath as the muscles in his neck tighten. "We joined The Society when we got married. Auctions are every three months and we are required to go to all of them and we host an auction once a year. We got out of going to the last auction because you've been sick."

"What about when I was kidnapped? Did they not know?"

He shakes his head. "No. They think you've been sick this entire time."

My mouth opens and closes. I don't know what to say or how to respond. "And this is something I agreed to?"

"It was your idea," he replies.

I stare at him, waiting for him to tell me he's lying or making this up. "Why would I want to do this?"

He runs a hand along his jaw. "So we could take them down from the inside."

How the hell did I go from that shy girl at Brighton to what he's describing now? I guess when your father sells you, it changes something inside of you drastically.

"And you don't think I'm ready?" I take a step toward him.

He exhales slowly as the muscles in his neck and arms relax. "I learned a long time ago to never underestimate you."

So, he's underestimated me at some point. Honestly, I can understand why he'd do that. I was always so shy and easily intimidated. "What makes you hesitant about this?" I ask.

"There are a lot of things you don't remember. What if a memory returns in the middle of it? What if someone asks you a question and you don't know how to respond?" Those are valid concerns.

"And you don't think we have enough time to prepare me for this?" He closes the distance between us and pulls me into his embrace. I cling to him as I try to process everything.

"I don't know. We'll try. There are ways we can avoid people, but there are things you need to know that I've avoided telling you."

I lean back to look up at him. "Like what?"

We fell asleep in the library after our long conversation last night. Untangling myself from Phoenix, I'm surprised I'm awake before him. Normally, he's the first one up. Last night was a lot. I never got to tell him about me remembering graduation day.

I remember seeing him on graduation day, but I don't remember having that conversation with him. He's known all along the things my father did. And it seems over the past several years we have attempted to bring him and The Society down. I think back to our conversation last night.

"After I bought you that night, you didn't speak to me for months. I didn't help matters. I pushed you away as much as I could. Made you hate me. But then you found out I was still going to auctions and you were pissed. You thought I was buying other girls and doing with them what I did with you."

I sigh as I turn the coffee pot on and watch as it begins to percolate. I could understand why I would have been pissed. I remember how I felt that night. Even though I was terrified, there was a part of me that was thankful it was Phoenix.

"You followed me to one of the auctions. Snuck into the back of the car. I was so pissed at you for putting yourself in danger like that. So, you told me to take you, too. I put you back in the car and drove you straight home. So, you didn't speak to me again until a few days before the next auction. What I didn't know is you had been planning and

scheming. The night of the auction, you waltzed into my office looking like a fucking goddess and told me you were coming."

I chuckle to myself as I pour my coffee and put creamer in it. He didn't argue. He gave me a silver mask and took me with him.

"You saw what really happened at those auctions, and a plan began to form. We were trying to turn it into something legal. Well, legal for our world. Instead of this being hosted at different people's homes. Have it located at one central place and the people who are up for auction doing it willingly. Many people did not like that and some of them have been trying to stop us. When news got out that we were married, they knew the best way to get to me was through you. I think your father used this to his advantage to get you back."

Phoenix walks into the kitchen looking sexy as hell with his bed head. He pads over, dropping a kiss on top of my head, before grabbing a cup and pouring himself some coffee. I wait until he takes a few sips before I bombard him with questions. He did the majority of the talking last night.

"You said last night that my father used taking me to get to you to his advantage. What did you mean?"

He runs his hand over his jaw, a slight shadow on his chin. He sits at the island, taking another sip of his coffee before he answers me. "Your father hates me. He knew I was out to destroy him. He heard someone else had taken you, but was unsuccessful in keeping you. I think he was determined to be the one who would be successful."

I think back to the day I had the memory of the person threatening Phoenix. I still don't think it was my father who kidnapped me.

"Phoenix, I don't ever remember seeing my father. When I would say my mantra, I always thought it would be my father that was the one who would rescue me." I begin to pace. "In fact, I thought that until the day I had the memory that he's the one that sold me."

He's quiet for a few minutes as he thinks. "You've admitted you don't remember everything while you were being held," he reminds me. "It was your father, Kenz." His voice holds no room for argument.

"Why are you so determined to put it on him? How do you know?"

He stands so quickly his chair falls over. I jump at the loud clatter. "Because I do. Trust me, I searched for you for months and things happened while you were gone that pointed to your father."

I walk to him and take his hands in mine. "What if that's what they wanted you to think? Does my father still go to these auctions?" The thought makes me sick. Phoenix nods slowly. "Okay. What do you think he'll think if he sees me at the auction this weekend? He'll know you got me back. He'll know you came for me."

He's quiet, but his chest is moving rapidly from how quickly he's breathing. "He won't be allowed to come to our auction. Anytime we host one, he's not allowed to attend."

That makes sense. I could understand why neither of us would want him here. "Okay. That's one thing we won't have to worry about." I go along with his thoughts that my father is somehow involved in kidnapping me.

"Is it possible he has people come to spy and report back to him?" It makes me feel slightly better that we host the auctions at his house downtown and not here. Over the past few months, this place has become my home, and I think an auction would taint that.

"It's possible. There is a certain anonymity with these auctions. But before joining The Society, there are certain criteria that must be met before attending an auction." I want to ask more questions, but I don't want to argue with Phoenix and it seems this is something he's determined is true.

"Okay. Well, what's the first thing we need to do to prepare?"

He sighs. "First, we're going to enjoy Thanksgiving. Then we'll begin planning tonight after everyone leaves."

I hop up at the realization that today is Thanksgiving. "Shit." He smirks at me. I grab his hand and pull him out of the kitchen.

"Where are we going?" he asks as he allows me to drag him through the living room and up the stairs.

"To take a shower and get ready."

He grabs me around the waist and lifts me so he's cradling me. "That sounds perfect," he murmurs as his mouth skims up my jaw.

"I wasn't thinking about that," I protest.

He scoffs. "What were you thinking?"

"I was thinking about saving time." He laughs as he takes the stairs two at a time.

"We will definitely not be saving time."

I lean back in my seat, smiling at everyone around the table. Rubbing my hand over my stomach, I sigh at how full I am. "Phillip, everything was so good."

He smiles around a forkful of my red velvet cake. After he gets done chewing, he lifts his fork toward me. "This cake is amazing."

Anna nods in agreement. "I told Dr. Chamberland and Tobias if I didn't get to eat anything else today but your red velvet cake, that would be okay with me." Anna just joined us a few minutes ago. She's still not strong enough to do much, but she was determined to eat some of my cake. She got a couple of bites in before she had to stop.

"Well, you were there for all the red velvet cakes that didn't turn out so well."

Anna laughs, turning to Rex then Phoenix. "She gave me food poisoning once."

I put my head in my hands. "I didn't know eggs could expire." The entire table erupts with laughter.

Phoenix wraps his arm around me, pulling me into his side. "I haven't heard this story." His nose trails up the shell of my ear, making my heart beat like a drum. I gaze at him, sharing a moment with him. It's nice being able to share something with him he doesn't know.

After everyone gets their fill, we all pitch in and help clean up so Clara can take some food to her mom and spend the rest of the day with her. I admire Phoenix and the way he treats his employees. I grew up differently. The help was to never be seen or heard. Here they don't feel like employees, they feel like family.

Anna's eyes droop and I can tell she's losing energy fast. Walking to her, I squat down in front of her. "Hey, if you're tired, I'll walk you to your room."

She nods. "Yeah, I was going to try to stay, but I may fall out of this chair."

I pat her hand. "I understand. It took me a long time to get all of my strength back and you were held longer than I was." Her mouth tips down in a frown and I hate myself for reminding her.

"Did you know Phoenix has a theater?" I ask, changing the subject as I help her up.

She arches an eyebrow at me as Rex and Phoenix come over to help if needed. "I didn't."

I hook my arm through hers, and we walk slowly to her room. At least she doesn't have to go upstairs. I think Rex would probably have to carry her. He remains close, though, and I can't help the slight tip of my mouth. He's different with her.

"He does. I think we need to have a girls' night and watch all the rom-coms we want." I tell her as we make it to her room. I help her get in bed and her eyes light up at the suggestion.

"We have to watch *The Proposal*!" she exclaims.

I laugh and nod in agreement. "To the window, to the wall..." I begin.

"'Til the sweat drips down my balls," Anna finishes. We both fall into a fit of giggles as Phoenix and Rex look at the two of us.

"Tomorrow," I promise her, trying not to think of the preparation that will still need to take place for the auction. She smiles and closes her eyes. I'm sure she'll be asleep before I make it to the door.

Rex stays as Phoenix and I walk out. "I have no idea what you two were talking about," Phoenix says.

I pat his chest. "Don't be jealous. Not everyone can be Ryan Reynolds."

He scowls as he grabs me around the waist and pulls me against him. He leans down so his mouth is against my ear. "And no one can fuck like me."

Chapter 23

"So, you're saying we've never had an auction here?" I ask. Phoenix shakes his head as he dresses so we can go to where the auction will be held.

"No. This is our home, and no one knows where it's located. People don't even know we have this property. They think we live near the historic district." He laid out an outfit for me to wear. I have to dress the part even as we plan the auction.

I gawk at the outfit as he puts on his cufflinks. "Come on, love. This outfit looks gorgeous on you," he encourages.

"I've worn this before?" I ask as I pick up the flimsy dress that looks more like lingerie than an actual dress.

"No. You never wear the same outfit twice, but you've worn others that are similar."

I grab the light blue concoction and head toward the bathroom, but I'm stopped with a hand around my waist. Phoenix pulls me so my back is against his chest. "You'll get dressed in front of me." It's not a request.

Tilting my head so I can see his face, I arch an eyebrow. "I will?" His large hands run down my sides to the edge of my shirt, lifting it. I raise my hands and allow him to pull it off.

"Yes. It's part of the fun and helps us get into character." Anxiety builds in my stomach like an unopened coke bottle that's been shaken. He cups my jaw, rubbing his thumb along my bottom lip. "It will help. I promise." He leans down, his lips brushing mine.

Just like that, anxiety turns into desire. His hand trails down until it's encircling my neck as he deepens the kiss. Kissing him is like magic, like a thrill ride at an amusement park, one of the best experiences of my life.

He pulls back, not allowing the kiss to get out of hand. Stepping back, he motions to me. "Get dressed." He uses that same tone with me again. It does things to me.

"Will you call me pet at the auction?" His eyes become hooded and his posture changes. My breathing picks up at his dark look as he steps forward. His hand grasps my throat as he lifts my chin to almost an uncomfortable position.

"I will. And do you know what you're supposed to call me?"

I stare at him, trying to rack my brain, not wanting to disappoint him with the wrong answer. "Master?"

His mouth slowly curves into a dangerous smile. "That's my good girl. Or, sir." I begin to nod, but stop myself because his hand is still grasping my throat.

"Is this the only time we do this?" I ask.

"Yes. It's our way of making it more enjoyable and tolerable." He releases my throat and kisses me on my jaw before stepping back and watching me.

Taking everything off, I stand before him in just my thong. He devours me with his eyes and it makes me feel like I could ask for anything and he'd give it to me. I probably could.

Pulling the dress on, I smooth it down over my hips, then walk to the floor-length mirror. Staring at my reflection, I'm surprised at how sexy I feel. The dress falls halfway to my thighs and hugs my curves. The light blue of the dress makes my hair look almost white.

He walks up behind me, wraps his arm around my waist and pulls me against him. His cock is hard against my back, but he doesn't try anything. Simply stares at me.

"You'll be asked multiple times if you can be shared. Even though your mask clearly shows you can not. The members test boundaries. Even those who have been firmly put in place." He turns me around so I'm facing him.

"Today we'll be planning, but there will be members present. Don't speak unless I give you the okay to do so." I exhale in relief. If that's a rule, it's fine with me. He won't let me speak if he knows I won't be able to answer something correctly. "If at any time you get overwhelmed or feel uncomfortable, put your arm down so your wrist is facing me." He takes my hand and turns my arm so my wrist is facing him. "Then take your index finger and your middle finger of your other hand and tap your wrist twice." He demonstrates it for me.

"That tells me I need to finish my conversation and excuse us. If you can't wait or you feel you're going to have a panic attack. Tap your wrist three times. That tells me to take care of you immediately."

I don't know how to respond to this. Swallowing, I glance down at my wrist, which he still has lightly grasped in his hand. I tap my fingers against the inside of my wrist and raise my gaze back to him.

"Like that?"

He nods as his thumb brushes over the pulse in my wrist. "Yes, perfect."

"Are we..." I look away from him, his stare becoming a little overwhelming. "Are we going to be expected to have sex in front of people?"

I don't think I can do that. Have we done that in the past? "No. The only time that's required is the first time someone is purchased."

"Someone? You mean women?"

"Men are purchased as well." I wasn't expecting that.

"Willingly or unwillingly?" I'm beginning to panic.

How am I going to pull this off? There's so much I don't know. People will be able to tell.

Phoenix grasps both of my wrists lightly and rubs circles on them with his thumbs. "Breathe, love. I know this is a lot. I hate I have to give you a crash course, but I promise to never leave your side. And if at any moment you need me to pull you away, I will."

"Okay," I whisper.

"To answer your question, there's a bit of both for men and women. Some choose to do it, others, as you already know, are forced into it. It's our goal to stop the practice of forcing those into it."

I'm speechless. Again. I thought we were trying to stop it all together, but we aren't. Things begin to click in my head.

"You said at the fights there are women there that offer services. But you have other legitimate businesses as a way for people to work if they don't want to do that. Are the fights a thing? Or were you really talking about the auction?" His mouth tips up into a smile.

"Smart girl." He wraps his arms around me, holding me close. "Yes. Some enjoy doing this. They like the thrill of it, but others have done it because it was their only way to get out of a dire situation. Usually financially. And many times, those who purchased them did not get them out of the situation."

"So, the fights?" I haven't thought about them much since he told me that, but I'm curious all the same.

"They are a thing. One day I'll take you, but I haven't yet because I didn't feel you were ready." I inhale deeply, feeling a little overwhelmed. This is so much to take in. "That's enough for now. Let's finish getting ready so we can go. We need to be there on time."

I nod and head into the bathroom. Putting my palms down on the cold counter, I lean forward and stare at myself in the mirror.

"We're doing this. We're really doing this." I take a few calming breaths before opening the drawer with my makeup. I have a lot of makeup. I'm assuming to keep up appearances for these auctions. Pulling out the various tubes of lipstick, they range from dark red to bright pink.

Who would have thought the girl who was nervous about wearing red lipstick on graduation day would be wearing a lot more than she ever thought? The aspect of Phoenix being Master or Sir at these events has me feeling things I didn't know were possible.

I thought this would be humiliating. But maybe it can be liberating. Maybe we took a bad situation and turned it around. I wonder what Anna would think if she knew about this. I'm not sure if it's something we'll ever tell her.

After I'm done applying my makeup, I brush my hair one more time to tame any strays. I have to look put together even if I don't feel it. It's all about playing the game. I think. That's what I'm gathering from what Phoenix has told me so far.

He appears in the doorway, looking amazing in his all black suit. My eyes roam over him as I walk toward him. "Is this always your outfit of choice?"

I run my palms over his chest to the collar of his shirt, fixing it slightly. Frowning, I rub my thumb over the fading hickey on his neck. He smirks, like he knows what I'm thinking. "Later, love."

He steps in front of the mirror and combs his hair. "Sometimes I wear a red shirt. Sometimes I wear a color that matches what you're wearing." He shrugs as he sprays some cologne, his ring catching the light.

An unexpected surge of frustration… maybe anger… rises in my chest. Something tickles at the edge of my brain, but it refuses to come to the forefront.

When he's done, he wraps his arm around my waist, pulling me close. Sighing, I melt into his embrace. "Kiss me, pet." Something stirs deep in my belly as I lift up on my toes and raise my chin. He meets me halfway, kissing me thoroughly.

He steps back, helping me get into my heels and leads the way downstairs. When we get to the bottom stair, I pull on his arm, stopping him. He arches an eyebrow at me. "Where's Anna?" I whisper.

"She's in her room. One of my security guys will stand watch at her door. She's pretty out of it from yesterday, so I doubt she'll want to leave her room today." *I promised her we'd watch rom-coms today. Maybe we still can when I get back.* Even if she falls asleep, the seats recline so she'll be comfortable. Phoenix leads the way to the kitchen and I stop at the sight of Phillip and Clara.

Clara offers a smile that doesn't reach her eyes. Phillip doesn't speak, which isn't like him. They don't like that we do this.

"Phillip, are you ready?"

Phillip grabs a black binder and kisses Clara on the cheek. "Yes, sir." Phillip is dressed in all black as well. He looks handsome as ever.

"You look nice, Phillip." I don't like the mood in the kitchen. Maybe a compliment will help. His eyes soften as he looks at me.

"Thank you, Miss McKenzie. You do as well." Clara offers a small wave. I return it as Phoenix puts his hand on the small of my back and leads me to the garage where Rex is waiting to drive us.

When we get in the SUV, there are masks on our seats. A silver one for me and a gold one for Phoenix. My heart begins to beat rapidly, unsure what I'm about to face.

When we get to the house, I stare at it, hoping it will look or feel familiar, but it doesn't. Phoenix hands me my mask. He puts his on, so I follow his lead. Rex exits the vehicle and opens my door. I'm surprised when I see he's wearing a blue mask, but I don't say anything. Placing my hand in his, I take a deep breath as I prepare myself for what's coming next.

Chapter 24

Phoenix steps out of the vehicle and places my arm on his as he guides me to the entrance. The house is beautiful. It's a few miles from the historic district. I'm amazed at how secluded it feels, even though the city is just a couple of miles away.

I still like our house on the lake better, but this house screams old money. Which is surprising, considering the fact that Phoenix and his father come from new money and is one of the reasons my father hates them.

"Is this where we lived before we moved to the lake?" I ask as we walk up the cobblestone stairs.

"It is. This house belonged to my mother." My steps falter. The mask is obstructing my view, so I have to turn my head to look at Phoenix.

"Your mother?" He nods as he opens the door and holds it for me. Stepping in, he disables the alarm as I look around. The foyer has marble flooring and a chandelier that could do some serious harm if it ever fell. There's a winding staircase that leads upstairs and several rooms on each side.

I glance inside them as I follow Phoenix and Phillip into the kitchen. This house reminds me of mine growing up. Cold and sterile. "Each room will be staged. The auction will take place in the ballroom. The ceremony will take place in the basement. There might be multiple ceremonies at once and we can section off the basement."

"The ceremony?" I ask.

"Yes. For those who were bought," he replies. I bring my hand up to my throat.

"Do we have to watch?" I ask. I don't know if I'll be able to do that.

"We don't have to do anything you don't want to do." I sigh in relief. "There will be two couples that are coming today to help with the setup process. Just to remind you, the white masks mean they're selling, the black ones mean they're buying. The red ones mean they're for sale, the black and red ones mean they're taken, but willing to share, the silver means they've been purchased and not up to sharing. Gold means they are an owner and aren't buying."

I'm thankful again that Phoenix doesn't share. I couldn't do that. The doorbell rings and I suck in a breath. I didn't think to ask who was coming.

Phoenix turns to me. "Are you ready?"

I shrug. "I guess?"

"Don't forget the signal if you become too overwhelmed." I nod. He intertwines his fingers with mine as we walk to the door to greet our guests.

It's two men and two women. One man is in a dark gray suit and his face is covered by his white mask. The only thing I notice is his brown eyes, his mask covers his entire face. The woman who is with him is wearing a black, skintight dress. I wonder if that's a requirement for those who are to be sold, since she's also wearing a red mask that looks identical to the one I wore.

The other man is wearing tan slacks, a navy button-up shirt that matches the dress of the woman he's with, and a silver tie that matches his mask. The woman is wearing a lace navy dress with long sleeves. She turns and places her hand on the man with her, giving me a glimpse of her bare back.

Their masks don't cover their entire face and from the look on the man's face, he has absolute devotion to her. She purchased him, but maybe it was an arrangement similar to Phoenix and I. *Did she save him from something as well?*

The other man is selling, and the woman is for sale. Everything in me wants to know if she's being sold willingly. Phoenix said some do it willingly. *Does that mean they sell themselves? How does that work?* I stay quiet as I put the questions in the back of mind.

"Welcome," Phoenix greets. There are no introductions. He places my hand on his arm and leads the tour, telling them what will happen in each room. I wish he had introduced them, but maybe I'm supposed to know them already. Or maybe introductions aren't done.

I keep eyeing the woman in the red mask. I want to know if she's afraid. I know I was afraid and I only remember being in the car with my father and having to go to the room to have sex with Phoenix.

When we get to the kitchen, Phillip goes over the menu and makes adjustments as needed. I barely pay attention. I feel like I'm walking through a fog.

Am I ready to do this? Why do I have to do this? Phoenix tried to stop this from happening. But why wasn't he successful?

Phoenix wraps his arm around my shoulder, pulling me into his side like he can tell I'm becoming overwhelmed. I know he told me to do the signal, but it's not to the point where I can't handle it. I don't speak the entire time and no one speaks to me. We walk them out. Phoenix says his goodbyes, and it's over.

After they drive away, I snatch my mask off and walk into the kitchen. Phillip hands me a glass of wine as I walk outside and sit on the patio. I sip my wine and stare at the fountain in the middle of the courtyard.

I have to come back to this place tomorrow and participate in an auction. I don't even know how the night will go. What all am I expected to participate in?

Disappointment settles in the pit of my stomach when I realize we were supposed to have our date tomorrow. I guess we won't be doing the Riverboat cruise this weekend after all.

Phoenix joins me outside with a glass of whiskey, his mask pushed up on his head. "You okay?" he asks as he sits next to me.

Sipping my wine, I shrug. "I just realized we won't be able to go on our date tomorrow." It's something so dumb to be focused on, but I was looking forward to having a day with just him. He doesn't respond, but I feel his eyes on me. When his finger trails from the crook of my arm to my wrist and back, I have to stop myself from pulling away.

"What if we go tonight?" he asks.

I turn to him in surprise. "Really?"

He cups my jaw, his thumb rubbing my bottom lip gently. "Really." That lightens my mood some as I take another sip of wine.

"No one talked to me. I don't know why I was expecting some kind of acknowledgement." He intertwines our fingers, squeezing my hand gently.

"It's the way things go at the majority of these. Whoever is considered the *alpha* is the one who's spoken to." I don't respond as I continue to sip on my wine.

Something feels off. Something has felt off since we left the house and I can't put my finger on what it is. I hate going into this, not knowing what to expect. Phoenix has prepared me the best he knows how, but I still feel at a disadvantage.

"Hey." He turns to me, releasing my hand, so I give him my full attention. He runs his finger from my forehead down to my chin. "Everything will be okay. I know this is scary, but I'll be by your side the entire time."

Staring into his eyes, I search for something that will give me answers. He grabs my hand gently, pulling me up and into his lap. Settling into him, his nose brushes the shell of my ear. "Is that a maze?" I ask as I look at the high greenery beyond the outdoor area.

He nods as he rubs his fingers up and down my arm. "Want to go home?" he asks. I nod immediately. *I can't believe we used to live here.*

"How long did we live here?" I ask as I get off his lap.

"Almost two years," he answers. When we walk into the kitchen, Phillip is cooking and preparing food. I frown as I look around.

"Are you staying here, Phillip?" He looks at me and shakes his head before he continues mixing.

"No. I'm going to do as much prepping as I can tonight before I come home."

"Will you be here by yourself?" I don't know why, but I don't like the idea. His lips lift into a soft smile.

"No, Clara is on her way. She's going to help get things set up for tomorrow. Then we're going by the restaurant to have dinner." I'm assuming he means the restaurant Phoenix took me to earlier this week.

Was that only a few days ago? It seems like ages. We say our good-byes and head to leave.

"Put your mask on until we get in the car," Phoenix instructs as he pulls his back down. I scrunch my nose wondering why, but follow his lead as I pull it back on.

"I'm being overcautious," Phoenix answers my question before I ask. "From the intel I've received, no one knew you were kidnapped, but we can't be too careful." He guides me to the SUV and helps me inside.

Once the door is shut and Rex pulls out of the driveway, we take our masks back off. "Do you think someone would try to take me again?" I ask.

"I think your father is capable of anything." He's right, he is. I learned that the hard way. I lean up and kiss his jaw, thankful he saved me. There's no telling where I'd be if he hadn't.

When we get home, Anna is still sleeping, so I decide to let her be and we can watch movies another day. Maybe the day after the auction. I'm sure I'll need the girl time after that. Phoenix tends to some business in his upstairs office, while I take a long bubble bath and read. This bathtub is amazing. It keeps the water warm, so I never have to refill it.

After forty-five minutes, Phoenix walks in and sits on the edge of the tub, staring down at me. I lick my lips as I return his stare. He's still in his black pants and black shirt, but the sleeves are rolled up, revealing his tattoos. "Are you done?" I ask. His eyes darken as he reaches his hand out and traces my collarbone with his finger.

"No." His finger dips beneath the water and encircles one of my nipples. I suck in a breath, my stomach trembling. "I kept thinking about you in here and I had to come see you." His finger trails to my other nipple. I swallow and arch into his touch, but I'm careful to not hit the tray holding my book.

He stands, leaving me wanting, and extends his hand to me. "Come on, love. We need to get ready to go." I'm disappointed his touches aren't leading anywhere, but I'm excited to go on this cruise.

He smirks at me as he helps me out of the tub, then helps me dry off. "Later," he promises as he leaves me to finish getting ready. I rub my thighs together in anticipation.

After the cruise takes off, Phoenix buys us some drinks and we find a secluded corner of the ship to look at the sights. He points out places to me he owns; restaurants, hotels, and a warehouse he holds the fights at.

"I used to come to River Street with my mom as a little girl almost every weekend. We'd do shopping, watch the tourists, and watch the boats. Besides baking with her, that's another memory I have of her that's my favorite." He doesn't respond, simply stares out at the water.

I nudge him slightly. "What about your mother?" I ask. He never talks about her. It makes me curious.

"I don't talk about my mother," he replies. His jaw ticks as he continues to stare at the water. I want to push, but tonight has been a carefree night so far, and I don't want to ruin it. Instead, I run my hand up his arm, to his shoulder, and rub my thumb along his fading hickey.

"I think I need to rectify this soon." He finally turns to look at me, his lips tipping up slightly. Shadows are still in his eyes, but he wraps his arms around my waist and pulls me between the railings and him. His knee pushing between my legs as I rub against him shamelessly.

"I'm not going to argue with that, love." He leans down and captures my lips, all thoughts of his mother dissipating with the desire simmering in my veins.

"If you don't come with me I'll kill you, but first I'll kill Phoenix and I'll make you watch." Fear settles in my mind at the thought of something happening to Phoenix.

"I knew you loved him."

I force my eyes open as I suck in a breath. Phoenix's arm is heavy on my waist. I roll over and straddle him. His arms come around me immediately.

"Kenz?" His voice is rough with sleep. Leaning up slightly, I stare down at him, assuring myself he's there. One arm wraps around my waist, the other grabs the nape of my neck.

"Nix." It's a plea as my lips find his. He pulls me down so I'm flush against him as his tongue finds mine. *He's safe. He's here. He's mine.*

He pulls back slightly, his gaze full of concern. "What's wrong?"

"I had a bad dream." His gaze softens.

I rock against him, and his chest rumbles with a growl. I'm wearing a T-shirt and thong. He's naked and I can feel him hard against me. I kiss up his jaw and pull his earlobe between my lips before making my way down to the spot next to his Adam's apple. Eyeing the hickey I left earlier tonight, I'm determined to make it darker.

As I suck and lick, he pushes my thong aside and lines himself up with me. "Nix, fuck," I moan. He eases into me as I suck his skin between my teeth.

He grabs my hair before thrusting into me. "Fuck." We both cry out at the same time.

"Ride my cock, Kenz." I do exactly as he says while I mark him. He's mine and no one can take him from me. Ever. Leaning up, I place my hands on his chest as I lift my hips and drop down on him over and over again.

"You're mine Phoenix. Forever," I moan as I lean back and put my hands on his thighs and ride him.

"Forever," he repeats. His hand rubs up my thigh and his thumb finds my clit. He rubs small circles as I ride him. My legs begin to tremble. Squeezing my eyes shut, I focus on the pleasure only he can bring. I love him. Everything about him.

He saved me and I'll do everything within my power to make sure nothing ever happens to him. He thrusts up into me and I cry out as my walls pulse around him. He groans as he pushes up in me and comes with me.

Collapsing on his chest, he wraps his arms around me and rubs his hand up and down my spine.

"You're mine," I whisper again.

"Always," he replies.

Chapter 25

We stand at the door, waiting to greet our guests. I'm wearing a black lace camisole and a long lace skirt with a split up to my thigh. My hair is pulled back in a low ponytail.

Phoenix is wearing black slacks, a black button-up shirt, and a burgundy vest that has specks of gold in it with a matching tie. He looks delicious. We both have on the same masks we were wearing yesterday.

He leans down, his breath skating over my skin, causing desire to settle low in my belly. Ever since I woke him up in the middle of the night, it's been hard to keep our hands off each other. We never went back to sleep. I was worried I'd be tired; instead nerves are making me hyper aware of what is happening tonight.

"Are you ready to tell me why you woke me up?" he asks. His lips graze the skin of my jaw. "Not that I'm complaining." His mouth moves against my skin as he smiles.

I told him it was a bad dream, but he's not buying it completely. It was actually a memory. I've had the memory before, but this time I remembered a little more and I'm trying to figure out what they meant by "I knew you loved him".

Before I can respond, cars begin to wind around the driveway and stop in front of the door. The valet step forward and do their job of opening doors and parking. I suck in a breath as men and women in various states of dress walk toward the door.

Phoenix wraps his arm around my waist and I'm pulled in tight against his side. "Just breathe, love," he whispers. I take a deep breath and let it out slowly. "What do you do if you become overwhelmed?" he asks.

"Tap my wrist."

"Good girl."

His praise does things to me as I lean into him. By the smirk he gives me, he knows it. I hold my breath as one of the employees Phoenix hires for these events opens the door. He's wearing a black and white tux with a blue mask.

Everyone has to wear a mask at the party. The only time masks are allowed to be taken off is if the couple is alone. It's to protect the identities of those who are present. But each person is wearing different types of masks.

Some are wearing masks that cover their entire face and some half of their face. But they're all enough to hide the person's identity. According to Phoenix, there are regulars we know. He told me if someone shows up that I know he will address them first, which will give me permission to address them as well.

The way guests are dressed varies. Some are dressed like they're going to a formal event, some are half naked, some are in jeans and a T-shirt. We greet each guest as they enter. Not many try to hold conversations, which I'm grateful for.

After half an hour of doing this, I get restless and bored. Leaning into Phoenix more, his fingers drift up to the exposed skin on my back. "Not too much longer," he promises.

I gaze up at him, surprised. It's weird how he can read my mind sometimes. His muscles go rigid against me and the grip he has on me tightens. Turning to face the door to see what caused this reaction, I study each person in line ready to be greeted.

At the end of the line there's an older man with graying hair in an all black suit. He's wearing a gold mask and the woman, who has to be twenty years younger than him, is wearing a silver mask. I can't take my eyes off the woman as they get closer. She looks familiar.

When they're finally in front of us, her eyes meet mine. Her blue eyes widen when she sees me. "Kenz, you're here," she whispers. I have no idea who she is. My lips tip up into a small smile. The man turns his attention to me, and Phoenix's hand tightens even more on my waist.

"Victor. Olivia," Phoenix greets them.

"How are you feeling?" Victor's deep voice washes over me. I glance up at Phoenix and he nods his head slightly, letting me know it's okay to speak.

"Much better. Thank you." He wraps his arm around the woman and offers me a smile before leading her away.

"Who were they?" I whisper.

"Later," Phoenix replies as the next couple steps up. I want to know now, but I endure the last few couples that are left. When everyone has arrived, I breathe a sigh of relief. I know it's not over, but maybe the worst part is. Only a few people greeted us by name, but I'm still curious about the older man and his date.

A man wearing a blue mask approaches us. "Everything is ready, sir." It's Phillip. I want to greet him, but I remind myself of what Phoenix told me. Don't speak unless he gives me permission. Several of the women have spoken to me tonight before they were spoken to. But maybe this is our agreement all the time.

Phoenix places his hand on my lower back and leads me to the ballroom. I come to a halt when the double doors open. My eyes snap to Phoenix. "We're going to watch the auction?" I thought the worst part would be greeting everyone.

"Yes, everyone watches." I suck in a shuddering breath and turn to face the room again. This is going to be so much worse. The first step we take is the hardest. Every muscle in my body is screaming at me to turn around and run. I want to tap on my wrist, but I don't think this is the place or time. This feels like déjà vu.

I stare straight ahead as Phoenix guides me to the front row. He sits down, spreading his legs slightly, and pulls me onto his lap. His hand latches onto my bare thigh, his grip firm and comforting as the auction begins.

The auctioneer steps forward and introduces the first person who will be auctioned. It's a twenty-one-year-old woman, virgin, with honey colored hair and dark brown eyes. I think. The auctioneer doesn't mention her eyes, but from where I'm sitting they look brown. There isn't fear in her eyes, though. I'm not sure if that's a good sign or not.

I remember feeling terrified. I pause at that thought. I don't remember the auction itself. I remember before the auction and after the auction, but not during. After her, I tune everything out. I don't want to see the one person who is terrified, that doesn't want to be here.

How have I been able to do this multiple times over the past several years? After what I went through?

Phoenix's fingers trail up the inside of my thigh and back down, but even that isn't enough to distract me. I glance around and pause at the woman standing in the back. She's staring at me, or maybe Phoenix. Her eyes narrow as our gazes connect. *Her eyes.*

"Pet, turn around." I want to argue, but turn around. Phoenix runs his bottom lip along the shell of my ear. "It's almost over," he promises. I adjust myself on his lap and wrap an arm around his neck, burying my head in the crook of his shoulder as I pretend to watch the rest of the auction.

As soon as the auction is over, we stand to leave and I search the room for the woman I saw earlier. Every time I see someone wearing navy, I do a double take, hoping it's her. She looked familiar as well. Sighing, I realize I'm not going to find her in this crowd. I don't remember greeting her, but there were so many people, I'm sure I don't remember everyone. The majority of the crowd is headed to the basement to watch the ceremony or whatever it is that takes place after the auction, but Phoenix turns us toward the stairs and we go to the second floor.

I only saw the rooms as I glanced in as we were touring everything yesterday, but he stops at a room that was closed yesterday. "What are we doing?" I ask. He removes a key from his pocket and unlocks the door. Pushing the door open, he turns the light on and my mouth drops.

The walls are black with gold trim. The bed looks bigger than a regular king sized bed. It has a gold comforter. On the wall behind it is a map painted in gold. "This is beautiful." He smiles as he closes and locks the door. When he removes his mask, I follow his lead and do the same.

"This is our room. We had it decorated when we moved out. We needed a place to be alone during this event." Walking further into the room, I take in every detail. There's an oddly shaped lounge chair next to the window. Walking toward it, I run my hand over the soft fabric. There's round hooks on each side at the top and some at the foot of the chair. Or bed?

"What is this?" I ask.

He chuckles as he comes to stand behind me. He pulls me flush against him. His lips trail over my shoulder. "How about I show you?"

I tilt my head to look up at him, but his hand wraps around my throat and holds me still. Sucking in a breath, he guides me until I'm standing at what I'm assuming is the head of the chair. It kind of looks like a recliner. It's not a piece of furniture I've ever seen before. Or, at least, I don't remember seeing it.

He grows hard against my back as his hand trails down from my throat, between my breasts and to the exposed skin of my abdomen. "You've been teasing me all night in this outfit. Showing me glimpses of your skin. It's driving me crazy." He rocks into me, his hard cock proving his point.

I'm sure this is a distraction from what's happening throughout this house, and as much as I hate to admit it, it's working. His index finger sneaks under my camisole, teasing my skin, and his mouth finds the sensitive spot on my jaw. Anticipation dances across my skin as he marks me.

"Nix," I whisper as he finishes and pulls my earlobe between his teeth.

"Bend over," he instructs. Bending at the waist, I'm surprised at how the chair curves perfectly and supports my body. It's like it was made just for me.

"You can hold on to the hooks or you can cross your arms and lay your head on them, whatever is more comfortable." I lay my head on my arms for now as his chest drags against my ass as he squats to the ground. I think that's what he's doing; it's hard to tell from my position.

His hand wraps around my ankle as he begins to run it up the inside of my leg, pushing my skirt up as he goes. Not knowing what he's going to do heightens every nerve ending in my body. His fingers brush over my knee right before his lips touch the back of my thigh. I try to control my breathing, but the harder I try to control it, the more erratic it becomes.

He pushes my skirt over my ass as his fingers send tingles all over my body. He runs his fingers up and down my ass as his lips trail higher and higher. "What will I find when I touch you?" he asks, just as he nips the bottom of my ass.

"Are you soaking wet for me, Pet?" I didn't think it was possible to get any more wet than I already am, but him calling me that turns me on. It's strange considering the reaction I had when he used it after the auction.

His thumb rubs against my pussy, and we moan at the same time. "Fuck. Are you my dirty little slut?" I press my hips against the chair at his words, looking for something. His teeth graze over my ass. "Answer me." He slaps two fingers against my pussy. I jump and yelp at the same time.

"Yes." Pulling my arms out from under my head, I grab the hooks on the side of the chair.

"Do you want my tongue or my cock?" My next breath rattles my chest.

"I—" He pulls my thong aside and runs his finger from my clit to my pussy and back again. "Can I…" I moan again when his finger swirls around my clit. "Can I have both?"

His chuckle is loud in the room. "So greedy." His tongue replaces his fingers. I cry out at the sudden pleasure that courses through my veins. He grabs my ass with both hands and he positions me so he has better access. I want to rock back against him, but the position I'm in and the grip he has on me prevent me from doing it.

"Please. Please. Please." It's all I can say. I don't know what I'm begging for, but I know he'll give it to me.

"Please, what, Pet?" I'm at a loss for words when he spears me with his tongue. He slaps his fingers against my clit again and I scream out.

"I need you." I'm not sure if he understands me. My words are a jumbled mess as he slaps my clit again. *What is he doing to me? I can't get enough.* Every time I want more.

"You need me to do what?"

I'm past caring what I sound like. "I need your cock. I need you to fuck me." He stands so quickly it takes me by surprise. His belt clanks as he undoes it. It sounds like he's ripping his clothes off just as he yanks my thong down my legs.

He lines up with me and slams into me. "Fuck," he moans as he stands perfectly still. I whimper at how good it feels. This position, the angle, how deep he is, everything is perfect. But he doesn't move and I become impatient. I try to rock against him, but his hand lands on my back to stop me.

"Have you figured out what this chair is yet?" he asks. Sounding perfectly calm and not at all like he's about to come unglued like I am. I try to focus on his words and not on how full I feel.

He fists my hair and pulls my head back. "Answer me, Pet." He's never been rough like this with me. I fucking love it.

"I haven't thought much about it since I asked. My mind has been occupied." He laughs, which causes a bit of friction, and we both groan. He leans over me, his chest against my back.

"It's a sex chair," he whispers. I clench around him at the thought and he grunts. "We had it specially made just for you. So it wasn't too tall or too short, so it curved at the right spot to give you the best pleasure when I'm inside you." He rocks against me slightly and my grip on the handles tightens even more. "These hooks are used to tie you up, or for you to hold on to when I'm fucking you."

Sucking in a shaky breath. "It's perfect," I reply. He hums, his lips latching onto the back of my shoulder as he rocks into me. His cock is rubbing against my inside wall so minutely, but it is making my stomach tremble and my legs shake. He doesn't pull out, just continues to rock.

I want to meet his thrusts, but I can't. I'm completely at his mercy. "You're close," he murmurs. I don't respond. I can't. The only thing I can do is focus on breathing. "Your legs are trembling. Your hair is getting damp at the nape of your neck. Your breathing is becoming even more erratic."

He rocks harder against me, and my eyes roll back in my head. "Your nerves are on fire with lust and all you want to do is come." I nod, desperate. He pulls out slightly and pushes back in. The added friction brings me even closer to jumping over that ledge. He stands, grips my hips and fucks me slowly.

"Nix." It's all I can say.

"There it is," he groans as he rocks into me one more time and my muscles tighten so much it doesn't feel like an orgasm at first. He pulls out, grunting, like it takes an effort. When he pushes back in, the muscles give-way and I dive headfirst off the ledge as my orgasm hits me like a freight train.

I scream, not caring if every person in this house can hear me. His thumb circles my clit as he slams into me over and over again, drawing out my orgasm for what feels like several minutes before he's shouting his release and collapsing on me.

I can't move. My muscles have turned to rubber. Kind of like when Professor Lockhart made the bones in Harry Potter's arm disappear. Phoenix slowly disengages from me, pries my hands away from the hooks and turns me so he can lift me. He cradles me as he walks to the bed and lays me down.

His hand runs through my hair. "You did so well. You were perfect." He continues to whisper my praises as I come down from my high. Finally able to move a little, I turn over on to my side and face him.

"You feeling okay to take a bath?" I nod as I bring my hand up and cup his jaw.

"Is it always like this?" I ask him again. Something like regret flashes in his eyes, but it's so quick, I'm not sure. He smiles at me as he leans forward and kisses me gently.

"Always."

Chapter 26

End of Auction Night

Three Years Earlier

Phoenix puts his jacket over me, grabs my elbow, and escorts me out of the house. I keep my eyes glued to the floor until a familiar pair of shoes steps in our path. "Move," Phoenix barks.

"Kenz," my father whispers, regret in his voice. I keep my eyes on the floor, refusing to meet his eyes. I can't look at him. He did this to me. "I'm sorry."

"Get out of the way." Phoenix's voice is laced with a warning. A warning I'm sure he'll back up. Raising my head, I glare into eyes I thought I could trust.

"No need to be sorry, Father. Not everyone gets to have the best sex of their life the first time they have sex." He flinches. Fuck him.

Phoenix grabs my elbow, and shoulder butts him as we walk out the door.

"Kenz!" my father yells out after me. I ignore him. "I had someone else who was going to buy you. They weren't going to take you to the basement. They were going to bring you to me and we were going to leave." My heart stops in my chest.

Phoenix pushes me into his SUV, follows behind me, and closes the door. Before I can respond, we're taking off. "Did you know that?" I ask him.

He doesn't respond. Instead, he takes his phone out and begins texting someone. "Phoenix?" He still ignores me. I want to hit him or shake him to make him answer me.

"Phoenix?" I try again, my voice desperate. His head raises, and he looks in my direction with a bored look.

"Did you know?" I ask.

"I did." Tears burn my eyes at his confession. He knew. Yet he bought me and had sex with me in front of all those people.

"I thought..." My voice cracks. "I thought you were saving me." I flick at a tear that falls. He leans across the space, getting in my face.

"This is a lesson not to trust anyone. Even me." I bite my tongue so hard I'm afraid it might start bleeding.

"Noted," I reply and turn away as I stare out the window. So, what will he do with me now? I was sure he was saving me. I'll never be that naïve again. From this day forward, I'll be on guard. Always.

When we pull up to his house, I instantly hate it. It's as hard and cold as what I grew up in. At least there it was mine. Here I'm a prisoner. The driver pulls into the garage. When he parks, Phoenix opens his door, grabs my elbow, and pulls me out. I want to punch him or kick him in the nuts, instead I let him pull me out. I'll play the long game here. He will regret the day he ever thought of buying me.

"So, why did you buy me?" I ask as he pulls me through a door that leads into a laundry room. The outside of the house looks like an old plantation home. It's beautiful, but definitely not my style.

"You don't want to know," he answers, as he leads me to the kitchen. There's a man in the kitchen making something that smells really good. He turns toward us, his face falling slightly when he sees me. "Phillip, this is McKenzie. McKenzie, this is Phillip. I asked him to make a late-night snack for you."

I want to protest, but the thought of Phillip doing that just for me makes me nod in appreciation. "Thank you." He places a plate with a bowl on the table. It has a grilled cheese sandwich and some tomato soup. A knot forms in my stomach that slowly makes its way up to my throat. My mom used to make that for me when I was a kid. It was my favorite feel good meal.

She'd make it for me when I didn't feel good or if I had a bad day. I miss her so much. If she were here, this would have never happened. Why did my father do this? If it was set up so someone else bought me at the auction, why? Glancing around the kitchen, I scrunch up my nose at how there's no character.

Sitting at the table, I pick at the sandwich as Phoenix sits across from me and continues to type on his phone. Sipping at the soup, I stare at him. I wish he'd go away. "I don't need a babysitter," I whisper. I wish I had more fight in me.

He arches an eyebrow at me, one side of his mouth twitching. He places his phone down on the table and leans forward on his elbows. "You might as well get used to it. I'm going to annoy the shit out of you."

I huff and pick up a piece of my sandwich to munch on it. "Why did you buy me?" I ask. Might as well try to get answers if he's going to stay.

Maybe if I talk enough, he'll leave. "And why did you have sex with me in front of all those people?" His face is blank.

"I bought you and I had sex with you because I wanted you." Heat races up my neck to my face. I try my best not to think about how he made me come an hour ago. How I begged him to make me feel good.

"You could have had me a different way."

He stares at me for several minutes before he leans forward. "No, I couldn't."

Looking away from him, I grab the spoon and stir the tomato soup. "I'm ready to go to sleep," I murmur.

He pushes away from the table and motions for me to follow him. And I do like a good girl. I follow him through the kitchen to the entryway and up a spiral staircase. When we get to the top of the stairs, there are three hallways. He leads toward the right.

He points at the first door. "That's my office." I follow him further and almost run into his back when he stops suddenly. He points to the right. "That's my bedroom." Then to the left. "That's your bedroom."

He's right across the hallway from me. What does that mean? Am I supposed to have sex with him whenever he wants? Will he sneak into my room unexpectedly? How long will he keep me? Question after question runs through my head as he opens the door into my room. There are a few suitcases on the bed.

"Those are your belongings that your father brought to the auction." I scrunch my nose.

"He said I wasn't leaving with anyone. Why would he bring me things if that were the case?" I ask.

"Either he was lying or he was trying to make it look convincing," he responds. "This is your bedroom. That door there is the bathroom, and this door is the walk-in closet. If you need anything, let Clara know and she'll get it for you."

"Clara?" I turn slowly in the room, taking in my surroundings.

"The housekeeper. She handles all the business of the house." He walks to the doorway before turning back to face me. "You'll meet her tomorrow. She's already gone for the night." He walks out the door and closes it.

I turn again, looking at the room. The bed is a four poster bed with a canopy; with wood so dark it almost looks black. The dresser is large and has brass handles that match the nightstand. There's a chandelier with lights that look like candles. I feel like I've stepped back into the early 1900s and I should be wearing a corset with a Southern Belle dress like Scarlett from Gone with the Wind.

The lump that's been forming all night is lodged in my throat. I have to focus on taking deep breaths so I don't hyperventilate. How is it the boy I had the hugest crush on at the academy turned into this? He always said he didn't want to turn into his father. So, what does he consider this? Tears stream down my cheeks as I grab each suitcase and roll them into the closet. I'm not unpacking because I don't plan on being here long.

I'll find a way out. He lives near the historic district of Savannah. I know Savannah; I grew up here so I can figure a way off this property. I doubt I'll make it out with all my suitcases, but I'll figure that out as I plan. Snatching Phoenix's jacket off, I open my bedroom door and throw it at his door. It's closed, but he'll see it at some point.

I tear the dress off I'm wearing, literally. I will never wear this thing again. Laying down on the bed in my panties and bra, I stare up at the canopy. This is ridiculous. I know this may be some people's style, but it's not mine. I feel like I've taken a trip back to the past. Everything in this house that I've seen seems dated.

I sit up at the knocking on my door. It takes me a moment to remember where I am. When the memories from last night assault me, I pull my knees up to my chest and place my forehead on them. If only it had been a dream, but this is more like a nightmare. Another knock at my door reminds me that's what woke me.

Pulling the blanket up to make sure I'm covered, I take a deep breath to prepare myself for what comes next. "Come in." A young woman with brown hair steps in, followed by Phoenix. His eyes rake over me and I swear I see a flicker of desire, but he can suck it. Last night was the one and only night he'll ever have me. I scowl at him and pull the covers tighter against me. I should have put some clothes on.

"Hi." The girl greets me. "I'm Clara." I nod at her. The girl Phoenix told me about last night. What is someone who looks so sweet and innocent doing working for a snake like Phoenix?

I don't greet Clara. I simply stare. She offers me a small smile, like she understands, but I ignore it. "If you need anything, just let me know and I'll make sure you get it."

"Can you help me get out of here?" I ask. Her eyes widen slightly and she glances up at Phoenix before looking back at me. I arch an eyebrow at her.

She clears her throat and runs her hand over her ponytail. "No, I can't."

"Then, obviously, you can't make sure I get everything I need." I know Clara isn't the one to blame for the predicament I'm in and I shouldn't be taking it out on her, but she's an easy target for now. I can feel Phoenix's glare, but I refuse to acknowledge it or him. He steps forward in an attempt to capture my attention, but I still ignore him.

"That's not a need. That's a want. And watch it or you won't be getting your needs met, either."

I roll my eyes. "Shocking," I murmur under my breath, but by Clara's quick inhale, I'm sure they both heard me.

"Leave," he barks at Clara, who scurries out. In two large steps, he's snatching the blanket off me and climbing onto the bed. I scramble back, but he's quicker as he crowds me. His knee is between my legs, pressing against my pussy, and he wraps his hand around my throat. His icy eyes are full of desire and it makes me sick that this is turning me on.

I force my muscles to remain rigid so I don't do something stupid like rock against his knee. "I can meet your needs, love." His lips trail up my jaw. I arch away from him, trying my best to get away from his touch. "Do I need to prove it again? Because last night you were screaming my name while thirty men were wishing they were me."

I squeeze my eyes shut at the reminder. I asked him to make me feel good, and he did. He made me feel things I've never felt in my life. A tear escapes the corner of my eye as I try to push back into the mattress, trying my best to get as far away from him as possible. His tongue slides up my cheek to the corner of my eye, shocking me so much I open them to come face to face with the devil.

The smile that curves his mouth is a warning. "If I lick it, it's mine." I swallow and he tightens his hand around my throat more. I can still breathe, but I can't move. "Your tears belong to me and I promise I'll be taking a lot of them."

He pushes off the bed and stalks out of the room. Clara comes rushing in, and I let her sit next to me and hug me.

"I'm sorry, Clara." She shushes me, making me feel even guiltier. I don't want to be a bitch, but Phoenix is bringing out the worst in me. It makes me hate him more. I want to cry and scream, but I sure as hell won't be giving him what he wants. So, I wipe the wetness from my cheek left there by my tears and his tongue and begin building my wall slowly. He'll regret the day he bought me. I'll make sure of it.

Chapter 27

Day After Auction
Three Years Earlier

I refuse to leave my room or eat for the next two days. Clara comes in each day with a tray of food, but leaves with that same tray of food. On the third day, Phoenix comes barging in with a tray of food glaring at me. I ignore his mood and glance around the room from the old love chair I'm sitting in. "Did you buy the house like this?"

"You will eat every bit of food on this tray yourself, or I will feed it to you."

He ignores my question. So, I ignore him. "Because the decor is extremely dated. I'd rethink hiring a different interior decorator because it's ghastly."

His hands ball into fists and his jaw ticks as his glare gets harder. I bat my eyelashes at him. "If you don't like your room, I will get someone in here to decorate it how you want. Now, eat your fucking food." He brings the tray over to me and my mouth waters at how good it smells. I'm starving. Everything in me wants to refuse, but by the look on his face, I know he's serious about feeding me himself. And I need to keep my strength up if I plan on escaping successfully.

So, I eat the grilled chicken, salad, and mashed potatoes. I have to force myself not to moan with every bite because Phoenix is watching me so closely. There's still a bit of mashed potatoes on my plate when I lean back.

"I can't eat anymore." He continues to glare at me, but removes the tray and walks out the door. I groan as I lean back on the couch. I can't stay cooped up in this room day in and day out. As fun as it is to piss Phoenix off, I need to begin coming up with a plan. Clara has been trying to coax me out of my room for days now. So, here goes nothing.

Stepping into the hallway, I stare at the closed door across the hall. I want to see what's on the other side of that door. Is his room just as dated as the rest of the house? Or did he change it up? Ignoring it for now, I walk toward the stairs and stop when I reach the door he pointed out to me yesterday that was his office.

It's slightly ajar, so I take it as an invitation and step up to gaze into the room. I'm not expecting to see Phoenix sitting at his desk. His head pops up and his eyes zone in on me. He leans back in his chair and brings his thumb up to his lip, rubbing it a few times before he smiles.

"Finally decided to venture outside of your room?"

I shrug and lean against the doorjamb. "I had to check the rest of the house to see if it's decorated just as horribly as my room." He grips the arm of his chair so hard his knuckles turn white. Every time I mention the decor, it pisses him off. "So, did you decorate the home?"

"No. My mother did." That answers my question. He takes me talking badly about the decor as an insult to his mother.

"Where is your mother? She wasn't at graduation." I remember him talking to me right before graduation. I asked him if his parents

were there and he said his father was. He never mentioned his mother. I wonder why.

"I don't know where she is," he answers, shocking me with his honest answer. I wonder briefly how old he was when she left. Or maybe she died, like mine did. I want to lash out at him and say something like maybe she got tired of looking at him every day, but I can't. I remember what it felt like when my mom died. It felt like my world was ending. And I wouldn't wish that on anyone. Even him.

"Alright, well, I'm going to explore the rest of this house." He pushes away from his desk and stands.

"I'll walk with you."

"No." I don't want him to come with me. He arches an eyebrow at me, an amused expression on his face.

"I wasn't asking." He stops in front of me and motions at me to turn around. "Let's go." I groan inwardly as I turn and walk back into the hallway. He closes his door and locks it, piquing my curiosity. What's in there that he has to lock the door? Huffing, I follow him downstairs and he stops in the main entryway.

I tilt my head back to look up at the chandelier. "Does every chandelier have lights in them that look like candles?"

He looks up and shrugs. "Yes."

My home growing up was modern. My father didn't have anything in it that looked remotely like old money, but Phoenix's home does. That was one of the things my father hated about the Stones. They were considered new money, *which is such an antiquated way of thinking. This house doesn't look like new money.*

"So, this was your parents' home?" I ask, fishing for more information.

"Yes. It's belonged to my mother's family for decades." Interesting. So, maybe Phoenix does come from old money. I want to ask why his father doesn't live here, but I leave it alone for now. I think I've reached my quota for questions.

"We can update the decor," Phoenix says as he leads me to a room to the right. Opening both doors, I step in and stare.

"A ballroom?" I ask. He nods and watches me as I walk around the room. There's a large fireplace on the left with a mirror over it. I love the fireplace. If there were some comfortable chairs in front of it, it would be a perfect place to read. Two chandeliers hang from the ceiling, with the same style as in my room and the entryway. On the right, the wall is made up of windows looking out over the estate.

Stepping up to one of the windows, I admire the large oak trees with the Spanish moss in them. One of my favorite things about Savannah. Stepping back, I turn in a circle, taking in everything about the ballroom.

"So, do you host a lot of parties?" I ask. He places his hands in his pockets and stares at me. He's answered all of my questions. Why won't he answer this one? His face is a mask. I'm beginning to learn that's his way of not revealing anything with his facial expressions. Understanding dawns on me as I turn around in the ballroom again.

"You host auctions." It's a statement that hits me in the stomach. Something that feels a lot like disappointment settles in my chest. I don't know why I'm disappointed. Maybe a part of me was still holding on to the image I had painted of him in school. I was so sure

he wasn't like the rest of the guys at school. Building my wall another row, I meet his stare.

"How often?" The veins on his forearms stand out as he crosses his tattooed arms.

"Once a year." His words are said matter-of-factly. Turning away from him, I stare out the windows. How can he do this to women? Why does he do it? My eyes burn with unshed tears that I refuse to let fall, because fuck him.

"Are there other women here?" I clench my fists and suck in a breath as I wait for his answer.

"No. You're the only woman I've ever bought." Relief washes over me. The thought of being held prisoner with other women I can't help would be my last straw. I was so close to getting out of this city and moving somewhere far away from my father, but here I am stuck with someone that might be worse.

"You should be flattered."

My head whips around at his absurd statement. "You're fucking kidding."

A small smirk forms on his lips and he shakes his head as he takes a calculated step toward me, then another. I step back, but he quickly has my back against one of the windows.

"I don't kid, darling."

I slap his face before I can even comprehend the action. His head turns to the side with the force of my hand. He looks stunned and pissed. Bringing my hands up to cover my mouth at the shock of my own actions, I wait to see how he retaliates. He turns his head slowly, so he's facing me again. Placing his hands on either side of me, he leans down until his nose is touching mine.

His face is slightly red from the slap and the creases around his eyes are so pronounced I could count them. "That will be the only time you'll ever hit me. Understand?" I nod. "Use your words."

"I... I understand." My heart is beating wildly in my chest, and a cold sweat has broken out over my skin. Will he hit me back? Will he punish me in another way? He leans back slightly and brings his finger to my forehead. I flinch, but he doesn't hit me. He runs his index finger down my cheek and to the pulse in my neck and back up.

Balling my hands into fists, I try to sink into the window behind me. I want to go back to my room. "I'm not going to hurt you," he speaks so softly I have to strain to hear him.

"But you already have," I whisper. He leans back slightly, giving me some space. He tilts his head, a question in his eyes that I refuse to answer. "I think I've had enough for one day. I want to go back to my room." He continues to stare at me for so long I begin to wonder if he'll let me go.

Finally, he pushes off the window and steps back. He's still close enough that his chest touches mine as I slide by and walk as quickly as I can out of the ballroom. Once I'm out of his line of sight, I take off and dash upstairs. Running down the hall and to my room, I close the door and lean against it. Slowly sinking to the floor, I pull my knees up to my chest and stare blankly into the bedroom.

He has the upper hand. I already knew that, but he still makes me feel things I don't want to feel. I'm pretty sure he knows it, too. Leaning my head against the door, I close my eyes. How am I going to survive this? Will I survive this?

"You will, McKenzie. You will."

Chapter 28

One Month After Auction

Three Years Prior

Over the next month, I memorized every room. I even found a hidden room. My excitement was quickly doused when I realized it didn't lead anywhere. I've been allowed outside, but only in the fenced-in backyard. I've learned Phoenix has a security guy named Rex, that goes with him everywhere. There are a couple of security guys that walk around the property looking important, but they don't scare me the way Rex does.

Phillip and Clara are the only staff I can tolerate. They seem nice enough, but I don't hold conversations with them. I refuse to get attached to anyone because I will leave here as soon as possible. Walking out of the bathroom in a towel, I stop at the sight of a nervous Clara and stoic Phoenix standing in my room.

Dropping my towel so I can pull on my clothes, I enjoy the gasp from Clara. But my attempt at making Phoenix uncomfortable backfires when his eyes rake over me. "Maybe next time knock."

He raises his eyebrows as he stares at me without a trace of guilt. "Why would I do that when this is my reward?"

I snarl at him as I grab my clothes and put them on quickly. "What do you want?" I ask as I yank on my sundress.

"You need to try on your dress." I pull my lips between my teeth and squint at him.

"What dress?"

He gestures at the bag Clara is holding, and she unzips it to show a beautiful white wedding dress. "I'm sure it will fit, but I need you to try it to make sure."

I look from the dress to him, back to the dress. "Why do I need a wedding dress?" Clara's knuckles turn white with how tight she's holding the dress.

"We're getting married," Phoenix says like he's telling me about the weather.

"I…" I take a step back. "No." I want to sound firm, but it comes out more as a gasp. Phoenix takes the dress from Clara.

"Thank you, Clara," he dismisses her and turns back to me. I step back again as Clara gives me a sympathetic look before leaving. There isn't anywhere for me to go.

"We're getting married, Kenz."

I shake my head. "I don't love you. You don't love me." My argument sounds stupid, even to me. For every step back I take, he steps toward me until my back hits the wall next to my nightstand. He cages me in and I swallow.

"You'll learn in our world love isn't a thing." As hard as I'm trying, my lips tremble and my eyes burn with unshed tears.

"This is your world, not mine." A tear escapes and he watches it slide down my cheek before he leans in and licks it. I squeeze my eyes shut

and place my hands against the wall, every muscle in my body wound tight.

"It's your world now too." I shake my head denying it, but knowing I won't be able to get out of this. He owns me and if he wants to marry me, then I have to marry him. I should have tried harder over the past month to escape.

"When?" I finally ask.

"In a month." I stare up at him. Maybe I can escape by then.

My stomach is full of butterflies as the lady Phoenix hired to do my hair pins the braid so it looks like a crown as the rest lays in soft curls around my shoulders. Phoenix likes my hair down. That's the only request he made for today. I can't believe this is happening. I can't believe I didn't find a way to escape. Phoenix's security has surrounded me since the moment he told me we were getting married.

It's like he knew I'd try anything to escape. If Phoenix wasn't around, Rex was there, Louis, or one of the other guys. I still don't understand why he's marrying me. He bought me. He owns me. Why isn't that enough? He has done some small renovations around the house, though.

He's replaced all the chandeliers, and he replaced the furniture in my bedroom. He's done some renovations in his room as well, but I haven't been in there. My stomach knots even more. Is he going to expect to have sex tonight? Will I be moving into his room? I haven't touched him and he hasn't tried to touch me since he told me about getting married. Except when he licked my tears.

I haven't cried since that day either. I refuse to give him the pleasure. The wedding is happening here on the grounds, so people have been coming and going all week to prepare. Once my hair is done, I stand and look in the mirror. I haven't had much input into the wedding. My only request was that it not take place in the ballroom. So we're having it outside. Thankfully, the weather is nice today.

A photographer enters, followed by Phoenix. This day is going to be documented? Why? I simply stare at him and wait to see what he has to say. I can't stop my eyes from roaming over him. He looks gorgeous in his black tuxedo. I hate it. His eyes trail over me as I stand before him in my robe.

"Everyone out." People scurry out of the room and I try to follow, but he grabs my wrist as I pass him. He stares down at me and I arch a perfectly shaped eyebrow at him.

"You did say everyone."

"Brat." I shrug. He's turned me into this person I don't like, but I have to keep my walls up or I know he'll break me in ways I can't imagine. "I want to take a few pictures before you get in your wedding dress."

I tilt my head at him. "What kind of pictures?"

He pulls me in front of him, his finger gliding from my wrist up my arm. "The kind that will loosen us up before the wedding. I need you to look like you want this." His fingers continue their path up my shoulder, to the back of my neck.

"You should have thought about that before today," I say, trying my best to calm my racing heart. I hate the way my body responds to him.

He gently grips the back of my neck. "You look gorgeous, McKenzie." I lick my lips and his eyes latch onto them.

"I'm not even finished getting ready." My voice is breathless as I bring my hands up to hold on to his forearms.

"It doesn't matter. You're always the most beautiful woman in the room." My heart lurches into my throat. Why is he talking to me like this? I want to believe him, but I don't trust him. "Will you take pictures?" I nod before I can even completely process his question.

How does he get me to drop my guard so quickly? Maybe it's good he hasn't been trying to do more over the past month, because just from this small interaction he's already got me bending to his will. He leans down and runs his lips up my jaw to my ear, goosebumps breaking out along my neck and arms. "Such a good girl."

I almost moan, but I catch myself. He slowly disentangles us as he walks to the door and motions for the photographer to enter. Under my robe, I'm wearing a white lace strapless bra and a matching white thong. Nothing fancy, but something that makes me feel sexy.

"Mr. Stone, can you take your jacket off?" The photographer asks.

Phoenix nods. "McKenzie, this is Fran. Fran, McKenzie."

She gives me a bright smile. "Nice to meet you, McKenzie. Thank you for letting me photograph your special day." I stop myself from scoffing. Either she doesn't know or she's a really good actress.

Fran walks over to Phoenix and touches his tie. I narrow my eyes at the interaction. "Can you remove the tie, or will that be too much of a hassle?" Phoenix shakes his head, and she begins to remove it. I lurch forward, placing myself between them. What the hell?

"I can do that." Fran's eyes widen, and I swear Phoenix chuckles.

"Of course." She looks down at her camera adjusting the settings. "Take his tie off and unbutton the top two buttons." I nod slightly, still irritated with her. I don't know why. She technically didn't do anything wrong.

Turning to face Phoenix fully, I look up at him. He's smirking down at me as I pull his tie free. "Jealous, love?" I hesitate. Jealous? And why is he calling me love? He normally calls me darling, but it's usually in a taunting way. This was different. Taking in a shaky breath, I release his tie and begin working on his buttons.

"No, but you're about to marry me. So, she doesn't need to touch what's mine." He wraps his arm around my waist, pulling me close. My fingers trace the outline of one of his tattoos. I can't seem to stop myself. His knee snakes between my legs as he pulls me tighter against him, causing friction. I gasp and his smirk grows wider.

"Pull her robe down, exposing her arm." I jump slightly, reminded that Fran is still in here. Phoenix's hand trails up my back and he grips the collar of my robe, pulling it down until my shoulder is exposed. He leans his head down and runs his lips over it. I want to rock against his knee, but I force myself to remain perfectly still.

"Come on, love. Loosen up." I allow myself to arch into him, causing a bit of friction. A whimper works its way up my throat. "That's it." His lips begin a path up my throat and he stops just below my ear, sucking slightly. I gasp at the sensation, and this time I can't stop myself from rocking against him.

He hardens against me and his chest rumbles. I'm glad I'm not the only one affected. His hand trails down my arm, over my waist and hip, to my thigh. Gripping my thigh, he pulls it up, causing the robe to fall away, exposing the lacy garter at my thigh. His other hand presses into my lower back, making me arch slightly and he leans forward, slotting his lips against mine.

I grip his shoulders as his tongue licks the seam of my lip, seeking entry. I open my mouth slightly and he takes advantage of it, his tongue quickly finding mine. "That's great. I got some good photos." Fran says. But Phoenix doesn't stop kissing me, instead he pulls me even tighter against him as the kiss turns heated. There's a soft click and suddenly I'm being spun and pressed against the wall.

Phoenix lifts my hands above my head and holds my wrists with one hand as his other hand trails down my body and he yanks the tie on my robe open. His eyes rake over my half naked body before he dips down and sucks my covered nipple in his mouth. I cry out as I arch against him.

"Should I make you come now? Or make you wait?" His voice is like gravel. I'm quickly brought back to earth. He is going to make me come at some point today. I close my eyes as his lips caress my collarbone, my shoulder, and throat.

He wraps an arm around me, holding me close, but still not releasing my arms. I slowly open my eyes to stare at him. "I'll make it good for you," he promises, and I have to swallow around the lump in my throat.

"I know you will," I whisper. And I do know that. He proved at the auction he's not a selfish lover. There is a part of him that wants to

protect me. But he also knows this is happening because he's making it happen. "I probably would have said yes if you had asked me to marry you."

He releases my arms, rubbing my wrists slightly to make sure I'm okay. He steps back and begins buttoning his shirt again before putting on his tie.

I pull my robe closed and tie it. "But you didn't even give me the chance. Now, you'll never know for sure if this is because you are forcing it or because I want it." He puts his jacket on and walks to the door.

"Get dressed. The ceremony begins in thirty minutes."

Chapter 29

Two Months After Auction

Three Years Prior

Walking toward Phoenix, I pretend like this is the wedding I used to dream about in high school. He's my one true love and I'm his. I don't recognize anyone except Phillip, Clara, and Rex. I wish Anna was here. When I stop in front of Phoenix, the priest doesn't ask who gives me away. Because no one is giving me away.

Phoenix is taking and there's nothing anyone can do to stop him. He lifts my veil and cups the back of my neck before bringing his forehead to mine. I suck in a breath and close my eyes, bringing my hands up to cling to his forearms. It's moments like these that make me think Phoenix isn't a terrible person.

He has some kind of plan, but he's not letting me in on it. "I promise I'll make this good for you, Kenz." I open my eyes and stare into his icy gaze. Does he mean the wedding or the marriage? "Both," he answers, reading my mind. I swallow and accept that he will stand behind those words.

"Okay," I whisper. Relief flashes in his eyes and he nods slightly before releasing me, and the priest begins the ceremony.

Phoenix does make the wedding good. Better than good. After the ceremony, we take a few more not so risqué pictures and then he escorts me to the makeshift dance floor where we have our first dance as husband and wife. He holds me close as we rock back and forth. It does things to my heart when he doesn't look at anyone or anything else except me.

"You look breathtaking," he murmurs before his lips brush against mine. I want to keep my heart in a cage, but he's making it so hard. I rake my fingernails up his scalp, hoping he'll deepen the kiss, but he doesn't. "Later, love," he promises. My stomach does a somersault, but I try my best not to let it show.

"You look amazing, too," I tell him as other people begin to join us on the dance floor. His hand lowers from the middle of my back to my lower back, his fingers grazing the top of my ass. "Phoenix," I whisper.

His chuckle is dark. "This is just foreplay, love." I stumble slightly, but he doesn't let me fall.

"Foreplay?" I ask. His lips skim the pulse on my neck as he hums.

"The anticipation of what's to come." So, he is going to make me come later. Before he can expand further or I can ask anymore questions, the song ends. We cut the cake, I throw my bouquet, and he removes my wedding garter with his teeth before throwing it. By the

time the reception is over and he's walking me into the house, I'm ready to jump him.

It's not fair how he completely disarms me, but at this moment in time I'm not angry about it. I'm ignoring the reality of things and riding the high only he can give me. He stops in the kitchen where a bucket filled with ice is chilling a bottle of champagne. He grabs it along with two glasses before grabbing my hand and leading me up the stairs to his bedroom.

He opens the door, but doesn't pull me in. "Stay here," he says as he goes in and places the bucket and glasses on the dresser. I glance around from the doorway as I wait for his next instructions. The walls are gray and the king size bed is covered in dark green bedding. It looks more modern than the rest of the house. The lighting is turned down low, creating a romantic ambiance.

Phoenix returns to me. Before I can ask him what he's doing, he's lifting me in his arms and carrying me across the threshold of his bedroom. "This is our bedroom now," he murmurs before setting me down on my feet. I'm surprised at his romantic gesture, but he did say he was going to make it good. I guess he meant it.

"I bought you something." He walks into the closet and comes out holding a white box wrapped with a white ribbon. He hands it to me and I stare at it for a few seconds before I begin to pull on the ribbon, but he stops me. "Go into the bathroom and open it. And if you want, come out wearing it."

He's giving me a choice. How very unlike him. I look from the box to him, my breath coming out in pants. "Okay," I whisper. He points out the bathroom door, but I stop in front of him and turn around. "Can you unzip my dress?" I ask. His breath tickles my neck as he unzips my dress. His knuckles graze my spine slowly.

Is this foreplay as well? I like it. Once I get in the bathroom, I quickly open the box and stare at the black lace. Lifting it out of the box, I smile at the thought of his look when I walk out of here with this on. It's a black lacy babydoll with a thong. I pull it on and stare at myself in the mirror. It's see through, but the lace covers my nipples, giving a little tease.

I take a deep breath and force myself to walk out of the bathroom. Phoenix is standing at the window, staring outside. He's stripped down to just his boxer briefs and I suck in a breath. He is gorgeous. Tattoos cover his arms and chest. I've only had glimpses of them up until this point. Seeing him almost completely bare makes me a little less nervous and a lot more ready to see where the foreplay is headed.

Phoenix turns to face me, his eyes take in every inch of me. My breathing quickens along with my pulse as he walks toward me until he's standing so close I have to crane my neck to look up at him. "Fuck, Kenz. I'm going to buy you one of these in every color." He wraps his hand around the back of my neck and hauls me against him.

I wrap my arms around his neck as his lips capture mine. This kiss is filled with lust and a promise of what the night holds. He wraps his other arm around me and lifts me. I grip his hips with my thighs as he carries me to the bed and gently throws me on it. He doesn't follow me. Instead, he stands at the edge and stares down at me.

I wish I knew how to be sexy. Is there something I should be doing? He grips his clothed cock and rubs it once, making me gasp. "Place your feet flat on the bed, love." I bend my knees and place my feet flat on the bed like he instructed. The lingerie falls to my waist, but my legs are closed so I don't feel exposed.

He places one knee on the bed as he licks his lips. "Spread your legs." I swallow twice before I'm able to get the courage to do as he said. He doesn't try to make me go faster, he simply waits. When my covered pussy comes into view, his eyes darken and a rumble works its way through his chest.

"Jesus." He grips one of my ankles and pulls me to the edge of the bed. I yelp in surprise. "Are you wet for me, love?" I nod. There's no sense in lying. His hand trails up my shin to the inside of my thigh before he rubs his thumb over the lace covering me. I gasp, arching slightly, wanting more.

He grips my thong. I lift my hips, allowing him to pull it down my legs. I keep my legs closed, nerves settling in my stomach. We've had sex, but all our clothes stayed on. Yes, he's seen me naked, but this is different. He shakes his head at me. "Don't be shy, love. I've been thinking about this all day."

His hands grip my knees and spread them. I squeeze my eyes shut, sucking in a breath. "Eyes on me, Kenz." I pop my eyes open. He smiles at me. "Good girl." His lips touch my knee, but he keeps his eyes on me as he trails up my inner thigh. I suck in a breath right before he sucks my clit into his mouth.

I cry out and grip the back of his head. He lifts his head slightly, grinning up at me. "That's right, love. Let everyone know who you belong to." Then he dives back in. He sucks and licks, pushing me closer and closer to the edge. I lift my hips, trying to ride his tongue. He pushes my legs further apart and I allow them to fall to the bed as he takes me higher and higher.

"Nix, fuck," I moan. He inserts a finger and rubs my inner wall. "Oh, god. Please," I whimper. He inserts another finger and licks me over and over before sucking my clit into his mouth. I explode and he continues to lick and rub until I'm so sensitive I push him away. He chuckles as he leans up.

Wiping his mouth, he crawls over me. He grabs the lingerie; I lift my hands and allow him to pull it off me. His eyes take in every part of my body. I don't shy away from his perusal. It makes me feel sexy because I see how badly he wants me. A surge of boldness overcomes me, so I trail my hand up his thigh and cup him.

He groans, but he doesn't stop me as I explore him. I grip him the best I can through his briefs and rub him. "Take them off," he demands. My eyes flick to his and he arches an eyebrow. Will I do it? I lean up, grip his briefs, and push them down. They don't get far because of the way he's kneeling on the bed, but it reveals his cock.

I knew he was large. I remember how it felt, but seeing it is a different experience altogether. He climbs off the bed and pushes them the rest of the way off before grabbing a condom off the nightstand and putting it on. I lick my lips as he crawls toward me, settling between my thighs.

"You ready?" he asks as he rubs the head of his cock through my pussy lips. I suck in a breath and arch against him. I clutch his biceps and nod. "I need to hear you say the words, love."

I swallow, trying to wet my dry throat. "I'm ready." He guides the tip of his cock to my entrance and enters me. The stretch feels so good.

My nails make divots in his biceps, but he doesn't seem to care as his hips meet mine.

He brings his forehead to mine. "You feel so good," he whispers against my lips before sucking my bottom lip between his. He pulls out until his tip is barely inside me, then thrusts inside. I rake my nails down his back and he groans.

"Fuck, yes. Mark me all up, love." He lifts my hips slightly, adjusting the angle so he hits all the sensitive spots inside me. I cling to him as he thrusts at a leisurely pace, making the build up slow, but so good.

"Nix," I whimper. He stops when he's completely sheathed inside me, rocking slightly, but every time he does, it's rubbing against the spot deep inside me that makes me want to implode. "Please," I beg, but I'm not sure what I'm begging for.

"I'm going to make you come so hard," he growls. He leans up on his shins, pulling me so I'm almost in his lap, but my back is still on the mattress. He begins to thrust harder and faster. His hands wrap around my hips as he pulls me into him over and over. "Touch yourself, love."

My eyes widen. I can't do that. "Come on," he encourages. I slowly trail my hand down my abdomen as he continues to thrust. I gingerly touch my clit and I suck in a breath. "That's right, love." At his encouragement, I circle my clit with my middle finger.

Crying out at the added pleasure. I want to close my eyes, but he told me earlier to keep my eyes on him. So, we stare deep into each other's eyes, making the connection even more intense. His eyes are filled with lust, desire, and something else I'm not sure of. What can he see when he looks at me?

Can he see how long I've wanted this? How long I've wanted him? How I used to daydream about him being my husband one day? His pace picks up and I cry out as my muscles begin to contract. Another thrust and swipe of my finger makes me explode. I suck in breath after breath as I ride out my orgasm. He continues to thrust, chasing his own orgasm.

He groans long and hard as he thrusts one more time. Phoenix rocks into me slightly as his orgasm takes over every muscle in his body. He's beautiful. He leans over me, wrapping his arms around me and pulling me so I'm straddling his lap. I wrap my legs and arms around him, basking in the glow of what we just did.

It felt like more than just sex to me, but I'm not sure if it's the same for him. My rings catch my eye and I swallow. Will this ever be more? Can it be?

Chapter 30

Three Months After Auction
Three Years Prior

The next month isn't as perfect as I had hoped after Phoenix said he'd make it good for me. He's rarely home, but when he is, he does eat dinner with me. But he hasn't tried to touch me since the day after our wedding. I think back to that night as I watch Phillip prepare breakfast. I want to ask him if I can help, but I still don't know my place here.

"It's time to wake up, Mrs. Stone." I try to hide my smile and pretend like I'm still asleep. He's on his side and his chest is pressing into my side. He runs his nose along my jaw before tracing the same path with his tongue.

I'm fighting a losing battle trying to keep my breathing even. "I know you're awake, love." He nips at my chin before covering my mouth with his. I give up all pretense and wrap my arms around his broad shoulders as he climbs on top of me and deepens the kiss.

My breath hitches as he rocks his hard cock against me. I can't believe I'm married to this man.

I sigh at the memory. I had hoped so much that's how he would be from now on, but it hasn't been. Being married to him is an emotional rollercoaster. I never know which Phoenix I'm going to get. Awareness skates over my skin. I turn and see Phoenix standing in the doorway of the kitchen, his eyes on me. I stand and walk to him, surprised to see him. He was gone when I woke up this morning. I expected him to be out on business.

"Hi," I greet him. He wraps an arm around me and pulls me into his chest. My heart lurches at the embrace.

He kisses the top of my head. "Hi, love." Tears spring to my eyes, but I shut it down. I still refuse to cry. I wrap my arm around his waist, needing the physical touch.

"Phillip, how long before breakfast is ready?" Phoenix asks.

"Around thirty minutes."

Phoenix pulls back and intertwines our fingers. "Come with me." I follow him as he leads me upstairs to our bedroom. I stop at the sight of a large box on the bed.

"What's that?" Unease skates down my spine when Phoenix doesn't answer right away. "Phoenix?"

He exhales. "It's a dress."

Inhaling sharply, I continue to stare at the box. "I don't like it when you buy me dresses," I say.

"You're going to look beautiful in it," he says like that's supposed to bring comfort.

"What is it for?"

"I'm hosting an auction tomorrow night."

"What?" My voice reverberates off the walls as I step away from him.

"I picked this dress out for you." He walks to the box and opens it, but I don't look. I laugh at him.

"You have lost your mind. I'm not going to an auction. I will stay in our room and no one will know I'm here."

He crosses his arms over his chest and arches an eyebrow at me. "It's not a request. You will go."

My mouth opens and closes like a fish out of water. "I won't. You can't make me." I want it to sound like a demand, but it comes out more as a plea.

His gaze softens. "You have to go, Kenz."

"Don't..." My voice cracks, so I turn away and walk into the bathroom. I will not cry. I will not. What will he make me do? Will I be put on display? I don't know what happens to those who have already been bought. Will we be expected to have sex in front of everyone again?

Bringing the palm of my hands to my eyes, I try my best to focus on my breathing. I will not cry. I suck in a shaky breath, trying to calm my nerves.

Fingers trail down my arm. I jerk away, turning around, and back into the counter. Phoenix stands over me. His eyes are soft and I hate it. He's looking at me the way I want him to look at me. How I've been longing for him to look at me since we got married.

"You belong to me. You will go." There's no room for argument.

"I hate you."

He chuckles darkly and leans in so his lips graze my earlobe. "I'm going to show you how amazing hate sex can be."

"Will we have to do that in front of people again?"

He sighs and steps away from me. "Yes."

I push away from the counter, walk out of the bathroom, walk down the stairs, and step out onto the back porch. I can't do this. The door slides open behind me, so I walk off the porch and into the yard. There's a large oak tree in the middle of the yard with a wooden swing.

Sitting on it, I kick off the ground and swing. Maybe it will break and free me of this misery. My heart is in pieces as I fly higher and higher. When I was little, we had a swing in the backyard that was similar to this and my father would push me on it. Will my father try to save me? Is he trying? It's been three months since the auction and I don't know if he's tried to get me back or not.

Will he come for me? Or has he given up? Does he know Phoenix and I are married? Allowing the swing to slow down and come to a stop, I lean my cheek against the rope. Phoenix steps in front of me. I wish he had done that when I was swinging. I could have done some real damage. He made me hope and now he's crushed it.

"Why are you doing this to me?"

He steps forward and grabs the rope leaning over me. "Believe it or not, I'm trying my best to protect you."

I scoff. "Don't lie to me."

He shakes the swing. I tighten my hold on the ropes, but I don't say anything. "I'm not lying to you, Kenz."

"Then don't let people watch us. If we have to, that's one thing, but why do they have to watch?"

He lets go of the swing and walks a few feet away before turning to face me again. "It's part of the initiation." I have no idea what that means.

"What initiation? Why can't we change it? It's being hosted at your house."

"I'm initiating to become part of the council. If you're just a member of The Society, you only have to do it in front of people publicly one time, but to be part of the council they watch one time as well."

I stare at him. We haven't had sex in a month. And the next time we're going to have sex will be in front of these people. I don't know what to say. He's proved over and over I'm his to bend. The worst part is I don't entirely hate it. He steps in front of me again and lifts my chin with his thumb and forefinger. "Trust me. I'll make them pay."

The dress fits perfectly. As much as I hate to admit it, it's absolutely gorgeous. I wasn't sure how the silver would look with my hair, but it's like the dress was made just for me. It has a deep set V, showing cleavage in a tasteful way. There's a split that ends halfway up my thighs and the lace of the dress teases my skin under it. I wish Phoenix wasn't so good at picking out clothes for me.

Walking out of the bathroom to a waiting Clara and Phoenix, I stand awkwardly with my hands at my side so they can look at me. I feel like a show dog or one of those little girls where the mom is living vicariously through her and makes her do all those stupid pageants.

"You look beautiful," Clara murmurs. My gaze flicks toward Phoenix, but he still doesn't say anything. He simply stares. I don't know what I was hoping for, but he could say something. Anything to make up for what he's doing to me.

"Clara, give us a minute," Phoenix says. Clara nods her head, walks out of the bedroom, and closes the door. He walks toward me, his steps calculated. I feel like a deer caught in the sights of a predator. I force my feet to stay rooted to the ground, even though every part of my being is screaming at me to run away. I know the moment he touches me I'll be putty, but I'll fight it as best as I can.

He stops inches away from me, but I keep my eyes glued on his chest. His thumb and forefinger grips my chin, lifting my face to look at him. I swallow at the lust and desire I see on his face. He rubs his thumb along my jaw before gripping the back of my head, his fingers carding through my hair.

"You're going to be the most beautiful woman in the room." My heart beats like a drum and hope flutters in my stomach. I bite the inside of my cheek, the pain grounding me a little. Don't give into his pretty words, McKenzie. He's said it before. I remind myself. But the way he's looking at me. It reminds me of the Phoenix I knew at school. The Phoenix that would sit at the same table as me in the library. The Phoenix who always wound up in the same classes as me. The Phoenix on our wedding night.

I was so infatuated with him for four years. And I always hoped that maybe he liked me too, because he always seemed to be where I was. But he never tried anything with me. I was never one of the girls he took under the bleachers. The one and only time he showed anything remotely close to having feelings for me was the day of graduation. He told me when I realized how awful my father was, he would be there to rescue me.

I'm still unsure about how awful my father is. Was he telling the truth about the arrangement? Phoenix didn't deny it. "I thought you said you would make this good for me."

His grip tightens slightly as he pulls me closer. "I'll make you feel good. You'll forget anyone is there." The hope that was fluttering in my stomach dies a quick death and I take a step back. He releases me reluctantly and takes a step back as well.

"Will you hide me like you did the first time?" I ask.

"I will." He crosses his arms over his chest, making his shirt tighten around his biceps. His shirt is rolled up to his elbows, giving me a glimpse of the tattoos on his arms. I have to find a way to make this clinical.

"So, how often do we have to do this? You said it's part of the initiation. How long does it last? Are there other parts of the initiation I need to know about?" I'm firing questions so fast, but he doesn't flinch.

"We already did it once at the auction I purchased you at. Then you're to do it at an auction you're hosting. It just so happens the one I purchased you at and the auction I'm hosting were scheduled back to back. You're also supposed to be attending every auction with me that is hosted by other people in The Society. We'll have another to attend three months from now."

"This is my life now, apparently. I am your property, right? And your wife." I scoff. "So, why spare me?" His smile is deadly and laced with venom.

"Now you're catching on. Good girl."

Chapter 31

Three Months After Auction

My hair is pinned back, so it falls in soft curls down my back. I'm finishing up the final touches to my makeup. Anna taught me how to do a smokey eye and she introduced me to red lipstick. I miss her. I wonder what she's doing. I haven't talked to her in almost a year. We drifted apart. Well, she stopped calling and texting me, so after a few attempts at trying to reach out to her, I finally gave up.

The last time I spoke to her, she said she met someone. I wonder if they're still together. Maybe that's what has kept her so busy. Studying myself one last time, I run my hands down my dress. Walking out of the bathroom, I stop at the sight of Phoenix. Why does he have to look so delectable? He's wearing an all black suit, but his tie has gold and silver designs on it.

He has two masks in his hands. One is gold, the other silver. He hands me the silver one. "You'll only have to wear it when we're around people." Turning the mask over in my hands, I admire its beauty. It will cover my nose up to my forehead. The way it's designed it reminds me of a crown. There's a jewel in the middle, the same color *as Phoenix's eyes. It has a black ribbon to tie it. As large as it is, I'm surprised at how lightweight it is.*

Phoenix's mask is identical to mine, except his is gold. "Why do I have silver and you have gold?" Phoenix pauses as he fixes one of his cufflinks. I'm not going to like this answer.

"Silver masks mean the person wearing it was bought, and the owner doesn't want to share. Gold masks mean the person wearing it is an owner and isn't going to buy or share." I probably shouldn't feel relief at his explanation, but I am. I don't want to be shared and I don't want to share. As toxic as that seems.

Clearing my throat, I turn to look at myself in the mirror so I can put on my mask. Phoenix steps up behind me and takes the mask from me. His fingertips brush my cheek as he puts the mask in place. My skin heats up at his light touches and the thought that tonight I'll be having sex with him again. My hands tremble slightly as I touch the edge of the mask.

"If you sit down. I can put yours on," I say as I turn to face him. I pull my bottom lip between my teeth as I gaze up at him. He brings his thumb up and pushes on my chin slightly so I'll release my lip.

"You'll mess up your lipstick," he whispers. He leans down until his lips are grazing mine. I stop breathing. He doesn't lean in further to turn it into a kiss. He looks into my eyes like he's trying to look into my soul. "That's my job." His lips brush mine as he speaks. My chest hitches as I suck in a shaky breath and look away. My face and neck heat up. I'm sure he can see the blush considering how low cut this dress is.

He backs up slightly, allowing me to breathe air that's not filled with his overwhelming scent, and sits down in the chair next to the window. I shake my head slightly and step up behind him. He hands me his mask over his shoulder. My hands are still shaking from that little interaction. I'm going to be a mess by the end of the night. Taking a steady breath, I place the mask on his face and tie the ribbon, making sure it's tight enough to hold it in place, but not so tight that it's uncomfortable.

He stands and offers me his hand. "Ready?"

"No."

He leans down and kisses the side of my forehead. I lean back and gape at him. Where has this side of him been for the past month?

"I'll be by your side the entire night."

I haven't left our room all day. Clara brought me breakfast and lunch, so when we get to the bottom of the stairs and I see all the decorations, I'm surprised. I glance up at the new chandelier. It's no longer the one that has lights that look like candles. It's a two-tier crystal chandelier. The top tier is smaller than the bottom tier with gold accents. In the entryway, there are black curtains draped from the ceiling to the floor, with lanterns and candles between each curtain. Phoenix leads me to the ballroom.

A man in a blue mask opens the door and we step in. It's like stepping into another world. Did the auction last month look anything like this? I remember being in awe when we stepped into the house, but when I was quickly escorted away from my father and the realization of what was going to happen hit me... Well, I don't remember much after that until Phoenix took me into a different room, gave me a different mask, and told me what was about to happen.

There are rows of chairs and an aisle to get to the front where there's a stage and podium. A black curtain hangs behind the stage with a large mask attached to it. The mask is red, and it looks just like mine and Phoenix's. On each side of the stage, there are large bouquets of red and black roses. The windows that didn't have curtains on them before but do now. I'm assuming to give the semblance of privacy.

"Who did all this?" I ask.

"Phillip handles all the logistics and planning and we hire people to make it happen." His hand grazes my lower back as he leads me back into the hallway.

"I like the new chandeliers." His lips twitch at the compliment, but he doesn't respond. There's a loud clang from the kitchen, making me jump. I rub my hand along my collarbone as I try to calm my racing heart and breathing. Phoenix wraps his arm around my waist and pulls me into his side.

"People will begin arriving in twenty minutes. We'll greet each guest, then we'll go into the ballroom and watch the auction. After that's complete, we'll go to the basement." I ball my hands into fists, my red fingernails digging into my palms. He maneuvers me, so I'm facing him. He wraps both arms around me, pulling me even closer.

"People will watch, but they won't be in the same room as us. They will be at a window. On our side, it's a mirror, so we won't be able to see them."

I sag slightly against Phoenix and press my forehead against his chest. He rubs his hands up and down my arms. "Will you still hide me?" I ask as I look up at him.

His fingertips trail up my arm to the column of my throat and back down. My whole body shivers at the contact, goosebumps breaking out over my arms. "I will. Contrary to what you might think about me, you are mine and I refuse to share. They might get glimpses, but over my dead body will they see any part of you I don't want them to see."

He leans down, so he's closer to me. "And if anyone attempted to, I'd gouge their eyes out and kill them slowly, drawing out their pain." He stands taller. "There are ten men that will not be here tonight because they crossed the boundaries I set the night I bought you."

My stomach flutters and my mouth gapes open. "What do you mean? What did they do? What did you do?"

"I had a certain boundary where they weren't allowed to get any closer than that spot. They crossed it, so they were quickly escorted out and held until I dropped you off at home and went back." I try to think back. I don't remember that happening. I don't remember the boundary or the men crossing it.

"What did you do when you went back?" He looks down at me, squinting his eyes. Is he trying to decide if I can handle what he tells me?

"I cut their dicks off, slowly. Then I put it in their mouth and sewed their mouths shut. I left them for about an hour. When I returned, I

covered their noses and let them choke on their own dicks if they hadn't already done so."

I drop my chin to my chest and gape at him. "That is..."

"Insane?" he asks.

"Brilliant."

He tilts his head at me in surprise, his lips lifting in a small smile. "There's hope for you after all, love." He places my hand on his forearm and turns us so we're facing the door.

"Don't speak to anyone unless I give you permission." I want to argue with this particular rule, but I don't because I'm grateful I won't have to hold a conversation with anyone.

"Are there any other rooms that have been decorated?" I ask, my stomach swooping at the slamming of car doors announcing the arrival of people.

"Yes, but we ran out of time, so I couldn't show you. Next time." There will be a next time. I don't know how I feel about that. As upset as I am with Phoenix, he seems to mean what he says about protecting me the best he can.

"Take deep breaths, love. If you get overwhelmed, tap your wrist twice with your index finger and your middle finger. I'll finish the conversation and escort you somewhere to help you calm down. If you feel like you're going to have a panic attack and you can't wait for me to finish a conversation, tap your wrist three times. I will have my eyes on you the entire night, so I promise I'll see you."

I grip his arm tighter. "Thank you," I whisper. Another man in a blue mask opens the front door and the first guest walks through the door and down the main entrance toward us. Phoenix leans down, his lips touching my ear softly.

"You belong to me. You are mine. You are my first priority. I will make sure you're safe. Always." Before I can respond, the first couple is standing in front of us. The woman is wearing the gold mask, and the man is wearing a silver one. I frown and purse my lips. I was under the impression that only women were sold. I guess I was wrong. The way the man is looking at the woman, he obviously has feelings for her. Unless he's a good actor.

"Ah, Phoenix, your pet looks absolutely breathtaking." I scowl at being called his pet. He called me that before, but I thought it was an endearment. Phoenix rubs the back of his knuckles over my jaw. Tilting my head to look up at him, I'm slightly taken aback by the brightness in his eyes. He has the same look the man has.

"She is, isn't she?" He leans down and kisses up my jaw to my ear. "Play along, pet," he whispers so only I can hear. Is the whole night a show? I allow my instincts to take over as I rub my hand up his forearm, to his bicep, and cup the back of his neck. Turning my head slightly, my lips capture his in the briefest kiss. He flicks his tongue, wetting my upper lip just enough for me to want more before he pulls away.

He hasn't kissed me since the day after our wedding. I hate a part of me wants more. The woman beams at me, but the man never looks in my direction. They walk toward the ballroom and we're greeting the next couple. I didn't have to speak to anyone, for that I'm grateful. But by the time the last couple walks into the ballroom, I'm beginning to believe the show Phoenix is putting on.

My thighs are slick with wetness because he instructed me not to wear anything under my dress. My palms are sweaty and my heart is beating as fast as a hummingbird's wings. The ballroom doors close and I inhale a shaky breath. I have no idea what comes next, but my gut is telling me to trust Phoenix.

Phoenix grips the side of my neck and turns me to face him. "Are you wet for me, pet?" I swallow and rub my thighs together. The hand not gripping my neck trails from my shoulder to between my breasts, his fingers pushing the fabric aside as he grazes his fingertips over my nipple.

I gasp as the need in my core gets so strong it almost hurts. He smirks. "Open your mouth and stick your tongue out." I obey immediately. He hums. "Such a good girl." His hand trails over my stomach to the split in my dress. I'm about to ask him what he's doing when the grip on my neck tightens and he places his thumb against my tongue.

"Suck," he orders as his lips trail from my shoulder to my collarbone and back again. I suck his thumb into my mouth at the same time his middle finger touches my clit. I moan around his thumb as he continues to lightly stroke my clit.

"So wet." He bites down on my earlobe. "I knew I'd have you a weeping mess before the end of the night." I suck in a breath through my nose. I want to beg him to add more pressure, but he continues to tease as I circle his thumb with my tongue. I'm about to pull off his thumb and beg when clapping erupts from the ballroom.

"That's our cue, love." He removes his finger from my clit, bringing it to his mouth and licks his finger clean. "Excellent." He removes his

thumb from my mouth and smirks. "That was practice for later." He winks at me and turns us toward the ballroom just as the doors open.

Chapter 32

Three Months After Auction

Throughout the entire auction, Phoenix distracts me with small touches. He wraps a piece of my hair around his finger. He trails his fingertip from my ankle up to my thigh and back down. Then he kisses my shoulder, neck, ear, and cheek. Leaning toward him until my mouth touches his ear. "If you keep this up, there's going to be a puddle on my chair."

His hand grips my knee as he pulls me so close I'm practically in his lap. "Good. Then everyone will know you belong to me." I scoff. Like he hasn't made it abundantly clear all night that I belong to him. He's been marking his territory since the first person stepped through the door.

A knot forms in my stomach. That's why he's doing this. Not because he cares. Not because he has a thing for me. It's because he bought me, it's because he made me marry him, I belong to him, and he's making it clear no one else can have me. I'm so stupid. I'm falling for his lies again. Leaning away from him, I cross my legs and pull my arm away from him. He allows me to pull away. Without his small touches and distractions, it gives me the opportunity to focus on the auction.

According to him, there are ten people up for auction tonight. Six have already been bid on. There are some people that look like they want to be here. But there are others that are terrified. One girl steps forward and my mouth drops. A mask covers her face, but I'm almost certain she was two grades before us at the academy.

"Did we go to school with her?" I ask Phoenix. He studies the girl for a minute before nodding. Is her father selling her too? Or her mother? How does this auction work, anyway? Who gets to sell and be sold and why?

I begin shaking my leg as her bid goes higher and higher. I wish I could bid on her, but I'm wearing a silver mask. I can't even ask Phoenix to bid on her because he's wearing a gold mask. She's terrified. I see it in her eyes, the gasping for breath, and how she shifts from side to side. The winning bid is for two million dollars. She begins to cry and is escorted off the stage.

Shifting in my seat, I have to stop myself from running after her. Closing my eyes, I know the look of fear in her eyes will be seared into my brain forever. Another girl is called up, and she looks just as scared as the previous girl, maybe even more so. I tap my wrist three times.

Phoenix wraps his arm around my bicep, stands, and walks us out a side door that leads to the kitchen. He guides me through the kitchen, down a hallway and to a room that's been locked every time I've tried to enter during my explorations. I come to a halt in the doorway. It's a sex room. The room is painted black with a king size bed. There's an odd shaped chair near the bed and there's a stand with various vibrators, and other things I'm not sure of.

"Is this where we're—"

"No," he interrupts. "It was the closest room I could get you to." My mouth forms an O as I walk around the room, taking in everything. Grazing my hand over the smooth leather of the oddly shaped chair, I glance over to Phoenix.

"What is this?"

He places his hands in his pockets. "A sex chair."

I squint at the chair before looking back at him. "What makes it a sex chair?" He walks over and runs his hand over it before grabbing me around the waist and pulling me against him, my back to his chest.

"Well, if you bend over the back of it." He pushes on my back until I'm bent over and my chest curves with the couch. It's more comfortable than I expected. "I could take you from behind and you would feel every inch, every ridge, every thrust." He pushes into me with his hips, his hardness pressing against me.

He lifts me and walks me to the front. "Lay down." I eye him before following his instructions. It's hard to do it without showing him everything under my dress. From the grin on his face, it's obvious he knows. Laying back, I place my legs on the raised part, trying to hold my dress from falling open.

But he grabs me by the thighs, pushing my hands away. He straddles the couch and wraps my legs over his thighs, still gripping my thighs. I gasp, knowing he can see everything. He stares without abandon as he pulls me until he can rock his clothed dick against my bare pussy. This is similar to the way he took me on our wedding night.

"On this side, I can angle you in such a way that I'll rub against your g-spot with every single thrust." He presses against me over and over again. I'm convinced I could come from just this.

"Nix," I gasp. He pauses for a second before sliding one hand up my inner thigh. His thumb slides through my folds, up to my clit and back. I jerk, wanting more.

"Do you know why I've been teasing you all night?" he asks as he continues to rub his thumb up and down my pussy lips.

"Why?" I try to lift my hips higher to encourage him to make his touches firmer. But his other hand grips my thigh and keeps me in my place.

"I knew tonight would be hard for you." His touch becomes more firm as my chest heaves. I grip the hand on my thigh, digging my fingernails into it, but he doesn't even flinch. "You needed a distraction, so I'm giving it to you."

It takes me a minute to comprehend what he's saying. It's true, the entire time we were greeting guests I was focusing on him because he kept flirting and teasing me. It wasn't until I pulled away from him I noticed what was actually happening. He pushes two fingers in me and begins to finger fuck me. I meet each of his thrusts

White hot pleasure courses up my spine, tingling my scalp as I clap my hand over my mouth. Squeezing my eyes shut, I cry out as my muscles contract around his fingers, giving me an intense orgasm that seems to go on forever. He draws my orgasm out by circling my clit until I collapse onto the chair and all the tension in my muscles gives way.

He brings his fingers to his mouth again, licking them, his eyes never leaving mine. "So good," he says. My heart pounds in my chest. I wish he was like this all the time.

He steps back, the outline of his cock straining against his pants. But he doesn't reach for it or try to push me to my knees after he helps me off the couch. He takes me to the en suite bathroom, grabs a washcloth to wet, pushes me down on the edge of the tub and cleans me. I jump at the first touch because of how sensitive I am, but I let him do it. I'm surprised I feel no embarrassment or shame.

After he's done, he holds his hand out to me and helps me stand on shaky legs. "They'll be done soon. We need to return. Will you be able to make it? There should only be one or two left."

"Can you keep distracting me?"

He wraps his arm around my waist and pulls me into his chest. "It will be my pleasure. Anything else?"

I pull my lips between my teeth as I stare into his icy blue eyes. "Can you kiss me?" As soon as the question leaves my mouth, I wish I could take it back, but I've been craving his kiss for weeks. Darting my eyes over his shoulder, I stare at his earlobe.

"It will be my pleasure," he rasps, gripping the back of my head with one hand and the side of my neck with the other. I close my eyes, counting every heartbeat before his lips touch mine. He licks the seam of my lips, seeking entry. Opening them in invitation, he captures my bottom lip between his and sucks before sucking my tongue into his mouth.

He groans as I wrap my arms around his shoulders, trying to pull him as close as possible. I'm drowning in him and I don't care. I want everything he has to offer me. Every touch. Every look. Every breath. He walks me backward until my back hits the door and lifts me. I follow his lead, wrapping my legs around his waist.

He wraps his hand around my throat, tilting my head just so as he devours me. I'm surprised I don't burn him with how hot I am. This kiss is more than I could imagine. My heart pounds as his kiss becomes laced with need and desire.

"More," he groans against my lips. I wrap my legs tighter around his waist and my arms tighter around his shoulders. He tilts my head, tearing his lips from mine, kissing up my jaw to my ear, down my throat to the crook of my shoulder, where he sucks my skin between his mouth and teeth. I gasp at every nip, suck, and lick. I never want this to end, but he's slowly lowering my legs to the floor and backing away.

He keeps his arm around my waist, supporting me so I don't fall in a heap on the floor. He runs his thumb across my bottom lip before kissing me one more time. "We have to get back." I can't speak, so I simply nod. He reaches behind me, opening the door and guiding me back to the ballroom.

We arrive in time to see the last bid. I ignore what's happening on stage and look around the ballroom. Phoenix has a possessive hand on my knee, his thumb rubbing comforting circles on the inside of my thigh. As I'm about to face the front, I spot a woman at the end of the aisle a few rows back staring at me. Through her mask, her eyes are in slits as she glares at me. I have no idea who she is and the longer I return her stare, the hair on the nape of my neck stands on end.

"What are you looking at?" Phoenix pulls my leg over his. Turning, I focus on the stage, not really seeing.

"That woman at the end of the third row. She's wearing a gold mask and a navy dress." I wrap my hand around Phoenix's, hoping he doesn't reject me. He doesn't; he intertwines our fingers and turns slightly so he can look behind us.

"There's no one there, Kenz." I turn again and sure enough, the chair is empty. Looking toward the back of the ballroom where everyone entered, there isn't anyone standing.

"I swear there was a woman there." He rubs his thumb over the back of my hand.

"I believe you. If you see her later, point her out to me." I glance around the ballroom again, searching for her. Where the hell did she go?

Chapter 33

Three Months After Auction

Phoenix leads me to a room on the other side of the house, a group of people following us. I rub my fingers together, trying to get rid of the tingling. I think I might faint. I wish we could get in the room and then the people can gather. Why do they have to follow us?

The room we enter is the same room where I found the secret entrance. He escorts me in and the people follow us into the room. I clutch Phoenix's arm as my breath hitches. He said they wouldn't be in the same room as us. He wraps his arm around me, pulling me close. "Relax, pet. They won't stay in here with us."

I look at him in confusion. Rex and another of his security guys enter and open the secret passage. "You all will watch from this room." Rex motions for them to enter. Some comply right away, but others aren't happy about it.

"What is this about, Phoenix?" The man takes a few steps in our direction, but Rex cuts him off.

Phoenix shrugs off his jacket and lays it across the chest at the end of the bed. "The bylaws state you can watch, but it doesn't say how. You will watch in the room or you won't watch at all."

Another man steps forward with a scowl on his face. "It has always been in the same room," he argues. A woman behind him moves slightly, catching my attention because her navy dress looks similar to the woman's in the ballroom. I try to catch a better glimpse of her, but the lighting in this room is dim, and she stays behind the man who's still talking. "You can't join and decide to make changes."

Phoenix begins to remove his cufflinks. "I can do whatever the hell I want. I've had the highest winning bid this year." That catches my attention. I tilt my head at him. He paid six million dollars for me. Is he talking about me? He said he hasn't bought anyone else, but what if he was lying? Right now I don't care. All I care about is him winning this argument because I do not want these people in the same room with us.

"If you keep arguing with me, I'll only let you hear what's going on in the room." The group erupts in murmurs. "Rex, please escort our guests into the room. If they don't go willingly, you can escort them out of my house." There are some more grumbles, but people begin to comply.

Phoenix rolls his sleeves up and I pull my bottom lip between my teeth as his tattooed forearms are uncovered. I lick my lips as he removes his tie and unbuttons the top two buttons on his shirt.

"Like what you see, pet?" Inhaling, my eyes snap to his. I was ogling and staring. He has a small smirk on his face, obviously enjoying the attention. How is it earlier today I loathed him, but within less than twenty-four hours, he has completely turned that around and disarmed me? He has a way of doing that. My heart beats heavy in

my chest. He's going to break me in so many ways, and it looks like I'm going to let him.

I don't answer him, but he doesn't seem to care. The door to the secret room closes behind me. "All set, boss." Phoenix steps into my space, putting an arm around me and pulling me in until my back arches and my feet are barely touching the ground.

"You ready?" My vision swims and my stomach rolls with nausea. This is happening. He cups the side of my neck and runs his thumb over my jaw. "You won't know they're there. I promise to make you forget." I nod slightly.

"You can move the curtain." Curtain? I try to turn when there's movement behind me, but Phoenix doesn't let me. I don't know why I didn't put two and two together the other day when I found that entrance. The curtain doesn't cover windows, well, not windows that look outside. The door gently shuts behind me, and I know this is about to happen.

"Open your mouth and stick your tongue out." He wasn't lying earlier when he said that was practice for later. I do as I'm instructed. He runs his thumb over my jaw again, his lips tipping into a grin that's half smile, half promise of what's coming.

"Such a good girl." He leans forward and licks my tongue with his. My stomach swoops like I'm riding a fast roller coaster. I didn't realize I'd like that. He does it one more time, our moans mingling together before he leans back and places his thumb on my tongue like earlier.

"Now, suck." I suck as his other hand wanders. It starts at my collarbone, tracing it with featherlike touches as my body tingles all over and a need only he can produce settles between my legs.

"Think you can handle my cock in that pretty mouth of yours?" he asks as he trails his fingers along the edge of the fabric of my dress. I can't talk with his thumb in my mouth, so I nod. "Have you ever done that before?" I shake my head.

He hums. "Seems like I get to experience all your firsts." And many of them have been in front of a group of people. His fingers dip inside my dress, caressing my breast as he circles my nipple before pinching it slightly.

I gasp as need, lust, and desire vibrate through every cell in my being. "Are you wet for me, pet?" I arch an eyebrow at him as I run my tongue over the pad of his thumb. What a silly question. I've been wet for him all night. He chuckles before slipping his thumb out of my mouth. Taking my hand, he leads me to the other side of the room, so the bed is between us and the window everyone is observing from.

He grabs a pillow and places it on the floor. "Get on your knees." I sink down onto the pillow, expecting him to unbutton his pants so I can suck his cock. "Spread your knees, but keep your toes touching." I adjust myself until I'm how he likes me. He squats down in front of me adjusting my dress slightly, so it's not in the way. Since I'm behind the bed, he's the only one that can see me. His hand grazes up my inner thigh and he swipes his finger through my wetness twice. I close my eyes and tip my head back at the small amount of pleasure.

"I'm going to make you feel so good, pet." I swallow as he stands. He turns and opens the drawer of the nightstand. When he turns toward me, there's a pink u-shaped vibrator in his hand. At least that's what I think it is. I want to clench my legs closed, but I can't with the way I'm positioned. He squats down again and shows me the vibrator.

“Have you ever used a vibrator?” he asks. Heat rushes up my neck to my forehead.

“Once,” I reply. His grip tightens on the vibrator, his knuckles turning white.

“With who?” His voice is low.

I lean my head back, squinting my eyes at him. “Myself.” His grip on the vibrator relaxes.

“And you only did it once? Did you not like it?” I sigh, not wanting to talk about this. Looking to the side, I avoid his intense gaze, but he won’t let me. He grips my chin with his thumb and forefinger, so I’m looking at him again.

“Come on, pet. If you didn’t like it, I won’t use it.”

I look at his nose, his cheek, his ear, anywhere but his eyes. “I did like it. A lot.”

“But?” he prods.

“It made me squirt,” I whisper as low as possible because I don’t want anyone else to hear. I’m so embarrassed I put my hands over my face. He gently removes them and cups the back of my neck with the hand not holding the vibrator.

“That’s nothing to be ashamed of.” I give him an “oh really” look. One side of his mouth tips into a smile. “They’re designed to give you pleasure.” He turns it on, making me jump at the sudden sound. He trails the vibrator along the V of my dress. Sucking in a breath, my stomach quivers at the sensation.

“I’m going to put this in you.” He circles my nipple with the vibrator. I pull my bottom lip between my teeth, tilting my head back. I whimper, wishing I had some friction on the pillow below me. He shows me a

small remote. "I'll control it. Turning it on and off as I wish. I'll also slow it down or speed it up as I wish."

"What if..." I trail off, my stomach flipping with anticipation and nerves. "What if I can't handle it?"

"Your mouth will be full, so you'll tap my leg twice." I stare into his beautiful eyes. "Trust me, pet. You're going to love this." He leans forward, kissing me slow and deep. He continues to trail the vibrator down my sternum, down my stomach, and between my legs. Bringing my hands up to cup his face, I kiss him like I've wanted to kiss him for weeks. He touches my clit, the vibrator still on, and I jerk.

I moan around his tongue as he moves in closer to me, his chest touching mine. He pulls back slightly, pulling my bottom lip between his teeth slowly. I love the way he kisses. It almost distracts me from what he's doing with the vibrator. That is until he pushes it inside me. I inhale sharply as my legs begin to shake. Before I careen over the edge, he stops it. I moan in frustration and he chuckles.

"All in time, pet." His words wash over me like a breeze on a hot summer day. He stands, undoing his pants. When he pulls his cock out, I bite down on the tip of my tongue. He's large. I look up at him. He's fully clothed and I hate it.

"Can you unbutton your shirt?" I ask him.

"If you want to see more, undress me." I suck in a breath at his command, but do as he says. His top two buttons are already undone, so I slowly begin undoing the rest. It's a tease when each button is undone as his tattooed skin comes into view. With the last flick of my fingers, his chest and abs come into view. His pants hang low on his hips, showing the V that leads down to his hard cock.

My fingers itch to touch his exposed skin, but I'm not sure if I'm allowed. Instead, I place my hands on my thighs. Tipping my chin, I look up at him. The look on his face breaks down the measly wall I've attempted at building and rebuilding over the past few months. He looks like he cares for me. Like this means more to him than a show or display for those watching us. I thought that on our wedding night too.

"You can touch, pet." The blue of his eyes is just a rim around his dilated pupils. I lift my hand and wrap my hand around his cock. He sucks in a breath, his eyes widening slightly, but he doesn't stop me as I rub up his shaft slowly. Releasing him, I trace my fingers along the indentions of his abs. Leaning up slightly so I can reach, I continue my exploration to his pecs before trailing my fingertips back down his abs.

I take my index finger and swipe off the bead of precum that is glistening on his tip. Settling back down onto the pillow, I bring my finger to my mouth, look up at him, and lick it off. His chest is moving quicker than it was a few minutes ago, and his eyes are even darker.

"So beautiful on your knees for me, pet." He cups my face and rubs his thumb across my lip. I almost believe he's doing this because he wants to. The vibrator turns on and I jerk forward. I place my hands on his thighs so I don't fall over any further.

"Oh god," I whisper. His cock is right there, so without thinking, I lean forward even more and suck one of his balls into my mouth.

"Shit." He wraps his hand around my hair as I move to the other one. I have no idea what I'm doing, so I allow instinct to take over. If his hand tightens in my hair, I know he likes it; if he also inhales or exhales suddenly, he loves it. I lick up his shaft, making sure to use as

much saliva as I can so he's good and wet before taking his tip into my mouth and circling it with my tongue.

I get distracted by the line that forms a V and pull off him. I wonder briefly if he's going to stop me, but he doesn't. My lips graze his skin and satisfaction blooms in me when goosebumps break out on his skin. When I reach my destination, I pull his skin between my lips. I've never done this before, but I want to mark him like he's marked me. I want to stamp my proof of ownership on him so no one else will ever get this side of him again.

"Are you claiming me as yours, pet?" I lift my eyes. His fingers run through my hair and he looks down at me with such devotion it almost makes me choke up. I want him to know he's mine and mine only. He seems to enjoy the fact I'm claiming him. When I'm done, I lean back slightly, inspecting my work.

Sighing, I return my attention back to his cock before taking him into my mouth again. "Fuck," he moans. He's long and I know he won't fit all the way in my mouth, so I wrap my hand around him as I slowly drop down on him. Just when I'm getting used to the vibrator and having him in my mouth, he turns it up. I moan around him, which makes him moan as well. I try to get friction again, but the way he instructed me to sit provides none.

I'm still a little hesitant about how fast he wants me to suck, but I'm learning how to suction my cheeks. "Look at me," he demands. I open my eyes and look up at him. "Make your grip tighter." I tighten my hand around him and he groans. "My pet is such a quick learner," he praises.

I swallow around him, and he closes his eyes for the briefest second before looking back at me. "I'm going to guide your head so you'll know how fast I like it." I nod slightly. His grip tightens around my hair as he begins to push and pull. He increases the speed on the vibrator again. I groan as I'm almost pushed to the edge, but he decreases it quickly, not letting me fall over.

I want to scream at him to let me come, but my mouth is full and I know it won't do any good. He'll let me when he's ready. Staring at him as he begins to thrust, he winks at me. "Such a good girl." He thrusts a few more times before pulling me off him. I'm a little surprised he didn't finish.

He pulls the drawer to the nightstand open, grabbing a condom before he kneels down in front of me. "I want to come in that sweet pussy pet, not in your mouth. I'll save that for another night." He turns the vibrator completely off and takes it out. I cry out at the emptiness, but he's soon pulling me to him so I'm straddling him, and guiding his cock in me. His hands are tight around my waist as I bring my hands up to hold on to his shoulders. He drops me inch by inch onto him. The stretch feels so good.

I lean my head back, my hair grazing the pillow as I concentrate on every ounce of pleasure he's giving me. "All they can see is your face and expressions. They know how good I'm making you feel." I had forgotten about the people watching us. He's really good at distracting me. "They see how good you're making me feel." I pull my head upright so I can look at him.

His face is flushed slightly and the edge of his hairline damp with sweat. He returns my stare as he wraps his arms around my waist, pulling me until I'm flush with his chest. "Ride me." The words are ripped out of his chest and I respond immediately by lifting up and back down. His forehead leans against mine as he runs one hand up my spine to cup the back of my head.

"So good." His voice is rough with desire. "So tight. So wet." I wrap my arms around his neck and cling to him as he touches every sensitive spot in me.

"Nix," I gasp. I'm going to come. I lean back slightly, placing one hand on the ground behind me and still holding onto him with the other hand. He holds on to the back of my neck as he leans back slightly and watches as I ride him.

"So. Fucking. Beautiful," he says every word with each thrust.

"Please," I moan. At this angle, he rubs a spot in me I didn't know existed until this very moment. As I fall back down on him, my muscles clench and I fall forward, my head landing in the crook of his neck as I come all over his cock. I scream his name as he thrusts up into me a few more times before he's holding me tight and coming too.

"Jesus, Kenz," he moans against my neck. He licks up the column of my throat before sucking my earlobe into his mouth. I shiver with another bolt of pleasure as he holds me for a few minutes. He helps me off him and I fall back as he removes the condom and throws it away.

He doesn't speak. He stands with his back to the window as he puts himself back in his pants and buttons his shirt. I guess there won't be any cuddling. Standing slowly since my legs are still shaking, I rub my hands down my dress to get rid of any wrinkles. Phoenix turns toward the door, still not acknowledging me, and an uneasy feeling settles in my stomach.

He pushes a button. "Rex, we're done. Please prepare to escort everyone out." Phoenix finally turns to me, extending his hand. I walk forward and take it as he opens the door and leads the way out.

"Do you need to use the restroom?" he asks as we pass Rex in the hallway. My stomach knots at the detachment in his voice. Tonight didn't mean anything to him. He made me believe it did. Just like our wedding.

"Yes, please." I hope he doesn't intend to go into the restroom with me. I need a moment to put my wall back up. He stops in front of a door, motioning for me to enter.

"I'll wait here." I exhale slowly as I walk into the restroom. Relieving myself quickly, I walk to the sink and stare at my reflection. I can't do this. I can not separate sex from my emotions; it's not within me.

Leaning forward on the palms of my hands, I take deep breaths as I imagine putting up one brick after another. Looking at myself in the mirror, I straighten my spine and lift my chin. "Turn it off, Kenz, or you won't survive this."

Taking one more deep breath, I open the door and allow Phoenix to lead the way back to the entryway to say farewell to all the guests. Phoenix doesn't try to distract me this time.

Chapter 34

Five Months After Auction

Time passes by unbelievably slowly. I've developed a sort of friendship with Phillip and Clara, but I still don't trust them completely. I keep waiting for Phoenix to acknowledge there is something between us, but I've barely seen him since the auction. Will we have sex again since we won't have to do it in front of others anymore? The next morning when I woke up regrettably sore from the previous night's activities, he was gone, and all the decorations had been completely removed.

Laying back on the bed, I stare up at the ceiling, bored out of my mind. Slapping my hands on the mattress, I stand and head to the kitchen. Phillip is there preparing dinner. He smiles at me when I enter. "Hi, Phillip," I greet him as I climb up on one of the chairs at the island.

"Hey, Miss McKenzie." Leaning forward, I watch as he begins layering a lasagna.

"You can call me Kenz," I tell him. His smile brightens, and he nods. "I love lasagna."

"Well, it will be just you tonight, so you'll have plenty." My stomach swirls with disappointment, but I try my best not to acknowledge it. Even though Phoenix doesn't talk to me a lot, we do usually eat dinner together. I don't respond. I wonder where Phoenix will be. I refuse to ask, though.

"Phillip?" He turns to me after he puts the lasagna in the oven.

"Yes?"

"Could I bake some cookies? I have a recipe I know by heart. If there're ingredients for it, could I make them?" He's nodding his head before I finish my sentence.

"Of course. I have a KitchenAid mixer, but we can get your own, since I use it a lot. But you can use it today. I'm sure we have the ingredients. I don't let us run out of things." I smile. It's the first real smile I've had in weeks. Telling him the list of ingredients he confirms he does have everything and shows me where it's all at.

I turn the second oven on so it'll begin to warm and start mixing everything. Just as I'm about to scoop the dough onto the cookie sheet, Phoenix walks in wearing a black suit and a black mask. He stops when he sees me. My heart drops then begins beating rapidly. It hasn't been three months. Is he going to another auction? Without me. And he's wearing a black mask. He was wearing a black mask when he bought me. Is he buying someone else?

My stomach dips in disappointment at the thought. "McKenzie," he greets me and I hate how I respond to him acknowledging me. I mentally berate myself. I know we haven't been on the best of terms since the last auction, but I want to know why he's going to an auction without me. And why is he wearing a black mask?

"I'm making chocolate chip cookies." He removes his mask, walks across the kitchen, and stops next to me. My heart stops with him. I inhale sharply, placing the cookie sheet in the oven.

"How long do they have to cook for?" he asks, standing too close to me.

"About ten minutes." I don't want him to go; I want him to stay home.

"Good, I'd like to try them." Why do I feel like I'm going to cry? I want to hate him so much, but it's not coming as easy as I'd like for it to. After the auction, he didn't acknowledge me or what we had done. He's tried to speak to me a few times, but he shattered my heart so he doesn't deserve my words. I'm no longer just his property. I'm his wife, but it's not different. It's not good like he promised me it would be.

There's an awkward silence that stretches between us as I watch the timer on the oven countdown. Why is he going to an auction without me? Is he going to buy someone else? Will he have sex with them in front of people too? Technically, he can do whatever he wants to do. But the thought of him being unfaithful shatters my heart even if our marriage is a sham.

The longer I think about it, the more my throat closes up and the harder I have to fight to not cry. I can't do this. I don't want to do this. For four years, I was infatuated with him, but it's never going to happen. Not the way I want it to happen. He stirs next to me, his arm brushing mine. I jerk away, giving him my back.

"Kenz?" He sounds like he's concerned, but it's a lie. I have to get away. It's the only solution. If he's going to an auction, I can use that time to try to create an escape plan. Married or not, I can't stay here

any longer. His fingers trail down my spine and I pull away again, but turn back to face him.

"Don't touch me. And don't call me Kenz." He steps back, leaning against the counter and crossing his arms over his chest. His eyes turn to slits as he studies me.

"I think you've misinterpreted what is going on here." His voice is a deadly whisper.

"No. I know where I stand with you. I'm your plaything when you want me to be, but you ignore me when you don't. And apparently you go to auctions and buy other girls. It hasn't even been three months since the last one." His lips tip up into a smirk as he pushes away from the counter and stalks toward me. I want to be brave and stay where I am, but I walk back until I'm against the kitchen table.

"Are you jealous?" he asks as he puts his hands on the table, caging me in.

"No. Why would I be jealous?" My fingers grip the edge of the table as he steps even closer to me. He trails his index finger from my hand to the inside of my elbow, up to my shoulder, leaving goosebumps in his wake.

"So, would you be okay if I went to an auction and bought another girl? Then had sex with her in front of a room full of people?" The image that provokes crushes my soul. I'm not dumb. I know he's slept with other women, but I don't want him to be sleeping with them now. I shrug, unable to answer, because I know my voice will give me away. "I don't like liars, McKenzie."

"Neither do I, Phoenix. You said I was the only woman you've done this with. And I thought they only happened every three months." His

finger trails up the column of my neck and traces along my jaw. I pull back slightly, but there's nowhere for me to go. I'm at his mercy. I hate it.

"You are the only woman I've done this with." His thumb rubs along my bottom lip. "And you'll be the only woman I'll ever do this with." My eyes brim with tears. I want it to be true so badly. "And it's happening a month earlier because the man who is hosting this time will be out of the country next month, so it was agreed he could move it up." I suck in a breath, trying to hold my tears at bay. He runs his thumb along my cheekbone. "Let them fall, darling." I shake my head as I hiccup.

I'm fighting so hard to keep them in, but one finally escapes. Tipping my chin down in shame, I know I won't be able to stop them now. He grips my chin with his thumb and index finger, lifting it. He leans forward and licks my cheek.

"They belong to me," he whispers. Then he's capturing my lips with his. I try to resist, but he doesn't give me a chance. He runs the back of his knuckles down my throat before he wraps his hand around it, holding me in place as he completely devours me. His tongue meets mine repeatedly as he wraps his other arm around my waist and lifts me onto the table.

"You belong to me," he murmurs against my mouth. "And not just because I bought you at some auction. You're my wife." His hand slips under the back of my shirt and runs up my spine.

"You don't act like I'm your wife," I whisper.

He breaks the kiss and leans back slightly. I bring the palm of my hand up to his chest and push. He leans back more, giving me the space

I need, but not completely moving away. "If I belong to you. If I'm your wife, why are you wearing a black mask?" Before he can answer, the oven timer begins to beep. He lets me slide out and take the cookies out, but as soon as they're on the counter, he has me caged in again.

I simply stare at him, waiting for the answer to my question. "There's a woman that needs rescuing and I'm going to attempt to do it." My heart softens a little, but he was supposedly rescuing me too.

"You said you were rescuing me, too," I remind him.

"Because of how much I paid for you and because we're married now, I have certain privileges. One of them is that I can purchase without doing with them what I did with you." I grab a cookie off the cookie sheet and hand it to him. He chuckles. "Is this my reward for telling you the truth?"

"Did it work?" He takes a bite from the cookie and hums.

"These are delicious, so absolutely." He pops the rest of the cookie in his mouth and takes another.

"Can I go with you?" My voice is low, but from his expression I can tell he heard me. He smiles lightly.

"Yes." My mouth drops slightly. I wasn't expecting that to be so easy. "You have some dresses. I'll get Clara to meet you in your bedroom to help you get ready. We have to leave in thirty minutes." Excitement stirs in my stomach, which is crazy, but I want to be included. I want him to prove I'm more to him than just his property. Maybe this is the beginning of that. That I can be a partner in whatever he has going on. That he can trust me.

Clara dressed me in a red satin dress with spaghetti straps. The bodice is tight and held up by the criss-cross in the back that ties into a bow in the middle of my back. The skirt flares out and shows off my legs. I actually had a fun time getting ready with Clara's help. Since I had to get ready so quickly, she straightened my hair while I did my makeup. I take one last glimpse in the mirror, happy with what I see.

I wish I didn't feel excited. I wish I could shut my emotions off. I wish this was a normal relationship. Why am I looking forward to tonight? I'm setting myself up to be hurt again, but I can't seem to stop it. Will we have sex again tonight? I shake my head as I walk down the last few steps. Don't do this to yourself, McKenzie.

Phoenix is waiting at the bottom of the stairs. His eyes rake over me as I descend each step. He extends his hand when I reach the last step. I take it as I step down, my heart beating rapidly at the look in his eyes. It's almost like he wants to eat me. He pulls me against his chest. I inhale sharply. "You look gorgeous, love."

His lips graze mine. I want it to be more, but he pulls back before it becomes more. His thumb brushes my chin before he hands me a mask. I stare at it. It's different from the one I wore before.

"It's beautiful," I whisper. I run my fingers over it. It's silver with a black attachment to the top that resembles a tiara with a silver jewel.

"I'm glad you like it." He doesn't say anything else as he places his hand on my lower back and guides me out of the house. Had he planned on taking me all along?

Chapter 35

Tonight we stand in the line to be greeted by the host. It gives me a chance to see the interactions between each couple. There are quite a few people here alone as well. The majority of them are wearing black masks, but some are wearing red and black masks.

"What do the red and black masks mean?" I ask Phoenix. He pulls me close to his side, his lips grazing my forehead. Why can't he be like this at home?

"It means they share. So, the other couples here wearing red and black will ask one of them to join." My muscles tighten. I remember seeing those at the auction he hosted, but I was so nervous about what was going to happen later that night, I didn't think to ask.

"Ummm... do you—"

"Absolutely not," he interrupts me, turning me so I face him. His eyes are full of an intense heat and something more. Possessiveness? "I don't share, love." He tips my chin up with his index finger and leans down until his mouth is a ghost over mine. "You're mine. Don't forget that."

He seals his declaration with a hard kiss. It's short, but he makes his point. He pulls away before I'm ready for him to, but the line is moving again. It's a long receiving line, but Phoenix distracts me like last time. He keeps me in front of him, my back to his chest. His hard cock pressing into the small of my back.

Every few minutes, his mouth will skim along the column of my throat, shoulder, or the back of my neck. Will he sleep with me again tonight? I don't know how to feel about this. We've barely had any interactions, but I can't deny how my body is responding to him. He pulls me tight against him as he takes my earlobe into his mouth.

"Are you wet for me, pet?" I swallow as his hand trails from my waist, up my torso, and stops between my breasts. He stretches his thumb to circle my hard nipple. I lick my lips as I push my hips back, grinding against him.

He grunts quietly in my ear. I get nervous at the thought of people seeing or watching. Glancing around us, I notice others are more focused on the person they're with.

"Nix," I gasp when he pinches my nipple.

"Do you know how long I've wanted you?" His lips trail down from my ear to the top of my shoulder, leaving goosebumps along the way. "I tried to fight it. The amount of times I wanted to bend you over one of those tables in the library? Countless." He rocks against me like he's imagining it.

He thought about me like that? I want to beg him to take me somewhere and take me exactly how he imagined back then, but we're next in line and before I'm ready, we're being greeted. Phoenix pulls back slightly, but keeps me in front of him. Maybe to hide his erection.

"Phoenix," the gentleman greets him, softly. He's wearing a traditional black tuxedo with a gold mask and the woman greeting with

him is wearing a black ball gown with silver embroidery and a silver mask. She smiles meekly, her eyes glassy. Every time the gentleman touches her, she sways away slightly.

"Lucas," Phoenix greets him in return before leading me toward their ballroom. We sit toward the back at the end of an aisle. When we're seated, I cross my leg, and he puts a possessive grip on my exposed thigh.

"You okay, pet?" I nod as I take a nervous glance around. I spot the woman who was wearing a navy dress at our auction. Even with a mask on, she's easily recognizable. She's glaring at me again. What did I do to this woman that she's looking at me like that? I almost say something to Phoenix, but decide against it.

The hosts walk in, the man's grip on the woman tight. "She doesn't like him," I whisper.

"Not many people do," Phoenix replies. My heart hurts at the thought of it. She's stuck with him day in and day out. There's no telling what he does to her.

"Will they..." I trail off. Phoenix turns to me, giving me his full attention.

"Yes, he bought her at the same auction I bought you and he's part of the council." That's why he addressed him by name. I pull my lip between my teeth, wanting to save her. He rubs his thumb along my chin, up my jaw, and grips the back of my neck. "Try not to think about it, pet. It will only make you sick." How does he do this so often?

"I don't want to watch."

He pulls my forehead against his. "We won't. We'll leave as soon as the auction is over." My shoulders slump and I exhale. "Then we'll go to one of my restaurants and have dinner and some drinks." I lift my hand to cup his cheek. Hope unfurls in my chest. Other than the auctions, he hasn't done anything with me outside of the house. Is it possible for this to be more? As much as I hate hoping again, I can't deny that I do.

"What about the person you plan on bidding on?" I want to know more about this person.

"Rex will take care of them." He doesn't expand further, so I drop it for now.

"So, if you're married, you don't have to have sex with the person you buy," I whisper low, so we're not overheard. He shakes his head.

"Not if you don't want to. Some married men want to." I stare at the side of his face. Does that mean he really does care about me?

The auctioneer announces there are eight people up for sale, then the auction begins and Phoenix pays close attention the entire time. His hand flexes each time someone is taken away and a new person is brought up. The first few people that come up I keep waiting for him to bid, but he doesn't. I learn as each person is brought up, if he shakes his head slightly, it's not who he's waiting for.

He's waiting for a specific person. Who is it? What is his connection with this person? How does he know about them? I want to ask all of these questions, but there isn't chatter during the auction. People are fixated on the auction. Bored and trying my best not to focus on what is actually happening, I let my gaze wander. The woman is watching me again.

She's wearing a light blue dress tonight with a white mask. That was the same color mask my father wore when he sold me. So, is she selling too? I look away, but can't help myself when I keep getting drawn back to her. Who is she? And why does it seem like she has such a fascination with me? After the auction is over I want to leave, but I have to go to the bathroom badly.

Phoenix leads me out of the ballroom. "I need to go to the restroom," I tell him. He nods slightly as we take a left out of the ballroom and into a hallway. His lips are in a thin line and his eyes are drawn tight. He stops in front of a door, but before he can say anything, I lift my hands and grip both sides of his neck.

"I'm sorry there wasn't someone who piqued your interest," I say, trying to be discreet. He sighs, wrapping his arms around my waist and pulling me close. I hold him tight, giving him the comfort he obviously needs.

"Go, so we can get out of here," he murmurs. I nod and turn to enter the bathroom. After I use the bathroom, I wash my hands and look at myself in the mirror one more time. A door clicks to my right and I snap my head in that direction. It's the woman that keeps glaring at me. How did she get in here? I thought that was a storage closet.

"Who are you? What are you doing in here?" Her smile is a threat as I back up.

"Who I am is none of your concern." She walks toward me until my back is against the wall and trails her long red fingernail from my cheek to my chin.

"You're a pretty little thing, aren't you?" I recoil from her touch. I want to scream for Phoenix, but at the same time, my curiosity is piqued. "Do you know how much Phoenix paid for you?"

I swallow and nod. "Yes, he told me." Her eyes narrow like she wasn't expecting that answer.

"Did you know it was because your father took his mother?" My heart stops in my chest. She clicks her tongue. "You didn't." I don't respond because I'm speechless.

"The moment you were dropped off at the academy, Phoenix swore he was going to take you like your father took his mother." I think back to all the times he was everywhere I was at. I had always hoped it was because he secretly liked me. He alluded to it earlier tonight. Did he lie? Is that why he only touches me when he has to? Is what she's saying true? Should I trust her? She's obviously jealous or angry.

She's older than Phoenix and I. Was she a teacher at the academy? I don't recognize her. Maybe I'd be able to place her better if she wasn't wearing a mask. Her eyes are different from anything I've seen before. Well, except for Phoenix. I narrow my eyes at her.

"Are you Phoenix's mother?"

She slaps my cheek lightly. "Such a smart girl."

"How has he not noticed you?" He comes to these auctions frequently.

"I don't attend these auctions. I didn't attend one until he hosted the one at his house. And I only did it then because he bought you. My curiosity was piqued." She finally steps away from me and I immediately eye the door. "And I dyed my hair. My son looks just like me. Hair and eyes." Her hair is an auburn color, so she dyed it from a dark blonde to that.

When she turns her back, I take a small step to the door, but she turns around immediately. "Nuh uh." She wags her index finger at me. Then she grabs me by the arm and pulls me into what I thought was a storage room, but it looks like a secret passage of some kind.

Right before she closes the door, Phoenix knocks on the bathroom. "Kenz?" I open my mouth to scream, but a large hand is placed over my mouth and I'm being dragged back so the shelves that should be there can return to their place. The person's hand is replaced by duct tape and a black bag is yanked over my head.

I want to scream. I want to cry. But I have to force myself to remain calm so I don't hyperventilate. "Let's see if my son actually cares for you." She grabs my upper arm and drags me along. I trip over my feet a few times and sometimes on the uneven ground.

"If he does try to find you and if he's successful at rescuing you, I need you to tell him I wasn't taken. I left."

Chapter 36

I sit up in bed; the moonlight shining between the cracks in the curtain. I'm drenched in sweat, but I'm shaking. Phoenix is asleep next to me. I cover my mouth with my hands, trying to hold in a sob. He lied to me about so much. I know I still don't remember everything. But he lied to me about why he bought me, our marriage, how he was rescuing me from my father, and his mom.

Slipping out of bed as quietly as possible, I tiptoe to the door.

"Kenz?" Phoenix's voice halts me and I have to suck in a breath and force myself to turn and face him.

"Sorry. I didn't mean to wake you. I just have to use the bathroom and get a drink of water." He hums and lays his head back down, so I leave quietly.

Standing in the hallway, I have no idea what to do now. I'm trapped here. The memory of the night with the secret room flashes before my eyes. Maybe there's a secret room here. I tiptoe across the hallway to my old room. There are a few things left that haven't been moved yet, so I put on some black leggings and a black hoodie.

Finding a bag, I grab everything else that's in here and quickly pack the bag. My heart feels like it's been put into a blender and pulverized. Grabbing a hair tie, I pull my hair up and lift the hood up to cover it. Glancing at the clock in the room, I'm surprised to see it's only two in the morning. *That dream felt so long. Or memories I guess.*

Stepping back out into the hallway, I hold my breath and ignore the nausea that threatens. I swallow a couple of times. I descend the stairs quietly. When I get to the bottom, I stay perfectly still and listen for any movement. When I'm sure no one else is awake, I slowly walk to the library. Entering, I lock the door and walk over to the window.

I place my bag on the floor and sit at the window seat, staring out at the lake. I try to think of a plan, but I can't stop thinking about how Phoenix has lied to me. He's made himself out to be this savior, and I fell for it. I think back to the intimate moments we shared as I play with the ring on my finger. I married him, but it wasn't willingly. But since I've been here, he's told me he loves me and we definitely have sex more than we did when we first got married. I still don't remember everything, though. I wish I could pinpoint exactly what is making my memories return.

He had to host an auction, or we did. It made me remember the first auction more clearly. I didn't argue with my father about the dress because I wanted to wear it. No, he made me wear it. Phoenix said he saved me from the headmaster buying me, but my father never said who was going to buy me, just that he had someone lined up.

If Phoenix decides to come looking for me, this will be the first place he'll look. I became too comfortable. I stopped looking for a way out and now I have no idea what to do. Phoenix said I was angry at him for not telling me what he was doing. He even said I didn't go to an auction in the beginning, but that's not true either.

I place my hands on top of my head and lean my forehead on my bent knees. I'm so confused. I have no idea what's going on and I wish I could still live in the sweet bliss of not knowing what I know now. A tear falls down my cheek and I wipe it away in frustration. He doesn't deserve my tears. My thoughts turn to Anna and leaving her here.

Was Anna the one he was looking for at the auction his mom kidnapped me at? Was he really looking for her at the auction he bought me? My stomach stirs and my chest constricts. I begin to feel lightheaded as my breathing quickens. Will this be how I die? I feel like I'm going to die.

I force myself to take a deep breath in and exhale slowly. I place my cheek on the cool window as I close my eyes and force all the thoughts and questions bombarding me from my mind. Once my breathing slows and my chest doesn't feel like someone is sitting on me, I form a plan.

The alarm is put on every night, but I know the alarm code. The only problem is when someone disarms the alarm, it immediately notifies Rex and Phoenix. So, if I unarm the alarm, I have maybe five minutes to make it to the rowboat on the lake. Even then, they'll probably get me quickly because of the jet ski or the motor boat they have.

Why is the Phoenix now different from the Phoenix who bought and married me? Did things eventually get better? Even if they did, he still had me eating out of the palm of his hand right from the beginning. Unless... Maybe his mom kidnapping me that time made me change my tune. I want to scream, but I force myself to stop before I have another panic attack.

With it being the middle of the night, how quickly will they react? I could get down to the boat and push it out on the water as a distraction. Maybe I could take the jet ski. I don't know it well enough to be able to do that. Or, I could go back upstairs, act like nothing has happened and the next time Phoenix and Rex have to go somewhere, I can run.

That's the answer. That's what I'm going to have to do. Sighing, I pull the pajamas I had on out of the bag, take off the leggings and hoodie, and put the pajamas back on. Stuffing everything in the bag, I open the storage area under the window seat and put the bag in it. I take one more deep breath before I leave the library and go to the kitchen. Grabbing a water, I lean against the counter and sip at it.

I don't want to go back upstairs. I don't know if I can do this. Pouring the rest of the water out, I place the cup in the dishwasher and turn to head upstairs.

"Jesus Christ!" I place my hand over my chest at the sight of Phoenix leaning against the doorway in the kitchen. "Don't do that!" I chastise him.

He chuckles as he pushes away from the doorway and walks toward me. I can't help myself when my eyes trail down his naked chest to his boxer briefs, to his legs and back up. My body betrays me with its reaction. "See something you like, love?" I tear my eyes away from his hardening cock to his face. The question reminds me of the memories that just assaulted me.

"Sorry, I woke up not feeling well, so I got some water." I ignore his question because if I admit to it, he might do something about it. And as much as I want to run away, I also know how much I care about him. He told me he loved me. Did he mean it?

"No need to apologize. When you didn't come right back, I came to look for you." He wraps his arm around my waist and pulls me close to him. "What's wrong?" He places the back of his hand on my forehead.

"I woke up sweating, but I was freezing. I'm not feeling the best." It's a half truth. I did wake up that way and I'm not feeling well. He purses his lips and his eyes crinkle slightly as he studies me.

"Did you take anything?"

"No, I don't know where that kind of stuff is." He turns toward a cabinet, opening it to reveal a First Aid Kit. He opens it, hands me the Motrin, and fills another glass of water for me. I take the Motrin and drink all the water. He takes my hand and leads me back upstairs.

He seems so concerned and I want to believe he is and this isn't an act, but I don't know what to believe anymore. "You're sure that's all that's wrong?" he asks.

"Yes," I whisper, hoping he doesn't try to grill me.

"If you're not feeling better in the morning, I'll call Dr. Chamberland to come over and check you out." I nod as he helps me into bed and lays down next to me.

"Are you cold?" he asks. I'm shaking slightly, but I don't know if it's from the adrenaline leaving my body or because I am cold.

"A little," I whisper. He pulls me close, adjusting me so my back is to his chest. He grabs the blankets, wrapping them tightly over us. I stiffen for the briefest moment before I relax into him. "I don't want to get you sick, if I'm getting sick."

He runs his lips over the back of my neck. "I'll be fine, love. Don't worry about me." I allow myself to be enveloped by his warmth and his smell before succumbing to my exhaustion.

Over the next several days, I keep my eyes open for opportunities to run, although I'm beginning to have second thoughts. Dr. Chamberland came to check on me and said I would be fine, but to make sure I stayed hydrated and to rest if I started feeling bad again. I bake, read, have a movie night with Anna, and go for walks to think through all my memories. I wanted to talk to Anna about them. I considered asking her if she'd leave with me if I do decide to run, but she's not strong enough yet.

Thankfully, because Phoenix is trying to give me space to recover, he doesn't try to sleep with me. He does stay at home to work because he wants to be close to me while I'm not feeling well. Each night we climb into bed, he wraps his arms around me, and he holds me close as we fall asleep. After the fourth night, I know if I don't do something soon, I'm going to fall back under his spell. What is it about him that makes him so irresistible?

Then it happens. I wake up one morning, and Phoenix is already gone for the day. He left me a note on my nightstand.

Had to leave early to do some business with Rex. Be home in time for dinner. Call me if you need me. Miss you already, Phoenix.

My heart clinches, still at war with what I should do. I get dressed in some warm clothes and comfortable shoes before going downstairs.

Should I leave or should I confront Phoenix? His mom could still be out there waiting to get me again. Did she kidnap me the second time too?

Phillip is finishing up breakfast when I walk into the kitchen. "Miss Kenzie, good morning!"

I smile at Phillip swallowing down the emotions threatening to spill over at the thought of not seeing him again. "Morning!" I reply. He places a cup of coffee down and a plate with eggs, grits, toast, and bacon. I hum. "My favorite. Thank you, Phillip."

He returns my smile. "We all want you to feel better and making sure you have proper nutrients is the first step."

"I'm beginning to feel better," I promise him. After I eat, Clara waltzes in and takes my plate, cleaning up the kitchen while Phillip goes into the pantry to make his grocery list.

"Will you be baking anything today?" Clara asks as she starts the dishwasher.

"I don't know. Maybe later, but I think I'm going to grab a book out of the library and go read outside for some fresh air."

Clara frowns. "It's chilly outside."

I glance outside, but shrug. "I'll grab the blanket in the library. I need some fresh air," I repeat. Clara finally nods.

"Alright, but don't stay out too long." Agreeing, I walk at a normal pace to the library even though I want to run. I grab my favorite book and the blanket. Opening the window, I drop my bag behind the bush. Making sure I leave everything how it should be, I look around the library one more time, memorizing each nook and cranny. This is my favorite place in the house. I sigh, still undecided if I'm going to go through with this.

Walking back to the kitchen, I'm relieved when no one is there. Making a last-minute decision, I walk to Anna's room, but she's still sleeping. I stare at her for a few minutes before deciding to leave her a note just in case.

Don't worry about me. I'll be fine. Love you.

Stepping outside, I continuously glance around to make sure none of the security that normally stays at the front of the house makes it around here. I grab my bag quickly and walk down to the boathouse, pulling my gloves on. My eyes stray from the rowboat to the motorboat.

Could I get away with taking the motorboat? How loud is it? How quickly would they come searching for me? Could I get away fast enough? Do I really want to do this?

Shaking my head, I drop my bag on the dock. I can't do this. I can't leave. As much as I hate to admit it, I know I'm safe with Phoenix. And with all my memories still not back, it's not smart to risk it. Looking out over the lake, I huff. *At least I can make it this far now without getting exhausted.* I climb into the rowboat along with my blanket.

This will give me some time to think. How do I confront Phoenix? I guess I never told him about his mom, because he still thinks it was my father. Why didn't I tell him? It looks like I had secrets of my own.

Closing my eyes I press the palms of my hands to my eyes.

I know if I go back to the house, it won't be long before I let Phoenix back in. I love him. I will always love him. How I wish I could just turn it off. Am I going to wind up like my mom?

I open my eyes and stand to get out of the boat, but quickly sit back down when the boat rocks, almost tipping me into the lake. My eyes widen at the realization that I've drifted away from the dock. Extremely far away from the dock.

How long were my eyes closed? What am I going to do?

I twist my head, trying to figure out where I'm at. *How did I get so far away from the dock?* I reach for my bag, but stop when I realize I dropped it on the dock. *Shit!*

I stare at the lake as I continue to drift. I can't keep sitting here, so I grab the paddles and row. Relief washes over me when I see a cabin. So, I do my best to row to the shore. My strength is rapidly decreasing.

There's a dock where I'm able to grab a rope to tie to the boat. *What happened to the rope that was tying the boat to Phoenix's dock?*

I climb out of the boat and come face to face with an old man pointing a rifle at me. My stomach drops as I raise my hands.

"Who the hell are you?" His voice is rough, just like everything else about him.

"Ummm... I'm McKenzie. I got lost." I motion to the boat. "I saw your cabin and was hoping I could get help." He keeps the rifle pointed at me, his eyes narrowing before he slowly lowers it. I sigh in relief.

"Alright. Come on. Is there someone I can call?" He turns and walks toward the cabin. *Does he know Phoenix? I'm pretty sure this is the same man Rex pointed out to me all those months ago.*

"Is your name Larry?" I ask.

He stops and turns back around, tilting his head at me. "How do you know that?" I twist my rings around on my finger. *Phoenix is going to be so pissed.*

"I'm McKenzie Stone." His eyes flare in recognition.

"Do you need help?" he asks.

Do I? It seems he knows the Stone name. Could I possibly stay here until I figure out what to do next? My ring catches my eye. *Maybe I can sell it and use the money to travel somewhere else.*

"McKenzie?"

I lift my eyes to look at him. "I don't know."

"You're safe here."

"If you don't come with me I'll kill you, but first I'll kill Phoenix and I'll make you watch." Fear settles in my mind at the thought of something happening to Phoenix.

"I knew you loved him." I glare at Phoenix's mom. She's right and I hate it.

"Come with me and nothing will happen to him."

"What did he ever do to you? He's been looking for you for years."

Her smile is deadly. "If I wanted to be found, he would have found me. Now, don't make me tell you again. Get in the boat." With one last glance up at the house, I climb into the boat.

She leans close to me as one of her men starts the engine and begins to navigate away from the dock.

"Let's see if he'll come for you."

I glare at her. "He will come for me. He always comes for me."

Chapter 37

Phoenix

Eleven Years Ago

I ball my hands into fists when the place we just finished searching comes up empty. She's nowhere. My dad punches the wall, his knuckles coming back bloody.

"We'll keep looking, dad," I promise him. He shakes his head and sits on the concrete steps in front of the building we know some of the girls for the auction were being held.

"She's gone, son. That son of a bitch has probably already sold her." I grit my teeth, wishing I had more power to do everything that's running through my head. Marcus Knight kidnapped my mother and sold her at one of his auctions.

"What about his wife? I thought he was married."

Dad scoffs as he pushes himself up. "He killed her. She hated his lifestyle, so he did away with her." We look at the building one last time before leaving. I don't want to believe she's gone. We'll find her and if we don't, I'll make sure Marcus Knight suffers.

Three Months Later

"Marcus Knight's daughter will be at Brighton," Dad tells me as I grab my bag off the conveyor belt at the airport. I pause.

"Will she?" I ask. We've learned things over the past three months. Many of the original members of The Society pledged their first-born daughters to be sold at an auction. So, he'll have to sell her. Eventually. I'll be there when he does it. I'll destroy his world like he destroyed ours.

"I'll get to know her," I promise him before I hang up. I'll make her love me. Then I'll break her.

The first day of school I look for her. She doesn't have social media, and I wasn't successful in finding a picture of her another way. So, I signed up to be her tour guide since this is her first year. I went to Brighton Junior High last year, so I know the campus pretty well already.

A girl walks toward the flagpole I'm standing at. She pushes her silver hair behind her ear. I wait for her to notice me. When she finally does, her brown eyes find my ice-cold eyes, and a part of me thaws. What the fuck?

"Phoenix?" she asks.

"That's me. McKenzie?" She nods as she adjusts her backpack. She's gorgeous. Too bad I'm going to break her.

Sitting in my office in downtown Savannah, an uneasy feeling settles in the pit of my stomach. I pack my things so I can go home and check on McKenzie. She seemed to be feeling a little better yesterday. It's the only reason I came to town. There were some things I had to take care of for the fight I plan on taking her to this weekend.

I need to show more of my true self to her. But the past several months have been what I wanted us to be all along. I hope she still loves me when she remembers. My phone rings, Rex's name popping up.

"Yeah," I answer as I walk out of my office and lock it. There's a beat of silence that has me pausing.

"McKenzie is missing."

"What?" My voice is deadly.

"Phillip and Clara said she went outside to read. When they hadn't seen her for a while and they couldn't find her, they alerted security. They found the rowboat missing. There was a bag with her things on the dock, and she left Anna a note."

"I'm on my way."

She's gone. More specifically, she left. But why wouldn't she take her bag? I should have been completely honest with her from the moment she woke up. Memory or no memory.

I have no idea what she remembered to cause this, but I do know this time she wasn't taken. I run my fingers through my hair as I break every speeding law there is to get home.

I don't change, instead Rex briefs me on what the plan is. We split up into three search parties. Five guys in each one. We track up and down the lake for almost an hour, but no one has found any trace of her. She didn't take the phone I gave her, but she never really used that, anyway. My phone rings and I answer it before it can ring a second time.

"Did you find her?" I bark.

"No, but we found the rowboat floating down the lake." I grip the phone so tight it cracks under the pressure. "Sir?" Rex asks.

"Look for her. She couldn't have gotten far." I hang up before he can say anything else.

"Call Rex, get the coordinates of where he's at so we can go meet him." I bark at my guys. What if we don't find her? What if she's hurt and we don't get to her in enough time? What if her father gets to her?

That bastard has been trying to take her since I won the bid on her. I sit and think back over the past seven years. My obsession with her started because I was determined to get back at her father. But it soon turned into more. The night I bought her and had her in front of all those men. That sealed our fate. She was mine. She'll always be mine.

I will find her. I will always find her.

To be continued...

Note From the Author

Ahhh!! I'm so glad you all have finally met Phoenix and McKenzie. I became obsessed with these two and they have been determined to tell their story. I can't wait to write the ending to their story and I promise it will be finished this year. I'm also excited to write more from Phoenix's point of view. I hope you all have fallen in love with Phoenix and McKenzie as much as I have. I know you all probably have so many unanswered questions, but they will be answered soon! Promise!

XOXO, Nicole

More by Nicole Abrams

The Coming Home Series:

Finding Caroline

Losing Ansley

Becoming Bailey

Claiming Becca

Liv's book coming soon!

Acknowledgements

My husband and son. You two are so supportive in everything I do. The nights I have to stay up late to write. The questions you ask about everything that goes into publishing a book. Thank you for supporting my dreams I love you both so much!

Ashleigh! I could not do this without you. Your constant encouragement, cheerleading, and honesty keeps me going. Even when you ask for spoilers. You know I'll ALWAYS give them to you. Thank you for being my friend and alpha reader. I'll love you always!

Scarlett. Thank you for editing and offering feedback. I'm thankful I met you. You've helped bring my writing to another level!

Brittany. You are amazing! You are supportive and willing to help wherever you can. Thank you for being a part of my team and helping me. I appreciate you!

My Hype Team and early readers. Thank you for sticking by my side. All of you mean so much to me and I appreciate your support, excitement, and encouraging words. Thank you for joining me on this crazy ride and spreading the word about Phoenix and McKenzie.

And to the readers! I appreciate each and everyone of you so much. Thank you for following along on this journey with me. I hope you loved the start of Phoenix and McKenzie's story and will finish it with me later this year.

About the author

Nicole Abrams is best known for her debut contemporary romance novel, Finding Caroline. Born in Georgia, she moved frequently with her military family, finally settling back into her home state as an adult. Always an avid reader, she eventually started journaling and writing short stories, which led to the creation of her first book. Nicole is a breast cancer survivor, beating her diagnosis in 2021 after undergoing surgery and radiation. She has an unhealthy obsession with the TV show Friends and when she is not writing you can find her spending time with the man of her dreams and their son.

Printed in Great Britain
by Amazon

56281943R00191